THE ANGEL OF THE GLADE

The first in a new historical mystery series featuring Dr. Clyde Deacon

Widower Clyde Deacon arrives in 1902 Fairfield, New York, to take up the post of doctor. Regarded with some suspicion by the town's inhabitants because he comes from Tennessee, he was also personal physician to President McKinley at the time of his assassination. A beautiful young actress is found murdered and Deacon is asked by the overworked town sheriff to assist him in the case. Gradually he discovers that the inhabitants of Fairfield are not as innocent as they seem...

THE ANGEL OF THE GLADE

A Dr Deacon Mystery

Scott Mackay

Severn House Large Print
London & New York

This first large print edition published 2012
in Great Britain and the USA by
SEVERN HOUSE PUBLISHERS LTD of
9-15 High Street, Sutton, Surrey, SM1 1DF.
First world regular print edition published 2009 by
Severn House Publishers Ltd., London and New York.

British Library Cataloguing in Publication Data

MacKay, Scott, 1957-
    The angel of the glade.
    1. Physicians--Fiction. 2. Murder--Investigation--
    Fiction. 3. Detective and mystery stories. 4. Large type
    books.
    I. Title
    813.6-dc22

ISBN-13: 978-0-7278-7986-8

Severn House Publishers support The Forest Stewardship
Council [FSC], the leading international forest certification
organisation. All our titles that are printed on Greenpeace-
approved FSC-certified paper carry the FSC logo.

Printed and bound in Great Britain by the
MPG Books Group, Bodmin, Cornwall.

To my mother, Claire

PART ONE

A Talent of the Stage

ONE

As I took my seat next to Mr Wilbert Robson, I knew the townspeople of Fairfield stared at me from behind their programs. They stared because I was their new doctor. I glanced toward the derbied gentlemen standing outside the high school fire doors who, in a discreet relay, passed a flask of whiskey around. They stared because I'd been next to President William McKinley in Buffalo last year when he'd been mortally wounded by that misguided anarchist, Leon Czolgosz. I looked at the newly installed electric footlights girdling the proscenium arch, pretending not to notice their interest. They stared because I was a long-time friend of the town sheriff, Stanley Armstrong. I opened my program and scanned the contents. Maybe they even stared because I came from Tennessee.

They stared for any number of reasons. But I knew they all asked the same question: Why, after a prestigious career as President McKinley's personal physician, would I

9

settle for a small parochial practice in an out-of-the-way place like Fairfield, New York?

The answer was as simple as it was complex: I hadn't yet forgiven myself for letting the President's life slip through my hands.

The play was *Angel of the Glade*, the 1896 melodrama by Booth Tarkington about a group of Americans on safari who, becoming lost, are rescued by a beautiful and mysterious jungle girl. Cast in the lead role was a lithe young senior wearing green tights, a skirt made of leaves, and a green lace-up shirt. The skirt of leaves did little to hide her athletic and alluring legs. Her chestnut hair was pinned underneath an unlikely-looking hat of feathers. As she explained to the hapless band of Americans that she was an angel sent to protect them from the dangers of the jungle, I watched her closely. She couldn't have been more than seventeen but she understood her stagecraft well. She had her audience mesmerized. Her voice carried to the back of the hall and her words came out naturally, not in the stilted monotones of her fellow high school players. She wasn't self-conscious in front of the audience, and in fact looked as if she enjoyed her audience, played to them, basked in their admiration. I could see she loved the stage, that she had a natural aptitude and talent for it. She was, in a word, an actress.

I glanced through my program and found her name: Charlotte Scott. I turned to Wilbert Robson's twenty-year-old son, Roger, who sat to my left.

'Do you know her?' I asked.

He leaned toward me. 'Who?' he said.

'Charlotte Scott.'

'Yes.' A vacuous smile came to the young man's face, revealing a spellbindingly white set of teeth. He seemed amused that I should take an interest in Miss Scott. 'She's the barber's daughter,' he said. 'Her old man's over there.' Roger lifted a lazy finger and pointed to a gentlemen three rows down. 'Howard Scott. An adequate barber, but a fool when it comes to money.'

'What's that on your face?' I asked.

I gazed at Roger Robson. He had a fading bruise on his left cheek. As a doctor, I was familiar with bruises of all shapes and sizes. This one looked as if it had come from a fist.

He raised his hand self-consciously to the injury. 'What?' he said. 'This?'

'Yes,' I said.

'I fell off my horse,' he said.

He was fibbing, I knew it just from the tone of his voice, but I wasn't going to press him about it. I turned my attention to Howard Scott, Miss Scott's father. He was thin, stork-like, with a full head of black and gray hair, impressive side-whiskers, and a dark mustache. He was in his late fifties. He'd been one of the men I'd seen earlier passing

11

the flask of whiskey by the fire doors. He gazed at his daughter as if she were an idol, as if she were indeed a celestial thing of the jungle. A fool when it came to his money. What did Roger Robson mean by that? I was curious. And why did he speak of the Scotts as if they were no more appealing than yesterday's trash?

Halfway through the third act a boy in bare feet, having slipped unnoticed into the auditorium without a ticket, excused his way down our aisle and tugged at my sleeve. I recognized him as one of Stanley Armstrong's brood.

'My ma's got trouble with her birthing,' he said, his ears turning red. 'Pa's sent me with the wagon to get you.'

I gazed at the boy, trying to recall his name, but Stanley had so many children I had a hard time keeping them straight. I leaned toward Wilbert Robson.

'I'm afraid I've got a country call,' I murmured. He raised his bushy eyebrows in enquiry. 'Camilla Armstrong,' I explained. 'The boy's come with the wagon.'

'Take my motor,' said Wilbert Robson. 'Haines has it just outside. He'll have you to the sheriff's farm in no time.'

'But how will you get home?' I asked.

'We'll walk,' he said. 'It's not more than a mile.'

I told Stanley's boy to drive home in the wagon, explaining that I would be able to get to the farm quicker in Mr Robson's motor car. The boy's eyes brightened. This was indeed an occasion for the fellow. The only motor car in all Fairfield was going to visit his home.

Haines was a tall, efficient fellow dressed in a mud-suit, driving goggles and a motoring cap.

'Glad to be of service, doc,' he said, tossing his cigarette aside. 'I'm about ready for a nice run myself.'

I climbed into the passenger seat of the 1901 Daimler.

'We'll have to stop by the surgery to get my bag,' I said.

'Sure thing, doc.'

He cranked the crankshaft and after a few rough belches the engine came to life. I wasn't immune to the novelty of a motor car ride. This was only my fourth drive in one. I clutched the edge of the seat as Haines jostled away from the school. We drove down Park Street. The wind snapped at my lapels, and the speed dial on the dashboard now reached the grand velocity of fifteen miles per hour.

'Don't you think you better slow down?' I suggested.

Haines gave me a devil-may-care grin. 'We're just getting started, doc,' he said. 'Don't you worry. I never lose control. Never have, never will.'

We jerked and bumped into town. My initial alarm gave way to pleasure. I likened it to a train ride, only one wasn't confined to the rails. One could go at locomotive speeds wherever one liked. The engine made a fearful racket. We reached the surgery in perhaps half the time it would have taken by buggy.

Once I had my bag, we set off for the sheriff's farm. A few passers-by stopped to stare. Some scurried on to doorsteps, afraid Haines might career wildly and strike them down dead in the street. The headlamps cast a diffuse beam on the road before us.

'If you don't mind me asking,' I said, 'how much did Mr Robson pay for this motor?'

'Ten thousand dollars,' said Haines. 'But this is the best money can buy. You can buy much cheaper ones.' He glanced at me. 'Are you thinking of buying, doc?' He had to shout over the noise of the engine.

'I paid thirty-six dollars for my buggy,' I said. 'I'm a while yet from a motor car.'

We drove southward along Tonawanda Road. The street was lined with shops and telegraph poles. A full moon shone above us, draping a creamy glow over the rooftops. We passed the Exchange Bank, the Post Office, and Wiley's Drug Store, where I saw the usual gang of rogues gathered around the soda pumps quenching their thirst. As we crossed the railroad tracks, the streets grew shabbier, and were lined with small paint-peeled bungalows and badly weathered tenement buildings. This was Hoopertown, the poorer section of town, so named because of the vicinity's main road, Hooper Avenue. The apparition of our motor car brought many residents to their windows. I glanced at the train yard, where a small locomotive with three Pullman passenger coaches sat steaming by the nearest shunt. No electric lights in this part of town, they still had gas jets.

We soon passed the outskirts of town. Tonawanda Road became nothing more than a rutted track. Up ahead we saw the sheriff's boy clip-clopping along in the wagon. Haines honked the horn. This was the sound of progress, like the sound of a bull moose searching for a mate. It was a sound, I thought, that belonged more in a circus, not on the open road.

The boy turned, startled, then shook the reins madly. The old nag, unimpressed by the approaching motor car, pulled the wagon two feet closer to the edge of the road. We sped past.

'Now I'll show you what she can really do,' said Haines.

He gripped a lever, pressed the pedal, all the while keeping his left hand on the steering wheel, and we lurched forward. With one hand I clutched my bowler, while with the other I held on to my seat. I glanced at the speed dial. Twenty miles per hour; as quick as a steam locomotive. The needle edged upward to twenty-five. We passed the Baptist Church at Reese's Corners. As we neared Lombard Hill I thought surely the man would slow down, that the motor couldn't take such a steep climb at such a breakneck pace, but we mounted the hill with ease. I glanced at the speed dial again. Blazes! The man was up to thirty-two miles per hour.

I looked at Haines. With those goggles over his eyes and that maniacal grin on his face he looked positively Mephistophelian. Proper caution should have prompted me to intercede. But I felt a lunatic grin coming to my own face. I now craved velocity the way some men crave opium. A hurricane of dust billowed behind us. The needle edged recklessly upward. Oh, glorious speed! I knew that some day, somehow, regardless of price, I would buy one of these marvelous machines.

But then Haines hit a large pothole.

The motor car jerked to the right and my heart leaped. Newfangled contraption! I let go of my bowler and grabbed my seat with both hands. How dare our legislators in Albany allow them on the roads? The motor car dodged to the left and my bowler flew off my head into the ditch. The devil take it! The Daimler lifted on two wheels then bounced back down on four. Haines struggled madly with the wheel. A man would have to be a fool to own such a dangerous conveyance! As much as Haines struggled with the wheel, he couldn't bring it under control. The critics were right, the motor car was nothing but a passing fad! The horse and buggy would remain supreme. As these thoughts stampeded through my mind, the Daimler veered into the ditch, plowed through a slough for thirty yards, covering us each with mud, and jolted to a stop. The engine choked, hissed, and finally died.

'Are you all right, doc?' asked Haines breathlessly. Steam rose from the bonnet. 'We ought to have Mayor Vanduzen do something about these potholes.'

'I would sooner face all the infidels in Christendom before I ride in one of these infernal horseless carriages again!' I said. 'You've ruined my suit. And I'll be lucky to find my hat.'

'There's a kerosene lamp in the boot, doc,' said Haines. 'I'll be happy to help you look for your hat. As for getting you to the sheriff's farm ... well...' He looked at the steaming bonnet skeptically. 'It might take a while. Maybe you should walk.'

'Walk?' I said. 'It's over three miles!'

I walked.

As Sheriff Armstrong's farm came into sight, I heard the clip-clop of the boy's wagon behind me. When he finally caught up with me and saw how I was all covered with mud, his eyes widened but he otherwise remained silent. My bad temper had long since gone. The grin had returned to my

17

face. I climbed on to the box next to the boy, and the boy shook the reins.

'I'm sorry, boy, but I've forgotten your name,' I said.

'It's Zachary, sir,' he said.

'Have you ever ridden in a motor car, Zachary?' I asked.

'No, sir,' he said.

My grin broadened. 'Then the minute I take delivery of mine,' I said, 'I'll come out to the farm and take you for a ride.'

When I entered the birthing room I realized I was too late. The child had been born and both mother and infant were doing fine.

Camilla Armstrong lay propped up on pillows holding the child, her twelfth, in swaddling. Stanley sat next to her on a milking stool while a young lady I'd not yet had the pleasure of meeting stood on the other side of the bed, wiping Camilla's forehead with a damp cloth. They all stared at me. I was covered with mud from head to foot. I became keenly aware of the bad impression I must be making on the young woman. As the area's new country doctor I had a standard to uphold. I looked as if I had just been wallowing in the dirt with pigs.

'I guarantee you,' I said, addressing the young lady directly, 'I had nothing to do with this mud. That fool chauffeur of Mr Robson's drove me into a ditch.'

A grin softened the young lady's becoming

18

features. She extended her hand in greeting.

'Dr Deacon,' she said, her voice warm and sure, 'it's a pleasure to meet you. I'm Miss Wade,' she added. 'Olive Wade.'

She had long golden hair done up in the usual way, a face with a full complement of pretty features, and a smile I found both disarming and enticing. Why did she have to be such a belle when I had to stand here soaked to my collar in mud? I took her hand carefully. I didn't want to get her lily-white fingers all dirty.

'The pleasure's mine, Miss Wade.'

'She's our midwife,' said Sheriff Armstrong.

'Well, well, well,' I said. 'I've heard of you, then.'

'And I of you,' she said. 'So this is what a presidential physician looks like.'

I sensed Stanley staring at me. He knew how badly I felt about President McKinley.

'I'm just a humble country doctor now, Miss Wade,' I said. I turned my attention to Camilla Armstrong. Her long black hair was laced with threads of gray, her face was pale, and black smudges of exhaustion shadowed her eyes. 'And how's our patient?' I asked.

'I'm fine,' she said. 'Miss Wade was an enormous help.'

'The cord was looped around the infant's neck,' explained Miss Wade matter-of-factly. 'I was able to safely untangle it.'

'That's just dandy, Miss Wade,' I said. 'And

19

the child?'

'A girl,' said Camilla. 'In fact, we've decided to name her Olive, after Miss Wade.'

'You couldn't have picked better,' I said. I turned to Stanley. We'd traveled as far west as Colorado together. We'd fought in Cuba together. Ten years ago, we'd been the only lawmen within a hundred miles of Cross Plains, Texas. 'And how's the father?' I asked.

The father looked up at me from his milking stool. He grinned, keeping a brave front, but I knew he was squeamish when it came to the birthing room.

'The father's just about ready for his whiskey jug,' he said.

'That sounds like a capital idea,' said Miss Wade, as if she were giving us an order. 'I'll bathe Mrs Armstrong and her child. I'm sure she'd like some privacy.'

Camilla gave a small acquiescent nod.

Stanley and I looked at each other. And we knew we had no choice. We had to obey. We had to do our duty.

We had to sit on the porch, drink whiskey, smoke cigars, and do absolutely nothing at all.

We settled on the porch. The moon was high, the crickets sang from the pond behind the house, and the musky smell of farm animals hung in the air. The scene was peaceful, restful, and for several minutes Stanley and I just sat there, smoking our

20

cigars and sipping whiskey.

After a while Stanley said, 'I don't know where I'm going to find the time for my new little girl.' He shook his head and took a deep breath. 'What with this Corn Mercantile burglary and the ironmongery fire, and not enough deputies to go around.'

I took a pull on my cigar and gazed at the full moon, which now settled westwards.

'Stanley...' I let the smoke drift from my mouth. 'Stanley, it's time you and Camilla stopped having children. Poor Camilla looks worn out.'

He nodded sullenly, leaned forward, and rested his elbows on his knees. 'We tried to stop, Clyde,' he said. 'We only ever wanted six. I never knew I was going to end up with twice that many.'

I flicked the ash from my cigar. 'I'd be happy to give you any number of prophylactic devices,' I said. 'I buy them by the gross for the surgery.'

'I don't need a box of French safes, Clyde,' he said. 'What I need is a few more deputies. And Camilla figures she's past the time when she can have more children now anyway. We figure Olive will be our last.'

Olive. I immediately thought of the comely midwife inside. 'That's not something I would count on, Stanley,' I said.

He shook his head again, looking exhausted. 'I'm going to have to make time for that little girl somehow,' he said. 'She's got to

21

know she has a daddy.'

I made no comment.

Stanley said, 'I'll wake Leroy when Miss Wade and Camilla are finished in there. He can take you and Miss Wade back to town. I reckon he won't run you into a ditch.'

Miss Wade. Was it whiskey euphoria I felt, or was it Miss Wade?

'I'm surprised Miss Wade isn't married,' I said.

Stanley gave me a sidelong glance, took a sip of whiskey, then wiped his mustache with the back of his sleeve.

'You're smitten by her, aren't you, Clyde?'

Various assorted children played behind us, up late because of their sister's birth.

'Don't talk nonsense, Stanley,' I said. 'I was just thinking ... I'm going to need some help at the surgery, and she seems ... well, competent ... and if she isn't married, and she needs the money, I can pay her more than what she's earning—'

'She doesn't need the money,' he said.

I paused. 'She has money?' I asked.

'The way you stared at her, why, a body would think you'd never seen a female human being before.'

'I wasn't staring,' I said. 'I was looking. Looking's not the same.'

'Your eyes were as big as silver dollars, Clyde.'

'I suppose she must be engaged,' I said.

He gave me another sidelong glance. 'I

22

don't know, Clyde,' he said. 'I've never seen her with anyone. She's new to Fairfield, same as you, and hasn't had the chance to make many friends.'

'You'd expect a woman like her to have friends flocking around her.'

'She's from Boston,' said Stanley. I suppose he thought that might explain why the young woman didn't have many friends. 'I understand both her parents died last year,' he continued. 'She came here to live with her aunt, Tabitha Stearns – I don't know if you know her. I guess you wouldn't, considering she's dead. Actually, Miss Wade came here to look after her aunt. Mrs Stearns died in March. I believe she was one of Doc Thorensen's patients. It's been hard on Miss Wade, losing so many loved ones so quickly. Maybe the reason she doesn't have any gentlemen friends is because she's been too busy looking after dying kinfolk. She lives alone now, up in that big house at the end of Poplar Avenue. You should run up and knock on her door some time. I'm sure she'd appreciate some gentlemen callers.'

'Stanley, I'm a widower,' I said flatly. 'I got to think of Emily.'

'Just because you knock on Miss Wade's door doesn't mean you got to stop thinking about Emily.'

'I don't have any reason to knock on her door now,' I said. 'If she's got all that money, why would she ever want to hire on as a nurse at my surgery?'

'She doesn't have to be a midwife either,' Stanley pointed out. 'She does it because she likes it.' Stanley took a sip of whiskey. 'And, who knows, maybe she might like nursing too.'

I pondered this notion.

'Well ... how much money does she actually have?' I asked.

'Seems Mrs Stearns left her everything. Then she's got everything her parents left her. I guess she must be worth pretty near twenty thousand a year.'

I harumphed. 'Then she's not going to want to be my nurse, is she?' I said. 'Some young gent's going to come along and propose to her, and that'll be the end of that.'

Stanley grinned at me slyly. 'I got a way you could prevent that,' he said.

'How?'

'You could propose to her first.'

I harumphed again.

We lapsed into silence. Stanley had it wrong. I had no personal interest in Olive Wade. Yes, I recognized that as far as ladies went she was prettier than most, and I certainly paused to consider her eligible status, but I wasn't going to let these two handicaps prejudice me against her professional capabilities. I was looking for help, I needed a nurse and, as Stanley said, if she liked midwifery, she just might like nursing.

I was thinking these thoughts when Olive

Wade herself stepped out on to the porch. Stanley and I both sprang to our feet.

'Are you all finished in there?' asked Stanley.

'Yes, sir,' she said.

'Then I'll go rouse Leroy.'

Stanley stepped inside. Miss Wade and I stood on the porch together. I tried to think of something to say, but for some reason my tongue felt as tied as a slip-knot.

Miss Wade glanced at me. 'Are you usually so talkative with new acquaintances?' she asked.

'I beg your pardon, Miss Wade, but I...' I trailed off. I looked toward the misty field of corn. I couldn't help thinking how I was still all covered in mud. I fumbled for the quickest dodge. 'I was ... I was just thinking of my son.'

'Oh,' she said. 'You have a son?'

'Jeremiah,' I said. 'He's at school. In Boston, as a matter of fact.'

'Ah,' she said. 'And your wife is in Boston with him?'

I continued to stare at the misty corn. The ghosts were out tonight. I sensed Emily all around me.

'No,' I said. 'My wife is dead.'

Miss Wade hesitated. 'Oh,' she said. 'I'm sorry.'

I steered the conversation away from Emily.

'The sheriff tells me you're from Boston,' I

said.

For the next five minutes we talked about Boston. I don't know why I found Miss Wade's presence so unsettling. But she seemed to bring to the surface feelings I had long ago buried. She gathered around her all the phantoms I'd tried so hard to forget. She reminded me so much of Emily, I nearly felt like crying. I was relieved when Stanley finally came out to the porch with a sleepy-eyed Leroy.

'Leroy's just going to run back to the barn and get the wagon,' said Stanley.

While Leroy was getting the wagon, a man of about fifty rode up the drive at a full gallop on a gray mare. Stanley peered across the moonlit yard.

'Why, it's Bertram Sawyer,' he said. He turned to me, a desolate look in his eyes. 'Trouble never rests, does it?' he said.

We only had to look at Bertram Sawyer to know he was as panicked as a spooked buck in deer-hunting season. He reined in next to the porch.

'Sheriff,' he cried, 'you got to come quick! There's been a drowning in the river down by the bridge.'

The man was still in his pajamas, and he was having a hard time keeping his horse under control. The waxed tips of his mustache pointed in different directions.

'A drowning?' said Stanley. His shoulders sank. 'Any idea who?'

Bertram Sawyer looked at me, then at Olive Wade, then back at the sheriff, his eyes catching the light of the kerosene lamp hanging from the porch ceiling. I thought the man might die of a stroke right there before us.

'Charlotte Scott,' he said. He swallowed a few times, his Adam's apple bobbing up and down. 'The barber's daughter.'

TWO

Charlotte Scott, the angel of the glade; the talented young actress.

Under different circumstances a moonlit ride in Leroy's hay wagon with Miss Wade might have been enjoyable. But because of our grim destination we were both subdued.

'That was kind of you,' she said.

We sat in the back of the wagon on some old feed sacks. Bertram Sawyer rode beside us.

'The sheriff needs time with his newborn and his wife tonight,' I said. 'A drowning is nothing a doctor can't handle.'

I tried to remember that stretch of the Tonawanda River near the railway bridge, struggling to recall if there were any particular hazards there, any deep pools or brisk rapids. I was so new to Fairfield that all I could remember was the picnic ground near the bridge.

'Did you know Charlotte Scott at all?' I asked Miss Wade.

The early summer corn in the fields around us glowed in the moonlight.

'I helped her with her singing,' said Miss

Wade. 'She came to my house often, and I accompanied her on the piano. She wanted to go to drama school in New York. Did you see her in the play tonight?'

'Yes,' I said. I recalled Charlotte Scott's performance in *Angel of the Glade*. 'For one so young, she has ... had ... a promising talent,' I said.

Miss Wade nodded. 'She did indeed, Dr Deacon. She did indeed.'

We arrived at the scene of the drowning a short while later.

'Are you coming?' I asked Miss Wade.

'No.' She looked upset. 'I'd prefer to stay here.'

I nodded. Having recently suffered the passing of her parents and aunt, she was bound to be in a delicate state. The death of Charlotte Scott, while upsetting to everyone, would be particularly trying to Miss Wade.

'Leroy,' I addressed the boy, 'stay with Miss Wade.'

'Yes, sir.'

I turned to Bertram Sawyer. 'Lead the way, Mr Sawyer.'

Mr Sawyer and I set off toward the river. Knots of high school students stood in a field at the bottom of a small slope. Some sat at picnic tables under box elders at the edge of the field. I saw food and drink, and a couple of smoldering bonfires. A man with a violin case stared at me as we walked past.

The hapless band of American safari hunters from *Angel of the Glade*, still in full costume, sat on a couple of old quilts that were spread out on the grass. They looked more lost than ever. Some older men stood on the road next to a buggy near the railway bridge, smoking cigarettes. I vaguely recognized one or two. Mrs Sawyer and her two young daughters, still in their nightgowns, their hair down, had come from their farm and were holding kerosene lanterns high above their heads. I heard the sound of the river just beyond a row of willows at the far end of the field. Mr Herbert Early, the high school drama teacher, stood next to one of these willows holding a lantern, peering at me as I approached through the dew-covered grass.

'Doctor?' he said.

He'd no doubt been expecting the sheriff.

'Evening, Mr Early,' I said.

He was a young man in his late twenties, but didn't look much older than some of his high school students. His brown hair was parted in the middle, he had out-of-date mutton-chop side-whiskers, probably meant to make him look older, and a narrow fringe of mustache. He wore a brown wool suit with a starched collar and bow-tie, and an Argyle vest that looked as if it had seen better days. His trouser legs were wet. The young man's eyes were wide, apprehensive; and, as I explained why Stanley the sheriff couldn't come, he nodded in a panicked, shaky way.

'Now, then,' I said, 'where's Miss Scott?'

'She's down there.' Mr Early lifted a tremulous finger. 'In those bulrushes.'

I put my hand on his arm, trying to steady him. 'Easy now, Mr Early,' I said. 'We've got a night ahead of us.'

His lower lip stiffened. He gave me a nod. 'It's just that I ... I should have...' He took a deep breath. 'I'm afraid it's my fault. I should have kept a closer watch on everybody.'

'It's no one's fault, Mr Early,' I said. 'It's just an unfortunate accident.'

He nodded. He lifted the lantern high and led us down to the river.

Mist clung to the shallows. An owl hooted in the distance. We startled some sleeping ducks that quacked their way into the water. The moon penetrated through the willow branches, mottling the river bank with a silvery light. I heard rapids upstream, a dream-like and repetitive sound, soothing and hypnotic; a sound that seemed to tempt the soul toward the calm and restful embrace of eternity. The Tonawanda wasn't a big river, but at this point it widened into a pool. I saw two changing-houses and a diving-board; this must be the local swimming hole. The ground grew wet underfoot, but I didn't care about my shoes. We splashed our way through the bulrushes and soon came to Charlotte Scott.

31

She was lying on her stomach in the mud with her legs trailing half in the water and her body up on the bank. The smell of swamp methane was strong, and the mud here was thick and black. She still wore her skirt of leaves and her lace-up shirt, but her hat of feathers was gone. Her hair was down, plastered in long snaky strands across her back. Her head was turned so that I could see only the right side of her face. Her cheek was covered with mud. I knelt beside her.

'Bring the lantern closer, Mr Early,' I said.

Mr Early crouched next to me and held the lantern directly above Miss Scott's body. Her hair looked dark in the wet. She smelled of alcohol.

'She was drinking?' I asked.

'Mr Murchison brought some sloe gin,' said Mr Early. 'And I believe Roger Robson had a flask of whiskey.'

'Who's Mr Murchison?' I asked.

Out on the river, I saw the ducks float by, a mother followed by six or seven youngsters.

'He owns the Parthenon Theater on Fredonia Street,' explained Mr Early. 'He helps us sometimes with our school productions.'

I stared at Charlotte Scott. I was no great believer in the Temperance Movement but I did wonder when the state might legislate a drinking age. I moved her hair from her neck and pressed my fingers to her carotid artery. No pulse. I took my hand away and sighed.

'Let's pull her out of the water and rest her up on that grass there,' I said.

Early and Sawyer each grabbed an arm. I lifted her feet. We carried her to the grass. The owl continued to hoot in the distance and I heard one of Bertram Sawyer's cows lowing on his farm. We laid her on the grass. I loosened the rawhide lace of her green bodice. Mr Early turned away. I put my ear to her breast and listened. No heartbeat, no breath sounds. I took out my handkerchief and handed it to Mr Early.

'Would you mind getting this wet, Mr Early?' I asked.

He took the handkerchief, walked to the river's edge, wet it, came back and handed it to me. I wiped the mud from Charlotte's face. I must confess, I was perplexed. She wasn't cyanosed, the way she should have been. Her skin wasn't blue at all; it was pink.

'How'd this happen?' I asked. 'Didn't she cry for help?'

Mr Early struggled for words. 'There was a fiddler,' he said. 'And there was dancing. We were all having such fun. We were celebrating the play. We were making a lot of noise.' He looked away. 'If she cried for help, none of us heard her. She came down here by herself for a swim.'

'She went swimming in her costume?' I asked.

'Everybody was swimming in their clothes. Look how hot it is.' He shrugged. 'It was all a big lark. They were all daring each other to go in.'

'Yes, but that's a theatrical costume,' I said. 'And it looks fairly flimsy to me.'

He looked at Charlotte Scott, his brow furrowing. 'I never thought of that,' he said.

'So she came down here by herself and she didn't tell anyone she was coming,' I said.

'I assume so,' he said. 'I was the first one to notice she was gone.'

He put the lantern on the grass next to Charlotte.

'And you found her right there, in those bulrushes?' I asked.

'Yes.'

I shook my head. 'She looks like a big strong girl. How could she drown in such a small bit of water like that?'

I was thinking of her pink face. Mr Early frowned. 'We didn't find her right away,' he said. He waved toward the bridge. 'We asked the ... the hoboes.'

I stared at the bridge. 'There were hoboes?'

I saw the remnants of a fire under the bridge, but no hoboes.

'Yes, earlier,' he said. 'They said they had not seen her.'

'How many hoboes?'

'Two. Or maybe three.'

'So you eventually found her in those bulrushes,' I repeated.

'Todd Rumsen found her hat floating out in the middle there. I imagine she drifted to

34

shore. The current's not that strong here.'

He stared at me, as if he were waiting for me to absolve him. I tried to reconstruct the scene. I had to conclude that Charlotte must indeed have come down here by herself, that all the others had been up in the field dancing, and that when she'd cried for help – if she had cried for help – none of them had heard her over the noise they'd been making. But how could an athletic young woman like Charlotte Scott so easily drown?

'Before she came down here by herself did she exhibit any pronounced signs of drunkenness?' I asked.

'No,' said Mr Early. 'I don't think she had much more than a few swallows of Mr Murchison's sloe gin.'

'And you say there were only two hoboes?' I said.

'Perhaps three.'

It didn't make sense. I lifted the lantern and held it to her face again. Pink. I leaned close and sniffed, but I smelled only alcohol. I looked at the bridge again. The bridge was a good distance away. Would the hoboes have heard her?

'Mr Early,' I said, 'would you oblige me by going over to that diving-board.' A furrow came to his brow, but I gave him no further explanation. 'Mr Sawyer, could you get some of the high school boys to gather poor Charlotte up and take her to the wagon.'

'Sure thing, doc,' said the farmer.

'What are you going to do?' asked Mr Early.

'I'm going to establish some possibilities, Mr Early,' I said. 'And I'll need your help. I'm going to the bridge. When I get there, I'll light a match. When you see that match, I want you to holler my name as loud as you can.'

He frowned again, but nodded. 'Of course, Dr Deacon.'

He retreated toward the diving-board. I set off downstream toward the bridge.

The bridge was fairly new, made of steel girders riveted together by sturdy bolts, set on concrete pilings. I saw the year of construction, 1893, carved into one of the concrete slabs. The embers of the hoboes' fire still glowed red. They couldn't have left long ago. Some whiskey bottles lay here and there, a few old crates had been up-ended to make chairs, and a rain barrel had been turned into a table with a square piece of plywood for a top. I saw the remains of five or six catfish lying about the fire. I took out my matches and struck one.

Mr Early hollered my name from upstream. I heard him loud and clear over the sound of the rapids. And I concluded there was no good reason why Charlotte Scott should have drowned here tonight.

THREE

It was well past two in the morning when Leroy Armstrong reined in his nag in front of the Scotts' modest wood-frame house on Milton Street. I had my arm around Bernice Scott, Charlotte's sixteen-year-old sister. She was a pale creature, slight and quivering, shattered by her sister's death. Her white shirtwaist with puff sleeves glowed in the moonlight. The hem of her violet skirt was wet from her searching through the shallows for her sister. The boater on her head sat askew but she didn't seem to notice. Her face was slick with tears.

Charlotte lay in the wagon under an old blanket. We'd let Miss Wade off at the corner. The parlor window of the Scott house was dimly lit. The moon, slanting from the west, cast fancy shadows through the house's gingerbread trim. I got off the wagon and helped Bernice down. As the girl and I approached the picket gate, a breeze stirred an American flag hanging from the roof-peak above the porch. Far in the distance I heard the clickety-clack of the nightly steam locomotive and, a moment later, its horn echoing like a lament over the town. The front door of the Scott house opened and out came Howard Scott, holding a lantern high above his head.

'Hello?' he called.

'Evening, Mr Scott,' I said.

'Is it Dr Deacon?' he asked.

'It sure is,' I said. 'And I'm afraid I have some tragic news for you, sir.'

I helped Bernice up the steps. She had a kind of shocked grin on her face now. Howard Scott was in shirtsleeves, but without collar or cuffs. His suspenders, now off his shoulders, hung in loose loops around either hip. He'd been waiting up for his daughters. He smelled of whiskey. I got right to the point.

'I'm afraid your daughter Charlotte has drowned in the river,' I said.

He seemed to freeze. He stared at me, then looked out to the road where Leroy waited in the wagon. The sound of the locomotive was growing fainter in the distance. A moth began to trouble itself around Mr Scott's lantern. The smell of fresh-baked bread drifted from the open door of the house. He stood there, as still as could be, then, in an instant, dropped his lantern. It crashed to the steps, and immediately the flames danced up from the spilled kerosene. I quickly scooped some dirt from the flower-bed and smothered the small fire. I saw the moth wing its way into the house.

'She's dead, Daddy,' murmured Bernice, as if she wanted to make sure her father understood.

She went to her father and clung to him. Mr Scott didn't put his arms around her; he left them hanging at his sides. He continued to stare at the wagon. He ran his hand distractedly through his thick graying hair, glanced back through the open doorway as Henrietta Scott came out of her first-floor bedroom, then turned toward the street and stared at the wagon again. He rested his hand on Bernice's shoulder, too stunned to say anything.

'Howard, who is it?' Henrietta Scott struggled on stiff arthritic legs to the porch, leaning heavily on her cane. When she saw me, she said, 'Oh, dear, what's happened?'

The barber turned to his wife, the dazed look still in his eyes. 'The doctor says our dear Charlotte has drowned in the river,' he said.

It was a simple statement of fact but, coming from the father, so much more. His world was gone. His life would never be the same. Mrs Scott looked first at her husband, and then at me, as if she hoped I might contradict him.

'I'm afraid it's true,' I said.

She stared a moment more, then fell into a swoon. Mr Scott simply watched her fall, too numb to do anything else. I took a few quick steps up to the porch and got my arm around her waist just in time. I lowered her gently to the varnished floorboards, then turned around.

'Leroy, bring my bag,' I called.

Leroy got my bag and hurried up the walk. I found some smelling salts in one of the side pockets and held them to Mrs Scott's nose. After a minute, she revived. I helped her to her feet and we all walked down to the wagon.

At the wagon, they stared at their daughter. With a sudden agility I wouldn't have expected from a man his age, Howard Scott leaped on to the back and pulled the blanket away. He knelt next to Charlotte. I pitied the man.

'Charlotte?' he said. 'Charlotte, please.' He touched her cold cheek. 'Wake up...' His voice came out choked. 'Please, Charlotte,' he begged. 'Please wake up.'

He was racked by a violent sob. I felt my throat knotting. Death came when it would. Howard Scott's angel was gone. Mrs Scott began to cry. Bernice stared at her dead sister with that same frantic and unnerving grin on her face.

It took me much time and effort, but I finally got them inside the house. Leroy Armstrong and I carried Charlotte up to her bedroom. I glanced around the room. It was large, had a big bed with a wrought-iron bedstead, a roll-top writing desk, ornamental umbrellas and fans, plaster busts of favorite playwrights, two wicker rockers, a coat rack, and a wicker sofa covered with decorative pillows. Bric-a-brac crowded every surface. A bouquet of thirty yellow roses stood on top of the bureau. I read the attached card and saw that they were from Mr Herbert Early, the high school drama teacher; a way of showing his appreciation for her work in *Angel of the Glade*. She had a whole bookcase full of dime novels. Walter Scott's *Ivanhoe* lay open on her bed and a pair of pretty pink ballet slippers was draped around the bedpost. Binoculars hung from a hook next to the window.

I moved the Walter Scott aside. Leroy had the cadaver over his shoulder. He was a brute of a boy, and often carried hundred-pound sacks of threshed corn for his father at harvest time. I pulled the quilt aside.

We laid her on her bed. I took another look around the room. She would spend one last night here, among the treasures of her girl-hood, and then she would sleep for ever in the Cattaraugus Avenue Cemetery.

We were just getting ready to leave when I noticed a box of matches on her bedside table – noticed it because of the words sten-cilled along the side: 'Parthenon Theater. Proprietor, Arnold R. Murchison'. Arnold Murchison, the same man who'd supplied the sloe gin at the picnic tonight. I took the matches and slipped them into my pocket. I took them because of Charlotte's face –

41

pink, not blue. I took them because Charlotte's few swallows of Mr Murchison's sloe gin might have proved lethal.

The thought nagged. An accidental drowning?

Selma Kligerman sat like a piece of granite in the chair before me. She was an elderly and rotund widow, dressed in an old-fashioned bustle skirt made of black silk,.

'This won't hurt a bit,' I said, and poked her thumb with a sharp needle.

I took out my pocket watch and, dabbing at the edges of the small wound with a stiff piece of filter paper, recorded Mrs Kligerman's bleeding time. Her eyes bulged, unnaturally so, and she sweated profusely. As I watched the second hand on my pocket watch, I again thought of Charlotte Scott. A drowning? It didn't make sense. I continued to dab at the small bead of blood on Mrs Kligerman's thumb. Forcing my thoughts back to the matter at hand, I turned to Charles Kligerman, Mrs Kligerman's fifty-year-old son.

'Have you noticed a change in your mother's moods, Mr Kligerman?' I asked.

He thought for a moment. 'Well ... her nerves have been acting up a bit, doctor,' he said. 'She's always had bad nerves, but they're pecking away at her more than usual these days.'

'My nerves are perfectly fine,' snapped the

old woman.

I glanced at my watch. Her bleeding time had gone beyond normal. I stopped dabbing and fixed a bandage to the small wound. I then gave her a cloth to wipe the sweat from her brow.

'You have a goiter, Mrs Kligerman,' I said. They looked at me as if I'd just pronounced a death sentence. 'Now, now, it's not that serious. Goiters can be cured. You just have to give them time, and you have to look after them.' I got up from my chair, walked around my desk and took out my prescription pad. 'I'll write a script for tincture of potassium iodine. That should make it better. Take three drops, three times daily. I don't care how you take it. In a glass of water would be fine.' I scribbled out the prescription and handed it to her. 'You should start feeling better in a week.'

I continued to sit at my desk after the Kligermans had left, staring out of the window. Finally I got up, walked to the outer office, cranked the phone and had Viola White, the town operator, put me through to Edmund Wilson, the undertaker.

The Wilson Funeral Home occupied a large but not particularly well-kept wood-frame house on Talbot Lane. Edmund Wilson had built a stable out back, which looked just as run-down as the house and, as I rattled up the gravel drive, I saw three of his five black horses grazing in the pasture down by the canal. A boy of nine, one of Wilson's assistants, bowed to me as I reined in. I got down off the box and he took my horse and buggy to the back. I mounted the steps to the funeral home, went inside, and gave another assistant my calling card.

'Mr Wilson's expecting me,' I said.

The assistant gave my card a morose glance and said, 'Come this way, doctor.' He put the card on a silver tray. 'Mr Wilson's in the mortuary.'

He led me to the top of the basement stairs and let me find my own way down.

I found Mr Wilson in the mortuary, a large cellar room fitted with special electric lights and several extra drains.

Edmund Wilson was a short man, broom-pole thin, but had long arms and hands, which gave him an ape-like appearance. He was a little older than me, in his late forties, and was dressed in a white apron and rubber gloves.

'I'm much obliged, Mr Wilson,' I said.

'Not at all, doc.' I could see that he was curious. 'And what might we be looking for?' he asked. 'I'm not a pathologist, but I do take an interest.'

His assistant, an obese man in his thirties, looked at me from the far corner, where they had Charlotte Scott lying on the embalming table.

I hesitated. 'I'm not rightly sure yet, Mr Wilson,' I said. 'I'll know when we find it.'

I was introduced to Mr Wilson's assistant, Lloyd Pearson. He seemed competent, and was thoroughly professional in his manner and attitude. They pulled away the sheet. Charlotte Scott was still in her theatrical costume. Mr Wilson took a pair of scissors and clipped away the skirt of leaves and the lace-up bodice. I looked for marks of violence. I saw some bruises but, other than those, nothing. Edmund Wilson took a scalpel and made an incision in the femoral artery behind her left knee to drain her blood. When I saw the color of her blood I immediately told him to stop.

'Mr Pearson,' I said, 'tie off that incision with a tourniquet. I'm afraid we can't go any further.'

Her blood was bright pink. While Mr Pearson tied off the incision, I turned to Mr Wilson.

'Do you have a tube or anything?' I asked. 'Or a hose with a hand-pump? Something I can stick down her throat?'

He looked at me quizzically, wondering what I was up to.

'Sure,' he said. He went to a cabinet and came back with a small length of hose and a hand-pump. 'Here you go.'

I stuck the hose down her throat, angling it along her windpipe.

I was surprised. I expected large amounts of river water, even sand, but there wasn't much trace of either. I withdrew the hose and inched it down her esophagus to her stomach. And that's when the smell hit me. Bitter almonds, a smell I remembered well from toxicology classes at John Hopkins. Mr Wilson and Mr Pearson were both staring at me.

'Doc?' said Mr Wilson.

I glanced at the undertaker. 'I'm sorry, Mr Wilson, but we're going to have to postpone Charlotte's funeral a day or two,' I said. 'I'm afraid the poor girl's been murdered.'

FOUR

The Sheriff's Office was on Court Street, one of the few brick buildings in town. It had a covered porch with a tin roof, and globe lamps on either side of the door with the word 'POLICE' on each one. A watering trough stood just beyond the edge of the boardwalk. I hitched Pythagoras to the hitching post, climbed the steps and went inside.

Stanley Armstrong sat behind his desk, hunched over the blotter, writing a report with a fountain pen, clutching the pen tightly, his lips twisted to one side. Of the five cells lining the back, one was occupied. Rupert Scales, the town drunk, was sleeping it off again. Stanley glanced up at me. A tentative smile came to his lips, but just as quickly disappeared when he saw the look on my face.

'Stanley,' I said, 'she was murdered. Poisoned with cyanide.'

He stared at me, his pen still poised above his report, his blue eyes lifting above his half-frame spectacles, his mustache drooping like a main-mast sail in dead-calm.

'Are you sure?' he asked.

Out the window I saw Cecil Fray, the blacksmith, lead a freshly shod horse from his shed. I closed the door. The little bell above the door tinkled. I glanced at Rupert Scales, who was snoring away peacefully.

'Stanley, her skin was pink,' I said. I took off my bowler, withdrew a handkerchief and wiped my forehead. It was another hot day. 'Her skin should have been blue – or at least grey.' He put his pen down, folded his hands and gazed at me matter-of-factly, ready to listen. 'She should have been cyanosed,' I said. 'But she wasn't. So I called Edmund Wilson. Lucky I caught him before he started work on her.' I contemplated Stanley's uniform: dark blue serge with big brass buttons down the front. 'I had a look at her blood while I was at the funeral home. Pink as well. I stuck a tube down her throat. And that's when I knew for sure. I could smell it. Prussic acid, as plain as day.'

Stanley turned away, looked out the window where Cecil Fray led a second horse from his shed. He rubbed his chin with his knuckles. I could see his mind already working, trying to figure it out, planning what he had to do. I couldn't help thinking, as I gazed at my old friend, that with so much work already he was bound to exhaust himself with the Charlotte Scott murder.

'A poisoning,' he said, as if he had to test the idea. He shifted his pen to one side. 'A poisoning,' he repeated. He glanced at me in a glassy way. 'Is there any way you can...?' His lips stiffened and he nodded to himself, adjusting to the news. 'I mean, how much poison would it take? Is there any way you can quantify—'

'I've got tests,' I said. 'I've got chemicals in the lab...' I saw in Stanley's face wrinkles and creases I didn't remember from Cross Plains, when we'd been lawmen together. I don't think I'd ever seen him so tired. Yet he seemed entirely ignorant of his condition, ready to push himself to his last ounce of strength to solve this crime. 'Stanley, are you all right?'

He put his hands flat on his desk. 'Sure, sure,' he said. 'I'm fine. I guess I'm going to have to make room for this. I'll phone Camilla and tell her I won't be home tonight.' I didn't like this, that he should put aside his family life for his work, especially when he had a newborn baby daughter. 'We'll get Judge Norris to sign for an autopsy.' He stood up, all business now. 'I guess I got a lot of legwork to do. How many people do you reckon attended the picnic last night?'

I stared at my old friend, thinking how every second of his day was loaded with work, how I myself still had time, hadn't fully established my practice yet, how my doctoring took me all of four hours a day.

'Forty or fifty,' I said.

49

'Then I better saddle Tessabel and set to,' he said, walking over to the coat tree to get his hat. 'I'm much obliged, Clyde.'

Rupert Scales stirred in his cell, looked up at me and gave me a wave.

'Howdy, doctor,' he called.

'Howdy, Rupert,' I said. I grabbed Stanley by the arm. 'You're going to talk to forty or fifty people?' I asked.

'I'll need witnesses, Clyde,' he said. 'This one's going to take witnesses, so I better not be lazy about it. Whoever did it got her down to the river bank first, out of sight. At least that's what I figure. Maybe I'll ask Herbert Early to make a list. Maybe he saw someone go down to the river alone with her.'

'And you're just going to drop the Corn Mercantile burglary?' I asked.

'The murder of a young woman takes precedence over a burglary, Clyde.'

'Yes, I know but ... why don't you let me help you, Stanley? You look tuckered out. You look plain exhausted, and you're going to make yourself sick if you don't watch out. You let me help you. I wouldn't mind doing the whole thing myself, if you'll let me. A case like this needs a lot of time right at the beginning, if you don't want it to go cold.'

'Clyde, you've got your own burdens to bear,' he said. 'And it's been a while since you been a lawman.'

'It's not something you forget, Stanley,' I said. Rupert Scales sat up and stared at us, now interested in our conversation. 'I've got the time. You don't. And what about your new little girl? Just the other night you were telling me you had to make time for her.'

He stared at me, squinting. 'Are you suggesting I deputize you, Clyde?'

I stared back. Nothing so official had occurred to me. But I now thought it might be a good idea.

'Why not?' I asked.

I saw him thinking. Finally he folded his arms in front of his chest, took a deep breath and sighed with some relief, as if he were starting to see the sense of my offer.

'The county can't pay you much,' he said.

'I don't want anything,' I said. 'I just want to help you, Stanley. I want to give you and Camilla a chance to be together with your new little girl.'

'Are you sure, Clyde?' he asked. 'I won't deny it, I could use the help, and you might be the best man for this particular case. You got your fancy chemicals for finding this cyanide in her stomach, and you know a thing or two about poisons in general from your doctor schooling. But I can't help thinking it's been a bad time for you lately.' The air seemed to thicken between us. 'I can't help thinking you've had a hard go since President McKinley's assassination, and that it's been a big change for you, coming to Fairfield, and that maybe taking on a case like this—'

'Maybe it's just the thing I need,' I said.

He again stared at me, looking at my proposition from all sides now, being a good sheriff. Then he walked around to the front of his desk, opened his drawer, pulled out a badge and put it in front of me.

'OK,' he said at last. I stared at the badge, a five-point star of tarnished brass with the words 'Fairfield Police' engraved into the metal. 'But I'm much obliged. If you need my help, just say so.'

I took the badge and slipped it into my vest pocket.

'I won't disappoint you, Stanley,' I said. 'I'll find Charlotte's killer. You can count on it.'

The next day I informed Howard Scott about his daughter's murder, then showed him my badge. A glass of whiskey stood on the table beside him.

'But who would want to do such a thing to my poor Charlotte?' he asked, his voice frail, high. 'Everybody loved her.' He leaned forward, his face turning red. At first he looked puzzled, as if his daughter's poisoning were more than he could understand. But then he shoehorned the fact into his head, and the effect was instantaneous anger. 'If I could get my hands on whoever...'

But speech failed him, and his grief came on like a dark wave, bringing tears to his eyes. He looked beaten. I wondered if the drinking was something new, or if he always drank in the afternoon.

'There were some hoboes down by the river,' I said.

His shoulders jerked and his eyes blazed, and I could see I'd inadvertently given him some scapegoats he could cling to. I'd merely meant to suggest that the hoboes might have seen or heard something.

'Hoboes?' he said.

I raised my hands. 'Now hold on a minute, Mr Scott,' I said. 'All I meant was ... and we have to find them first.'

'Find them?' he said. 'Where have they gone?'

I shrugged. 'I guess they've moved on,' I said.

'Running, more like,' he said sullenly.

'No, not running,' I insisted. 'Let's not go pointing fingers just yet. Just because there happened to be a few hoboes down by the river at or around the time your daughter was murdered doesn't necessarily mean they're the ones who did it.'

'You think someone from around here did it?' he said, incredulous. 'There's no one around here would do such a thing to my sweet Charlotte.' He lifted his hands, using them to convey the innocence of Fairfield's inhabitants. 'I know the whole town.'

'That doesn't strike me as a good reason for singling out the nearest darn vagrant,' I said.

'I know, but they've gone, doc,' he said, his voice hardening, as if he thought I was a fool for not seeing the obvious. 'Why would they run off like that if they didn't kill Charlotte?' He lifted his whiskey, drank it in one gulp and settled a bit. He didn't seem to understand that the hoboes could have moved on for any number of reasons. Or that it was preposterous that they should kill the girl with cyanide. He didn't want to believe that one of his own neighbors might have killed Charlotte. 'They're running, doc, mark my words.' He seemed completely satisfied on this point. 'And the only reason they're running is because they killed Charlotte. We've got to track them down,' he said. 'And we've got to do it fast. Before they get too far.'

Because an autopsy precluded the original plan of an open-casket funeral – Charlotte's face wouldn't look exactly right after an autopsy – Howard Scott came to see his dead daughter one last time later that day. He showed no emotion, as if he had dried up inside. Edmund Wilson had dressed Charlotte in a plain white gown, had combed out her hair, and had folded her hands over her stomach. I gazed at her. She had full lips, wide cheek-bones and delicate eyebrows that were like strokes of artist's charcoal. She was a typical American beauty. As Howard Scott stared down at her, a puzzled look came to his face.

'Where's her locket?' he asked.

He looked up with blank eyes at Mr Wilson and his assistant, Mr Pearson, then turned to me. Though he was fifty years old, he looked like a schoolboy, blessed with a trusting ignorance.

'What locket?' I asked.

He blinked, the same way a horse headed for the glue factory might blink.

'The locket I gave her for her fourteenth birthday,' he said. 'She always wore it.' He turned to Mr Wilson. 'What have you done with it?'

Mr Wilson looked at Howard Scott sadly, as if the barber had gone mad.

'I haven't done anything with it, Howard,' he said. 'She wasn't wearing any locket.'

'Sure she was,' said Howard Scott. Around him floated a miasma of alcohol fumes. 'She wore it all the time. It had a Greek archer on it. She never took it off. Not in the three years she had it.'

I spoke up. 'Maybe it fell off in the river,' I said.

'Nope,' he said. 'She had to unclasp it to get it off her neck. The chain was only so long.' He turned back to Mr Wilson. 'Did you take it, Edmund? Did you pocket it for yourself?'

I stepped forward. 'Mr Scott, you're badly shook up,' I said. I rested my hand on his shoulder, but he pulled away.

'I'm not shook up,' he said. 'I just want to know what happened to her locket. It wasn't just some two-bit piece of junk, Dr Deacon. It was real jewelry. Cost me a month's wages. I had to travel all the way to Buffalo to get it. It had a fourteen-carat gold chain.' He looked at Edmund Wilson and Lloyd Pearson, his lower lip protruding, his shoulders rising, his forearms flexing. 'And I wouldn't feel right burying her without it, is all.'

I nursed a glass of bourbon as I sat alone in the surgery. The breeze coming through the window ruffled some papers on my desk. I was pensive, weary of human folly. The autopsy was over, and I was overwhelmed by the unexpected results.

'Charlotte Scott,' I said to myself, 'you are one complicated girl.'

Outside, a horse came to a stop in front of the surgery. The horse whinnied, but it was as if the sound came to me through a dream. Then I heard Stanley calling me from the front walk. I rose from my desk and, keeping my bourbon in hand, walked to the window. The wind bent the bridal lace out of the way, and in the winking of the electrical street lamps I saw the sheriff in his blue serge uniform and bobby hat; eastern police attire, so different from the stetson and riding chaps he'd worn in Cross Plains. I walked to the front door and opened it. The June air was warm, moist, and from my garden rose the sharp smell of marigolds.

Stanley approached me, waving. He was

shuffling. I'd never known Stanley to shuffle before. Would I shuffle when I turned forty-eight? Why did the fifth decade have to be so ruinous?

'You ought to eat more, Clyde,' said Stanley as he climbed the steps to the porch. 'You're wasting away.'

'I will when I find a cook,' I said.

I led him into the examining room, where I poured a glass of bourbon for him. He sat in one of my Windsor armchairs, held the glass up to the light and inspected it the way a jeweler might inspect a gem.

'The good stuff?' he asked.

I nodded. 'Ten dollars a keg,' I said.

He sniffed the bourbon, lifted the glass in my direction and said, 'Here's how.'

He drank it all, then looked at me. His eyes were keen, prepared, and for a moment I saw some of the old Stanley; the Stanley of Cross Plains, the Stanley who had the tempered strength of a new buckboard spring.

'So, was it cyanide?' he asked, as if eager to hear me confirm the worst.

I got up, walked to a shelf and lifted a beaker full of murky blue liquid.

'These are Charlotte's stomach contents,' I told him. 'I added this and that to them, chemicals to tag the cyanide, and the prussic acid's shown up this blue color.' I nodded at the beaker, impressed yet cowed by its potential danger. 'There's enough poison in here to kill everyone on Culver Street, and then some.'

This was the plain and obvious result of the autopsy, but by no means the most stunning. I walked back to my desk and sank into my chair. I put the beaker down and stared at it.

'What else?' asked Stanley.

Prussic acid, yes, but something else as well; a secondary result, one I now felt curiously shy about, as if I'd mistakenly blundered into a young girl's secret world and had to display what I'd found like crêpe dressing in a haberdasher's window. Stanley was now staring at me the same way he used to stare across the plains, his eyes no more than slits. I felt sad. I looked at him over the rim of my whiskey glass. The room seemed too bright. I took a sip of my whiskey. I looked out the window as thunder murmured far to the north-west. A storm was brewing over Lake Ontario.

'Stanley,' I said, 'the girl was three months pregnant.' I lifted my chin, took off my eyeglasses and watched pity steal over Stanley's face. Bad enough a seventeen-year-old girl should die, but the murder had reached to an unborn child. 'I found a dead little baby inside her,' I said. 'Looks like our killer actually killed two people instead of one.'

FIVE

The *Fairfield Newspacket* had a story about Charlotte's murder the next day. As I sat in my parlor sipping my morning coffee I grew dismayed by the paper's vigilante tone. It quoted Howard Scott extensively. Scott spoke of the 'dastardly vagrants' who'd been under the bridge, told the *Newspacket* that a 'sheriff's posse' should be organized right away to catch these 'no-good fiends' and that any trains passing through Fairfield should be checked for 'rail-riding hoboes'. The perpetrators of this 'heinous crime' had actually had the 'audacity' to steal Charlotte's locket.

Sheriff Stanley Armstrong was quoted as well. He explained to the *Newspacket* that Dr Clyde Deacon had 'valiantly volunteered' to investigate the crime, that the doctor's knowledge of poisons, as well as his previous law enforcement experience, made him ideally suited, adding that in the recent Cuban conflict I'd single-handedly 'neutralized' an artillery position on San Juan Hill. Sad as Charlotte Scott's murder seemed, I couldn't help thinking, as I stirred another lump of sugar into my coffee, that this newspaper story might harm my investigation more than help it.

Several other sources were quoted as well, mostly high school students who'd been at the river the night of Charlotte's murder. Horace Muncner, treasurer of the chess club, reported 'three unsavory fellows' under the bridge, while Jennifer Price, president of the senior choir, said she'd seen a whole camp of gypsies, 'thirty or forty at least!' The *Newspacket* was more interested in printing hyperbole and sensationalism than getting the facts straight, and I was afraid that as I untangled my case my greatest enemy might be the unwitting ignorance of Fairfield's townfolk.

At noon, after a morning of patients, I rode my bicycle to Fairfield High School and arrived just as the lunch bell rang. The squat two-storey structure made from red brick had ivy climbing up the sides and a steepled bell tower where the tarnished bell lurched back and forth as it rang. The bike rack was a tangle of bikes both old and new. The maple trees were in thick leaf.

I climbed the flagstone steps and entered through the main doors. The corridors were crowded – town youngsters heading home for lunch, farm youngsters bustling to the lunchroom with satchel bags. A sign told me that all visitors should report to the main office, but I'd arranged a discreet meeting with Mr Herbert Early in his classroom.

When I got to his classroom, Mr Early wasn't there.

'Can I help you, doctor?' a voice called behind me.

I turned around. It was Prudence Gooderham, the grade ten teacher. She was around thirty, wore a pale green skirt and a shirtwaist with puff sleeves, and had her hair pinned above her ears in the popular fashion. She'd made her own attempt at the Gibson Girl, only she was too tall, too meager around the hips to successfully emulate the feminine ideal of our modern age. Despite her relative youth she reminded me of a dried out bundle of sticks. She was, I believe, a born spinster, coping silently and stoically with her eternal loneliness.

'Afternoon, Miss Gooderham,' I said. 'I have a meeting with Mr Early in his classroom at twelve.' I pulled my pocket watch from my vest. 'I believe I'm a little late. I've had a busy morning at the surgery.'

'Mr Early's in a meeting with the school trustees just now,' said Miss Gooderham. She glanced down the corridor toward the teacher's parlor and gave her hands an excited but nervous rub. 'And I think the news is good.'

My eyebrows rose. 'How so?' I asked.

A playful look came to her eyes. 'You've not heard, then, Dr Deacon?'

'Not a thing,' I said.

From down the corridor a group of grade

61

nine girls shrieked in sudden laughter.

'Principal Small retires at the end of this month,' she said. 'The trustees have been considering several replacements. Mr Early is one of those under consideration.' Her eyes grew earnest and she clasped her hands together in nervous anticipation. 'He may be young, but he's ever so dedicated. He's been working hard for this. Fairfield is one of the most prestigious high schools in Genesee County. He's had his eye on this post ever since he came here five years ago. If anybody deserves it, Herbert Early does.'

Her enthusiasm was infectious. Nothing pleased me more than good news. I took out a calling card and handed it to Prudence Gooderham.

'Then maybe you can let him know I was here.'

'He insisted you wait,' she said. 'He said he didn't think he would be long.'

'Well...'

She took me by the elbow and led me into the classroom.

'You sit anywhere you like,' she said. 'We all understand the importance of what you're doing. I believe you wanted a list of those in attendance at the midnight picnic on Thursday night.'

'Yes,' I said, sitting in the first desk of the first row.

'Let me see...' She fussed among the papers on Herbert Early's desk. 'I don't see it,' she said. 'But if you could just wait a few minutes ... I know you must be terribly busy ... but this meeting with the trustees, it was entirely unexpected.'

'I suppose I could wait a little while,' I said. 'And you don't have to go bothering for me so much, Miss Gooderham.'

'I'm sorry, but I do feel ... a little breathless...' She glanced at the classroom door and an odd light came to her eyes. 'I feel so happy for Herbert.' I was surprised by her sudden familiarity with Mr Early's Christian name. She rubbed her hand absently along the back of his mahogany chair, seeming to forget that I was in the room. 'Forgive me, Dr Deacon ... but if you understood just what this means to Mr Early, how he's been longing for it, how he's devoted himself to it, you might more readily understand the suspense I'm at present forced to endure.'

'I understand completely, Miss Gooderham.'

I wasn't at all sure what Miss Gooderham's stake in Mr Early's appointment could be, but by the way she was acting it seemed considerable.

'I'll just trot down to the staff parlor and see how they're getting on,' she said.

She left the classroom.

I contemplated my surroundings. The high school was far different from the one-room schoolhouse in Clifford's Bend, Tennessee I'd attended as a boy. I remembered the

63

benches and the dirt floor, and the slate tablets we learned our lessons on. I remembered the school-marm, Miss Reyburn, a slight young girl who wore her reddish hair in braids, tied with blue ribbons, and whom I fell in love with long before I learned my alphabet. Then came the Civil War, and my father took me out of school and hired private tutors for me. He was a man of means, with considerable land. But all that was lost when the South fell.

I heard footsteps out in the corridor. Herbert Early appeared at the door. He was smiling from ear to ear.

'I think the news is good,' I said, rising.

'Capital news, doctor,' he said, 'simply capital.'

He shook my hand vigorously. I allowed my wrist to be rattled about in its socket.

'Congratulations, Mr Early,' I said.

He let go of my hand and surveyed me with irrepressible confidence. 'I dare say, Dr Deacon, if anybody deserves it, I do,' he said. 'I don't think there's been a single teacher in the history of the school who's had a better rapport with the students. Education's more than just the teaching of the curriculum. It's about finding the best in your students. It's about encouragement and intelligent direction.'

'A noble philosophy, Mr Early, and I wish you the best of luck with it.'

He glowed. This was his day, and he didn't

see any reason to be humble about it. I glanced at the clock above the blackboard. I prodded Mr Early.

'If I could get that list from you, Mr Early,' I said.

He became an engine of efficiency. He marched over to the filing cabinet, opened the top drawer, and came back with a two-page list, the names written in his own cursive script.

'Here you are, doctor,' he said. 'I hope you find it useful. The names on this first page are students.' I glanced down at twenty-two names, then flipped to the second page. 'The names on that second page, well, that's everybody else. At least, everybody else I can remember. There were a lot of people there, so I'm sure I've missed a few.'

Two names on this second page had been put into a separate column: Arnold Murchison and Frank Jaslowski. I of course recognized Arnold Murchison's name, still had the box of matches bearing it from Charlotte's room, but I was unfamiliar with Frank Jaslowski.

'Who's this man you've got circled with Murchison?' I asked.

Mr Early glanced at the names. 'Frank Jaslowski. He works for Murchison.'

'At the Parthenon Theater?'

'Yes.'

'I don't think I've passed by there yet.'

A wry grin came to Mr Early's face. 'It's

not a particularly reputable theater, Dr Deacon,' he said. 'I'm afraid they present all manner of ragtime and vaudeville.' His grin broadened. 'Even some burlesque. But Mr Murchison is generous whenever I mount a school production, and possesses theatrical expertise, of a sort, even if it's purely technical. He helped me find a bargain on the new electric footlights. And he gives me all the pancake and make-up I need.'

'Isn't that dandy?' I said. 'And this name over here? Richard Lip?'

'He was one of the hoboes under the bridge. The only one I recognized.'

'Lip,' I said. 'That's an odd name.'

'He's Chinese,' said Mr Early. 'He's been haunting Fairfield for years now.'

'Chinese, you say.' I folded the list and put it into my bag. 'I thought you might have time to answer a few questions,' I said.

'Of course, doctor.'

'I hate being crude, but I was wondering if you might shed some light on ... on Charlotte Scott's various ... her various *amours*, as the French say. That is, if she had any you knew about. The Scotts are too upset to talk about Charlotte just now, and I was hoping you might know something.'

I was thinking of Charlotte's secret pregnancy. In my experience as a lawman in Cross Plains I'd learned a most distressing fact: sweethearts often killed each other. So my line of questioning was entirely reasonable. Mr Early's brow settled and he folded his hands on the blotter. He stared at a plaster of Paris human skull on the desk. Was this poor Yorick?

'Charlotte was a pretty girl,' he began, 'but not the prettiest girl in the school. There are perhaps three or four others whom...' He looked at me with that wry grin again. I knew what that grin meant. We were men; we were talking about the charms of a young woman. 'But if she wasn't the prettiest, she was certainly the most willing.' I took his meaning clearly. 'I'm not exactly sure how many young men she's gone with ... but I'm sure if we were to count them, our number would be in the double digits.'

'And were there any...' I struggled to find the least offensive words, '...did she ever have any serious suitors?'

Mr Early gazed up at the ceiling, thinking for a moment.

'She had a childhood sweetheart, Morley Suggett,' he said. 'A great lug of a farm boy who lives out in West Shelby. His father took him out of school last year and I guess that's when he and Charlotte stopped seeing each other.'

'Was he at the picnic last Thursday?' I asked. 'I didn't see his name on the list.'

'No,' said Mr Early, 'he wasn't.'

I nodded. 'Did she have any other young fellas who liked her?' I asked.

'I believe she was more than moderately

entangled with Michael Sims.'

My brow furrowed. 'Michael Sims?' I said. 'I'm sorry, I'm not familiar with—'

'He's a clerk at the Exchange Bank,' said Mr Early. 'A slight young man, he couldn't weigh more than ninety-five pounds soaking wet. You'll see him sometimes walking through the Green with his nose stuck in a book. I believe Charlotte and he were an item this past ... this past March, I think. But that's ancient history, at least in a school-girl's life. And then more recently there's been Roger Robson.'

'Roger Robson?' I was surprised. 'Wilbert Robson's son?' I thought of young Mr Robson's tawny good looks, his devil-may-care attitude, how he'd pointed out Howard Scott to me with casual disdain the night of Charlotte's performance. 'I can't see him with a barber's daughter. Not with all that money.'

'Roger Robson's a rogue,' said Mr Early. 'You can't imagine how delighted I was when he finally matriculated.'

'And do you think Miss Scott and Mr Robson were...' I looked at the globe of the world that sat in the corner. I had to press on. I had to blunder through a young girl's secret world. 'Do you think they knew each other in the ... the Biblical sense?'

The color rose in Mr Early's face. 'Good heavens, how should I know?' he said. 'But look around you, Dr Deacon,' he said, gesturing out the window, where across the playing-field I saw the pretty white wood-frame houses of Talbot Lane and Garden Street climb the slope beyond the river. 'You think you see an innocent small town basking in the sunshine. But even in Fairfield we have our share of teenage girls who ruin themselves.' He shook his head. 'Not that Charlotte was a girl who...' A frown came to his brow. 'In many ways, she was a difficult girl. I'm not sure if I ever entirely understood her.' I couldn't help thinking of Mr Early's yellow roses in Charlotte's bedroom. 'And I don't mean just in her ... her *amours*, as you call them. She was demanding. I might even say she was headstrong and manipulative. As for *Angel of the Glade* ... well, sir, I should be awarded the Medal of Honor for my patience. Whether she knew Roger Robson in the way you're suggesting, I just don't know.'

'Was Roger Robson actually serious about her?' I asked.

He pressed his hands flat against the table. 'Not likely,' he said. 'Roger Robson's not a serious fellow. When you first meet him you admire his charm and wit, but then you realize he's a creature of whim. Not only that, he likes the girls, Dr Deacon. Charlotte wasn't his first, and she won't be his last.'

'And Roger Robson was at the picnic Thursday night?'

'Yes.'

I now tried to establish some possibilities.

'Did Mr Robson at any time go down to the river alone with Charlotte Scott last Thursday night?' I asked.

Mr Early glanced out the back window, where a few pigeons preened themselves on the ledge, and where, through the lofty greenness of the elder trees, I saw the spire of the Congregationalist Church thrusting skyward.

'Not that I recall,' he said.

'Did anybody at all go down to the river with Charlotte Scott alone?' I asked.

He tugged absently on his left mutton-chop side-whisker. He continued to gaze past my shoulder. 'No, not that I recall,' he said.

'Think, Mr Early,' I said. 'This is important.'

Two warm spots of pink climbed into his smooth cheeks.

'No,' he said. 'I'm afraid I didn't see anything untoward, Dr Deacon.' An apologetic grin came to his face. He leaned back in his chair. 'I wish I could help you, I really do, but I honestly didn't see anything even remotely sinister.'

So I left him. I went over the names in my head. Morley Suggett, the lug of a farm boy, Charlotte's childhood sweetheart. Michael Sims, the clerk at the Exchange Bank, the man with his nose in a book. Roger Robson, son of the richest man in town, a rogue and a rascal. Would any of them turn out to be

70

suspects? What about Arnold Murchison, the owner of the Parthenon Theater? And the man who worked for him, Frank Jaslowski? Finally, there was Richard Lip, the Chinese hobo. Did he hear or see anything on the night of Charlotte's murder?

Charlotte Scott's funeral was held the next day at the Fairfield Congregationalist Church on Park and Court Streets. The Reverend Eric Porteous officiated, and in attendance were not only Mayor Henry Vanduzen and Mrs Vanduzen, but also many of the town's most prominent citizens. So deep an impression had the murder of Charlotte Scott made on the town that the church was seated to capacity. A crowd of several hundred more, many of them high school students, paid their last respects from the granite steps outside, despite the continuing rain. I saw Arnold Murchison in the crowd, recognized him now, dressed in a Sunday suit that looked ten years out of date. I saw Mr Herbert Early escorting his wife Alice in a wheelchair. Stanley Armstrong was there, and so were his three regular deputies, Ernie Mulroy, Raymond Putsey, and Donal Loughlin. I saw the Robsons. I saw Prudence Gooderham, the grade ten teacher. I saw practically everyone, but I couldn't see the person I was looking for. I couldn't see Olive Wade, the midwife.

The service ended and Edmund Wilson's

assistants bore the casket to the hearse. The four black horses stood waiting on Riverside Drive, their coats gleaming in spite of the rain. Mr Wilson's assistants, dressed in stove-pipe top hats, morning coats, and freshly blacked boots, eased the casket into the hearse. The hearse had brass fittings, glass sides, and black crêpe trim. Mr and Mrs Scott were led out by Mrs Scott's sister, Mrs Beulah Frith. The barber was bent double, and tears streamed down his cheeks. Mrs Frith held an umbrella over the stricken man's neatly pomaded head. I felt my own eyes clouding with tears. Here was death's sad parade again.

As I left the church, I looked around. Olive Wade was nowhere in sight. I got on my bicycle and followed the procession across the river and down Cattaraugus Avenue toward the cemetery, slaloming around the puddles, careful not to mire myself in the treacherous gravel at the side of the road. At the cemetery, among a multitude of black umbrellas, mourning dresses, top hats, bowlers, and bonnets, I finally spied Olive Wade standing next to Mr Everett Howse, son of Mr and Mrs Daniel Howse. The Howses owned the Exchange Bank, where Michael Sims worked. Everett Howse was a junior assemblyman in Albany. Miss Wade wore a mourning bonnet with lace, and a mourning spray of black satin flowers. Though her face was suitably composed, I found it nonetheless ravishing. She was holding Mr Howse's arm. I couldn't understand why Mr Howse was here. Didn't the State government still have another week before its summer recess? He was certainly no intimate of the Scott family. He was impeccably dressed. Yet to wear a Prince Albert suit to a funeral, even if it was in black wool, struck me as badly overdone. His sidewhiskers were affected, and he was far too young to wear a monocle. I turned away. I didn't know why Miss Wade had her hand resting on Mr Howse's arm. I took an instant dislike to the man. And I realized that for the first time in as long as I could remember, I was actually jealous.

I watched the Scott family gather at the graveside. I looked at Bernice Scott, Charlotte's sixteen-year-old sister. She was the only one in the crowd who wasn't wearing black. Instead she wore violet. An assortment of artificial bluebells and forget-me-nots adorned her pie-plate hat, and she had a violet shawl around her shoulders to protect her from the rain. The hem of her violet skirt was wet from dragging through the grass. She wore a camera around her neck, one of the new Kodak 'Brownies'; an odd, even inappropriate, accessory. Who took pictures at funerals? She touched the camera nervously, as if it were a talisman.

I was just moving closer when I felt someone tap my elbow. I turned around and beheld Olive Wade.

'I saw you standing here by yourself,' she said, 'and I thought I might...'

She stopped. I was both delighted and mortified to see her. I fumbled for words.

'Can Mr Howse bear to part with you?' I asked, casting a glance at the junior assembly-man.

My words were ill-chosen.

'Indeed, he could not,' she said. 'But Mr Howse should attend to his parents. They hardly ever see him.'

Her voice thrilled me with its quiet rectitude and confidence. Her bearing was as regal as ever. Yet beneath her composure I now detected that same fragility I'd noted on the night of Charlotte's murder. I couldn't help wondering if Charlotte Scott's funeral had brought to mind yet again the all-too-recent passing of her aunt and parents. The wealthy heiress from Boston had her sad moments.

'Have you known Mr Howse long?' I asked, using a bland and formulaic enquiry I felt embarrassed about even as it left my lips.

She glanced toward the graveside, where the Reverend Eric Porteous prepared to deliver the final blessing.

'The Howses have been very kind to me,' she said.

I didn't think I'd ever seen such fine skin or such spell-binding blue eyes.

'Doesn't Mr Howse spend most of his time

74

in Albany?' I asked.

She glanced at me with a beguiling grin. 'You seem inordinately concerned with Everett Howse.'

'He seems a familiar fellow.' I was unable to stop myself.

'And you object to that?' she said, still with that grin on her face.

I tried to moderate my tone. 'He doesn't strike me as serious,' I said, 'that's all. I wonder what suffering his wife might put up with.'

'Oh ... but Mr Howse isn't married.'

I felt my cheeks warming. 'And his parents let him prowl the female population of New York State freely?' I attempted a joke.

'You shouldn't have such an uncharitable view of the man.'

She seemed truly amused by my discomfiture.

'On the contrary, Miss Wade,' I said, 'I'm being as charitable as I can.'

The Reverend Eric Porteous began his final blessing by the graveside. Throughout the whole length of the blessing – and with Eric Porteous, these things ran full measure – I kept taking furtive glances at Miss Wade. What could be said about her character? She was forthright. Brazenly honest. Intelligent. Playful. All the things I'd found most charming about my poor dead Emily. At last Eric Porteous finished. I noticed Miss Wade staring at somebody.

'Who are you looking at?' I asked.

I followed her gaze.

'I'm looking at Roger Robson,' she said. I contemplated the young man with interest. A rakish lock of light brown hair hung like an inverted question mark over his broad forehead. He seemed bored by the funeral. 'And I'm thinking how sad it is that he hasn't shed a single tear over Charlotte.'

When the funeral was over, and Olive Wade had ridden off with the Howses, I walked my bike through the rain up to the Talbot Lane footbridge. I kept thinking about Miss Wade, trying not to make too much of the way she had sought me out at the funeral, or how she had teased me so gently about Mr Everett Howse. But as I walked past the old yew trees just immediately before the footbridge, with the rain coming down steadily, I couldn't help thinking that Stanley might be right, that whenever Miss Wade was around my eyes went wide like silver dollars, as if I'd never seen a female human being before, and that I was, in fact, smitten by her.

SIX

I was just putting the newspaper aside the next morning when I heard pounding on the surgery door. Not knocking, not tapping, but pounding, as if Paul Bunyan himself stood out there. I put my coffee down, pulled on my corduroy vest, took off my eyeglasses, and went to the hall to answer the door.

The man standing there was well over six feet tall, had broad muscular arms, a large flat face, a square jaw, small blue eyes, and bunches of straw-colored hair sprouting from beneath the brim of a farm hat. He looked about nineteen, wore blue dungarees, a checkered shirt, and had the smell of horses about him. Hitched to the post out front was a large brown dray.

'Are you Dr Deacon?' he asked. His voice had a flat country twang to it.

'I am,' I said.

He nodded gruffly. 'The sheriff says you ain't caught them hobo fellers who kilt Charlotte Scott yet. He says yer looking after it.'

He was red-faced and sweating, looked as

if he were angry with the whole world. He could have been the Strong Man from the Ringling Brothers' Circus. The sleeves of his shirt were far too short for his thick arms and his left leather boot had a hole in the toe, revealing a besmirched red sock.

'And who are you?' I asked.

He drew back, affronted, as if I should know who he was. His chin dipped and he gazed at me as if he didn't know what to make of me. Then he seemed to remember his manners and took off his hat.

'My name's Morley Suggett, sir,' he said. 'I'm Luke Suggett's son? We got a hunnert acres out by West Shelby. We grow the best corn in the county.'

So this was Morley Suggett, Charlotte Scott's childhood sweetheart. I stared at him. I now vaguely recalled Morley Suggett. On Sundays, crammed into a black suit, he passed a big silver collection plate from pew to pew in the Fairfield Congregationalist Church.

'Mr Suggett, my investigation has just begun and I—'

'The more time you give them hobo fellers to get away, the harder it'll be to catch them.'

I heard a great deal of animosity in his voice. I was polite but firm. I thought my best course was simply to ease Morley Suggett from my doorstep as kindly as I could. Now was not the time to ask him any questions. He looked as wound up as a spool of thread.

'Mr Suggett, I understand you were Charlotte's close friend, and I'm sorry about her demise, but rest assured, I'm doing everything I can to apprehend her killer.'

I gave him a smile, tried to close my door, but he pushed it open.

'Not by giving them hobo fellers a big head start, you ain't,' he said. 'I aim to see them vagrants brought to justice. And we ain't never going to bring 'em to justice if we don't get a move on and catch 'em.'

Then, to my great surprise, he turned from me, as if suddenly he didn't have the wherewithal to face me any more. Tears sprang to his eyes like water from two artesian wells. I had the sense I was witnessing not so much a farm boy breaking down as a calamitous act of nature. His shoulders heaved, the way a mountain might heave just before a landslide. His face contorted, and a great sob escaped from his thin lips, a bellowing sound, thick and primordial, terrifying in its rawness.

'Mr Suggett?' I said.

He looked at me. 'I was her beau,' he said, his voice now small, whelpish.

'Yes, I realize that, but...'

I must confess, I was at a loss. I didn't know what to do with him. I knew there was nothing I could say to make him feel better, but I tried anyway.

'Miss Scott's passing was sad for everyone,

Mr Suggett,' I said.

He screwed up his eyes. A mean look came to his face, as if he thought it was my fault. Under other circumstances, I might have been offended. But I saw Morley Suggett needed kindness.

'Then are you going to raise a posse or ain't you?' he asked. 'I got half the fellers in West Shelby rustled up and ready to go.'

This was rural America. Even a place as settled as Genesee County needed an occasional posse, especially when regular constabulary in such places consisted of no more than five or six men. But the posse as a tool of rural law enforcement had always made me nervous, and though through the years I'd organized dozens of them in Cross Plains, I always felt it was like giving a loaded revolver to a four-year-old child. Sometimes I got lucky and the posse behaved itself. More likely, the apprehended fugitive wound up dead.

'I don't rightly believe a posse would be the best course just now, Mr Suggett,' I said.

He leaned forward, the largeness of his head blocking out the sky. 'Well ... the town can wait just so long, doctor.' He'd put his hands on his hips, his chin dipping in a quick chop of a nod, as if the common sense of what he was saying were indisputable. 'You need a posse, Dr Deacon, that's a fact, and sooner or later you're going to get one.'

★ ★ ★

The following day I went to Wiley's Drug Store.

The young clerk, Bruce Farrow, had gone to fetch Mr Wiley. I stood by the soda fountain looking around. Gordon Wiley ran a well-stocked establishment, and as a doctor I'd grown to trust his ability as a chemist over the last month or two. He was superbly organized and kept catalogues of every medicine available. Over and above those dubious tonics of cocaine and alcohol, he stocked medicines I'd found to be truly effective. The marble counter-tops gleamed. Bottles of Paine's Celery Compound were lined up like soldiers behind the dispensary wicket. Boxes of Wine of Cardui stood shoulder to shoulder with jars of Aruica Salve and cartons of Carter's Little Nerve Pills. The globe lamps were of the softest pink. The soda fountains sparkled and the smell of fresh-brewed coffee hung in the air.

Gordon Wiley emerged from the storeroom with a leather-bound inventory book in his hand.

'Sorry to keep you waiting, doc,' he said. 'I'm just going through the inventory now.' He turned to his clerk. 'Say, Bruce, why don't you rustle up Doc Deacon a lime soda. It's a mighty hot day out there, and he looks as if he could use some refreshment.'

I gave him a small bow. 'I thank you kindly, sir.'

'Oh, now, doc, you don't have to be quite

so courtly with me,' said Mr Wiley. 'Though I suppose growing up on a plantation you're used to courtly manners.'

As Mr Wiley continued going through his inventory book, Bruce came back with my lime soda. I took a long, deep drink. Mr Wiley was right. The day was warm and I was wearing my thick professional coat and my black bowler. I sighed in gratification as the drink's effervescence lifted my spirits.

'Now, then,' I said, 'd'you have a sample?'

He looked up from his inventory book.

'If you'd come right this way, doc,' he said.

He led me to the prescriptions cabinet at the back.

'I keep it in here,' he said, opening the cabinet.

He produced for me a four-ounce vial of Scheele's Prussic Acid, a cyanide compound used externally for the treatment of varicose veins. I no longer prescribed the treatment myself, finding it of little benefit, but several doctors, including my competitor, Dr Olaf Thorensen, did. Mr Wiley took a pencil from behind his ear and, tapping each vial, began counting them off.

'...nine, ten, eleven,' he counted. 'They come in boxes of fifteen.' He looked down at his inventory book. 'So I've sold...' But he trailed off as his brow furrowed. Then he looked at the vials and counted them again. He stared at the vials then looked down at his book. 'Wait a minute ... according to my inventory, I should still have twelve vials in here. But there's one missing.' He turned around. 'Hey, Bruce, you ain't sold none of this prussic acid without marking it down, have you?'

The boy shook his head. 'No, sir.'

Wiley straightened his shoulders. He was a full-chested man, about thirty-five, square-jawed, wearing a plaid bow-tie and plaid suspenders. His white shirt was crisply starched.

'I don't never make a mistake like this, doc,' he said. 'Isn't that the dangdest thing?' He counted the vials again, tapping each of them with a swing of his pencil. 'Now let me see. If I remember correctly ... there was Clara Cox, I think she's one of Doc Thorensen's patients, lives over on Ontario Street ... and then there was Melba Kennicott, she's got the veins bad, her legs are nearly purple with them ... and then there was...' He tapped his pencil against his lips. 'Oh, yeah, there was Mr Early, from the high school, bought some for his wife.'

This was indeed interesting. 'Mr Herbert Early, the drama teacher?' I asked.

'Yes indeed, sir,' he said. 'He was in here a week ago Monday. I got the date written down in my book.'

'And his wife suffers from varicose veins?'

He smiled pleasantly. 'I wouldn't know, doc,' he said. 'I'm not acquainted with his wife's legs. But everyone knows she's sickly.'

'And was this the first time Mr Early bought the Scheele's?' I asked.

'As far as I recall.'

I thought for a moment.

'And you have no idea what happened to the other vial?' I asked. 'The one that's missing?'

He looked down at his inventory book. 'I'm not sure,' he said. 'But this was shipped by Villar and Pouncer in Cleveland, and they've been known to ship short before. I reckon that's what happened. I just wrote fifteen vials down without opening the carton. I'm real careful with the stuff. It's always locked in this cabinet and no one can get at it without asking for it first.'

I found Roger Robson and some of his friends hanging around the thin elm tree in front of the Arlington Avenue Cigar and Gift Shop smoking cigarettes and drinking bottled cola, a regular gang of dandies ranging in age from seventeen to twenty, all dressed in cuffed trousers, straw boaters, and loosely knotted ties. Roger had a pair of fancy dongolas on his feet. As I rode up on my bicycle his back was toward me. He leaned against the tree, his legs crossed in a careless pose of ease, a cigarette dangling from his fingertips. I rang my bell. He turned around, saw me, and immediately dropped his cigarette. He crushed it into the ground. Roger was the tallest among this swank crew. They slinked their hips this way and that as I got off my bicycle. Some put thumbs through belt loops while others slid hands into pockets. All composed their faces into expressions of insolence or boredom; all except Roger, who strode toward me, a toothy smile on his face. I was, after all, his father's doctor.

'Hello, doc,' he said. 'A mighty fine day for cycling. The fellas and me are just hanging around watching the girls go by in the Green.'

He waved a lazy hand at the town common across the street. The large park sloped gently toward the river, and was in fact the field from which Fairfield had derived its name. Several young women strolled along the walkways holding umbrellas or parasols above their heads to protect them from the sun. I saw a few row-boats on the river. The opposite bank rose sharply to Cattaraugus Avenue. Puffy white clouds floated in the sky, their undersides tufted with wisps of grey.

'You've got yourself a nice spot of shade here,' I said.

'Say, doc, you're not going to tell my father about that cigarette, are you?'

I pondered his bonny vacuous face. His teeth continued to gleam at me.

'I wouldn't think of it,' I said.

He nodded. 'Thanks,' he said. 'I like a good smoke now and again. Care for one?'

'I prefer a cigar,' I said.

'I suppose there's nothing like a good cigar, too. My mama says a cigar can cure a bad case of catarrh.' Athena Robson had her own notions of medicine, most of them bizarre. I pulled out the badge Stanley Armstrong had given me. Even the dazzling sunlight couldn't seem to diminish the badge's brassy darkness.

'You knew about this, didn't you?' I said. 'You knew I was looking into Charlotte's murder.'

The smile remained pasted to his face, but I sensed a dimming of his eyes.

'My father told me,' he said.

'I hate to spoil your afternoon,' I said, slipping the badge back into my pocket, 'but why don't we go for a stroll so we can have a pow-wow about poor Charlotte?'

He glanced at his friends. 'You fellas wait for me,' he called. 'The doctor and me are taking a walk.'

As we walked out on to the grass the heat intensified, and the smell of the fresh-cut lawn thickened around us. Two young women walked by, tugging along a cocker spaniel. They glanced at Roger, and then giggled, as if the nearness of such a handsome charmer were cause for nervous hilarity. Roger stared after them, put his fingertips to the brim of his hat, nodded toward them, and then slid his hands into his back pockets.

86

'I swear, we got more female beauty in this town than we have in the whole state,' he said.

'Roger, I understand you and Charlotte were...' High above the cemetery I saw a hawk circling on a warm updraft. 'That you had an attachment of sorts,' I said.

He looked at me speculatively. 'An attachment?' He kicked a clump of cut grass out of the way. 'I don't know about that, doc,' he said. 'I bought her sodas, I took her for rides in my dad's motor car, and we had some picnics together.' His hands came out of his back pockets. 'But an attachment?' He shook his head, baffled by the word. 'I don't know.' The hawk disappeared behind the rim of the hill. 'We had this ... I don't know what you'd call it.' His shoulders sagged. 'She was a real gay bird, doc, that's all.'

I had to peck away cautiously. I didn't want to scare him off with my suspicions.

'Was she in trouble of any kind?' I asked. 'Did she ever tell you something that didn't sound quite right?'

He had to think about this. He curved his right hand into a claw, nestled it into his left palm, and cracked a few knuckles. A young married couple pushed a baby carriage over the grass toward the bandstand.

'She lived for trouble, doc,' he said finally. And he cracked his knuckles some more.

'Any trouble in particular?' I asked.

He stopped cracking and stared at me.

87

'I think Mr Early might be the one to ask,' he said.

'Mr Early?'

A frank grin came to his face. 'Love blossoms in the strangest places, don't it, doc?' He let me infer what I might from this. I couldn't help thinking of the thirty yellow roses Mr Early had sent to Charlotte. 'Whether you'd call it trouble, I don't know. Mr Early has people in New York. Some cousins who live in New Rochelle. And Charlotte wanted to go to New York. You know ... the acting. She wanted to go to school there. She thought Mr Early might help her.'

I stared at him. 'And that's trouble?' I said.

He glanced over his shoulder. We continued to walk. The smile slipped from Roger's face as he gathered his thoughts.

'Mr Early's the nicest man in the world,' he said. 'But I expect he gets lonely now and again. And Charlotte ... well ... you know ... she wanted to go to New York...'

I grasped his meaning clearly.

'But Mr Early's a married man,' I said.

'Have you met his wife?' he asked.

I was unprepared for the casual cruelty I heard in Roger's voice. 'I haven't had the pleasure,' I said.

'You have to wonder how a reasonably handsome man like Herbert Early wound up with someone like Mrs Early.' On the river before us, a mallard duck skidded to a stop among some water lilies. 'She's stuck in that wheelchair all the time.' He shrugged. 'She's as plain as they come. And then there's Charlotte.'

I could see how Mr Early, struggling all these years with a sick wife, might in a moment of weakness let down his guard, especially when he was surrounded all the time by young female students. When we finally came to the river's edge, I asked Roger, 'Weren't you jealous?'

'Of what?' he said.

'Of Mr Early.'

'I'm too young to be jealous,' he said. 'I had my fun with Charlotte, that's all I ever wanted.'

My face settled. 'Did you ruin her?' I asked bluntly.

He found the question amusing. 'Doc, we're living in the modern age.'

I stopped. 'You don't have to worry, Roger, I won't tell your father.'

He shrugged indifferently. 'There was nothing there to ruin,' he said. 'The road was well traveled long before I ever got there.'

I found the notion monstrous. 'Let's go back to the night of the picnic,' I said. 'When did you get to the river?'

'Oh ... about ten thirty,' he said. 'Just after the play.'

'And did you go swimming?'

'I was the first one in. Nothing makes the ladies strip faster than the prospect of a midnight swim.'

He reckoned himself an expert, and was quick to dispense this boastful tip.

'And Mr Early said you had a flask of whiskey,' I said.

He looked at me defensively. 'So what if I did?'

'I understand there was some sloe gin as well.'

'Arnold Murchison brought the sloe gin from the Parthenon Theater.'

'Charlotte smelled of alcohol,' I said. 'I've been told the sloe gin wasn't that strong.'

'It varied from bottle to bottle. The home-made stuff always does. I'm sure the bottle Murchison and his boys were drinking had to be a hundred-proof.'

'And did Charlotte have any of your whiskey?'

'She had a sip or two, sure,' he said.

We turned around and began heading back. Some boys in knee pants and paddock caps had launched a kite into the sky and were teasing it in the updrafts.

'Don't you think she's too young to be drinking?' I said.

'I never forced her,' he said. 'She asked.'

'Did you see anybody tamper with any-thing she drank?'

'No.'

The hawk had returned to the sky above the cemetery and was circling closer and closer to the boys' kite.

'I guess there was hardly anybody down by the river when she got murdered,' I said.

'Most of us were finished swimming by that time, yes, that's right,' he said.

'Did you see Charlotte go down to the river with anybody at or around the time she got murdered?'

He stopped. He slid his hands into his back pockets again, twitched his hips to the right, then to the left, and looked at me from under his forelock of light brown hair. 'I don't want to get no one in trouble, doc,' he said.

'Roger, we're talking of a young woman's life here.'

He looked down at the grass, where a few dandelions grew in the burgeoning clover.

'Well ... doc...' he said, his voice breathless, as if he were getting ready to jump off a bridge, '...the only person I saw her go down to the river with was Herbert Early. Whether he had one of those bottles of sloe gin in his hand, I just cansay.'

Wilbert Robson, Roger's father, escorted me around Robson Metalworks, the largest, most lucrative factory in town, with the deliberate gait of a monarch who surveys his realm. His hefty stomach preceded him with a pomp all of its own, and his freshly lit eight-inch cigar was poised confidently between his first and middle fingers. The noise was horrendous. Steam-powered choppers, crimpers, clampers, benders, and extruders

91

shaped, molded, and cast raw steel, brass, nickel, tin, and iron into finished products. Within the cavernous vault of the factory, horse-drawn wagons pulled bundles of wire, electrical fixtures, saw blades, hammer heads, anvils, and lead piping. Grime and sweat covered the workers, and their clothes were black with the soot from the boilers. At the far end, five or six men poured molten steel into molds, the hot metal glowing bright orange as it sparked and sizzled in the gloom.

Robson shouted over the din. 'We get our steel delivered straight from Pittsburgh,' he said. 'Never mind these middlemen. They pick your pocket any way they can.' He raised his eyebrows. 'And we make some of our own alloys. It's cheaper that way. Next week we convert that extruder over there. We've got an order for a million feet of railroad track from the Brazilian government. We'll be doing that right through Christmas.'

We continued through the noise and smoke. 'I see you have hammers and saws over there,' I said.

'We make anything, so long as we have an order for it,' he said. He gestured toward a door just beyond a waist-high mound of horseshoes. 'This is what you wanted to see.'

We passed through the door and entered an adjoining room. The din outside immediately grew muffled.

'This is where we do our housewares,' he said. Ten rows of trestle tables sat end to end in the housewares room. I did a quick employee headcount – twenty women and an equal number of children. 'This is all silver plate,' continued Robson. He lifted a card-holder from the nearest table, a small tray with an ornate handle for calling cards. 'We do our own engraving. Right now we're doing card-holders, gravy-boats, and bon-bon trays because they all have the same handle. We got raised ornamentation here. Of course, it's not as heavy as actual silver, but it sure looks like the real thing. We dip them in that lacquer over there, and when they're dry we have the children polish them up.'

'And those are the various polishes over there?' I asked, pointing to some shelves.

Several of the containers were marked with the skull-and-crossbones sign.

'Yes, sir,' said Wilbert Robson.

I took a step closer, examining the polishes. 'Tell me, Wilbert, what kind of polishes do you use?'

He scratched his head, thinking. 'Well ... we use a good many petroleum distillates, a number of oxides, a few carbides, and a whole heap of—'

'I mean specifically.'

'Specifically?' he said, his bushy eyebrows rising. 'Let's see ... we use ferric oxide, jeweler's rouge, potassium cyanide, corundum, tripoli—'

'And you just leave these polishes out here on the shelves like this? They're all poisonous. Shouldn't they be locked up somewhere?'

A frown came to his face. 'Now, Clyde, I know what you're thinking, and I understand your concern. But I got these young ladies looking out for these children, and they know how to handle the polishes carefully and with respect. I've got that big vent down at the end. I look after my employees. The last thing I need in here is a gang of sick, whining children not pulling their weight.'

I stared at the polishes. Potassium cyanide, sitting in a big glass jar, as blue as a Mediterranean sky. Here was a source of cyanide, on open shelves; a source of cyanide easily available to ... to whom? To Roger Robson?

We were just about to leave the housewares room when in came the young man himself. His face was a picture of trepidation. I stood by and watched Wilbert's face settle, not sure what was going on.

'Haines said you wanted to see me, sir,' said Roger to his father. Roger seemed positively terrified of his father. He turned to me, as subdued as I'd ever seen him. 'Good afternoon, doctor,' he said, rather formally.

I nodded.

'What's this I hear about you and your chums stoning a stray dog to death?' asked

Wilbert Robson.

Roger looked at the floor of the house-wares room. 'We were just having a bit of fun ... sir,' he said.

Wilbert took a few steps closer to his son. He clenched his fist and held it in front of his son's face. Wilbert gave me a wink, as if it were a joke between us.

'Maybe I should have my own bit of fun with you,' he said. 'They say you tied the poor creature up.'

'It looked rabid, sir.'

'So you stoned it to death.'

'It wasn't dead when we put it in the ditch, sir.'

'But it's probably dead now.'

Roger hesitated. 'I don't know, sir. We thought we were doing a public service, sir.'

'Maybe I should give you a few knocks on the nose,' said Wilbert. 'That might be a public service.'

Roger simply hung his head. Wilbert's face settled with disgust. He let his fist sink to his side.

'Go on, get out of here,' he said, as if Roger were the vilest creature on earth. 'I'll deal with you later.'

SEVEN

Had I spent my whole life in Clifford's Bend I might have considered Fairfield, with its population of 9,237, its five churches, its two miles of concrete sidewalk, its four hotels, two banks, and one department store a bustling metropolis of the first magnitude. But I'd lived in Washington, DC. Still, Fairfield had its urban amenities. Most notable among these was the Tonawanda Road Electric Tram Car Service, which replaced the old horse-drawn service in 1894.

I now rode south in one of the town's three tramcars. I wore a blue pin-check blazer and a linen crash hat; cool summer attire, casual, anonymous, and comfortable. The tram ventured over the tracks into Hoopertown. Here was the crowded, noisier part of town. Even at this late hour the streets were clogged with livery buggies and farm wagons. As I alighted at the corner of Hooper Avenue, a Negro gentleman played the banjo and sang in front of a saloon. His little dog pranced around on two legs, dancing. A girl waif sold flowers on the corner. The gutters were thick with horse manure. A whole section of plank sidewalk had been torn up, preparatory to the laying of new concrete, leaving a muddy trench in front of a row of shops. I turned left on Hooper and walked two blocks east till I came to Fredonia. The air was smoky, thick with the burn of locomotive engines in the train yard. It was here on this corner, in perhaps the noisiest part of town, that I found the Parthenon Theater, a sprawling wood-frame structure of mauve clapboard and purple trim.

The theater's show windows featured photographs of young women in harem pants, can-can skirts, and filmy cheesecloth dresses. A legless man on a pushcart sat just outside the entrance begging for coins, the stub of an extinguished cigar stuck in the corner of his mouth. An alley choked with horse manure and garbage led to a stable in the back. The front steps of the theater were slick with the expectorations of inveterate tobacco chewers.

As I opened the door and entered the establishment, I was struck by the smell of stale beer and cigarette smoke. A player-piano churned on an old automatic roll, a ragtime ditty I'd heard numerous times but now couldn't name. On stage, five chorus girls with laurel leaves in their hair danced in skimpy Roman togas. The bill card said 'VENUS AND HER SORORITY'. Waiters in white shirts and black bow-ties moved through the dim cabaret with trays of beer;

the bartender was busy pouring whiskey into shot glasses; and a native Indian, a Cree, stood by the far door with a broom in his hand and a white apron around his waist. I went up to the bar and asked for Arnold Murchison.

'He's got someone with him right now,' said the bartender, jerking his head toward a door at the back. 'You'll have to wait. Can I get you something?'

'Bourbon,' I said.

The bartender poured bourbon into a shot glass. I slid a quarter across the counter. I was about to hoist myself up on to a bar stool when I heard someone call my name. I turned around and saw Rupert Scales, the town drunk, sitting at a table all by himself against the far wall under a lithograph of a racing horse. As an occasional occupant of the sheriff's jail, Rupert Scales had periodically joined Stanley and me on Tuesday nights for a poker game. When he wasn't drunk, he was a formidable cartwright, and earned a good living.

I waded through the tables to the other side of the theater. 'Evening, Rupert,' I said.

'Evening, doc,' he said. 'Is someone sick?'

'No,' I said. 'I'm here to see Arnold Murchison, about the Charlotte Scott murder case.'

He nodded. 'He's got Frank Jaslowski in there right now,' he said. 'Sit yourself down. It might be a while. There's some sort of ruckus going on.'

I sat down. 'Is that a fact?' I said.

Frank Jaslowski was one of the names on Herbert Early's list, the man who worked for Murchison.

'It's always a fact around here,' said Rupert Scales. 'I'm actually waiting to see Arnie myself. He owes me money for work I did on one of his racing traps.'

I raised my eyebrows. 'Murchison races?' I said.

Rupert took a sip of his beer. 'He was a regular at Saratoga Springs until last year.' He sat back, draping his arm over the back of the empty chair beside him. 'He got in a scrape with his bookmakers, something to do with doctoring the odds on one of his horses, and he's had to bow out for a while.' Rupert looked positively pleased about this. 'His bookmakers lost a lot of money, and they want it back, and the Track Association is sniffing around, and if Arnie doesn't pay it back soon they just might...' But Rupert suddenly lost interest in Murchison's racing difficulties as he watched me take a sip of bourbon. 'Say, doc, could you buy me a drink? That bourbon looks mighty good, and I'm a little short tonight. Like I say, Arnie owes me money for that racing trap.'

Before I could reply, Murchison's office door opened and a tall man with one leg shorter than the other, a full black beard, and a bowler hat crammed over his head lurched into the theater, his shoulders jerking back and forth like an oil rig, his left leg dragging a half second behind his right one. This, Rupert informed me, was Frank Jaslowski. Arnold Murchison appeared behind him. Even over the din of the player-piano I heard Arnold Murchison's voice clearly.

'I don't care where you look!' bawled the theater owner. 'Look everywhere! But for the love of Christ, find him!'

Rupert Scales grinned. 'Looks like Frank caught it this time,' he said.

I hardly listened; I was watching Murchison. He was about forty-five, of medium height, stocky but not corpulent, wore a brown bowler, a burgundy vest, a white shirt with the sleeves rolled up, and had red hair and a red mustache. He watched his companion go. When Jaslowski was gone, he surveyed the theater, his eyes grim, suspicious, as if every man here were a personal enemy. Finally he spotted me and Rupert and his eyes widened. He looked mortified to see us both sitting at the same table together – I don't know why. He hurried over. By the time he reached us he was smiling, his mortification gone, or at least hidden.

'Evening, doc,' he said. 'Good to see you. I knew you'd show up sooner or later.' He gave Rupert a look of unconvincing hospitality. 'Why don't we get you away from Rupert here,' he said. 'I bet he's already asked you for money.'

100

'The blazes I did,' protested Rupert. 'I asked him for a drink.'

'It amounts to the same thing, don't it, Rupert?' said Murchison.

I slid my half-finished bourbon across the table to Rupert. 'That's the best I can do for now, Rupert,' I said.

And I got up and followed Arnold Murchison to his office.

The walls in Murchison's office were covered with photographs and prints of racing horses. At least half a dozen sepia-toned stills of Murchison himself standing in the winner's circle at Saratoga Springs with the winner's wreath around his neck hung above the fireplace against the far wall. Racing forms lay scattered all over Murchison's desk. Stacks of racing magazines sat on an old captain's chest in the corner. As we took our seats, Murchison pulled out a bottle of whiskey and a couple of shot glasses. He poured two generous drinks. His face was livid with freckles and his small grey eyes looked harried.

'I'm sorry about Rupert, doc,' he said.

'He was telling me you owed him money for work he did on a racing trap.'

Murchison looked to one side, annoyed by this. 'I wish he'd keep his big mouth shut,' he said. He quickly changed the subject. 'I guess it's Charlotte you want to talk about.'

I took out the box of Parthenon matches. 'I found these on Charlotte's bedside table,' I said.

He stared at the matches sadly. 'Such a tragedy, ain't it?' he said.

'You knew Miss Scott well?' I asked. I was glad to see he was willing to talk about her.

'Oh, sure,' he said. 'Came here after school two or three times a week, asking me things. You know, about theater. Really wanted to learn.'

'And you saw her in *Angel of the Glade?*' I asked.

'I was helping with the lights,' he said. 'She was first-rate in that, wasn't she?'

'A remarkable talent,' I agreed.

'You don't see that too often in someone so young. That kind of dedication, that kind of discipline. She did a bang-up job, that's for sure.'

'And were you at the picnic afterwards?' I asked.

'I was up on the road with the boys.'

'I've been told you supplied the party with some home-made sloe gin,' I said.

'My wife Pauline makes it.'

'Charlotte was poisoned with cyanide,' I said.

'I read it in the *Newspacket.*'

'And she was drinking your sloe gin.'

His eyes widened as he got my meaning. 'I suppose she was,' he said. 'But she was also drinking Roger Robson's whiskey. And I believe she had some lemonade as well.'

He leaned forward, folding his big square

hands on top of all the racing forms. We stared at each other. He remained affable, accepting my probing. He knew I had a job to do.

'I suppose you had a good view of the picnic ground from up on the road,' I said.

'I did.'

'Then you might have seen Charlotte go down to the river with someone at or around the time she was murdered.'

'I saw Richard Lip,' he said.

I leaned forward. Richard Lip, the Chinese hobo Herbert Early had on his list of names.

'She went down to the river with Richard Lip?' I said, not sure if I understood.

'No,' he said, 'but he was down by the river about the time she was murdered.' From beyond the closed door, we heard applause for Venus and her Sorority. 'I should know. I was the one who chased him away.'

'You chased him?'

Murchison took a sip of whiskey and sat back in his chair. He stared at me, his eyes squinting, observing me the way he might observe a distant object.

'He came up from the bridge,' said Murchison. 'I'd seen his fire earlier. I knew he'd be up sooner or later. To freeload. So I kept a lookout up on the road. About eleven o'clock he prowls into the picnic ground. He sniffs around, looking for food, looking for a drink, and he finally goes over to those picnic tables on the far side. Bernice Scott is sitting there all by herself. You know, Charlotte's sister. I didn't want Lip bothering no young girls so I go down to the picnic ground and chase him away.'

I took a deep breath, thinking this over.

'And he went to the river afterwards?' I asked.

Murchison nodded. 'Must have been quarter past eleven by the time he headed for the river. He disappeared through those willows and headed downstream.'

'Did he have anything in his hands?'

'A bottle of sloe gin. Bernice Scott gave him a bottle.'

I pondered this new information. I worked through the scenario: Richard Lip goes down to the river, Richard Lip spots Charlotte Scott all by herself, Richard Lip laces the sloe gin with cyanide, Richard Lip gets Charlotte Scott to drink it. A frown came to my face. It didn't work. Why would Lip kill Charlotte? Did they even know each other? And why would he carry cyanide around with him?

'Did you see anybody else go down to the river with Charlotte?' I asked.

I was trying to confirm Roger Robson's story about Herbert Early.

He shook his head. 'No, sir.' He shrugged. 'But I saw Richard Lip fine.'

I had a small girl in front of me, Mary O'Riley, six years old, from Hoopertown.

104

Her mother, a thin woman in a faded print dress, watched me anxiously as I performed my examination. I put my palm to the child's forehead. She ran a fever. 'And whereabouts in Hoopertown do you live?' I asked Cecelia O'Riley.

Mrs O'Riley looked surprised by the question.

'At Fredonia and Mohawk,' she said.

'Then you must see a lot of trains,' I suggested.

'Hear them, more like,' she said. 'We've got no windows on that side.'

I reached behind Mary O'Riley's ear. She had a lump there.

'And is your husband working right now?' I asked.

'He works as a machinist at the metalworks.'

Out in the hall, I heard the bell above the front door ring. Another patient.

'Mrs O'Riley, your daughter has the mumps,' I said.

'Oh, dear.'

'Keep her home from school for a few days, make sure she gets plenty of rest, and get her to drink as much as she can. You can put ice on the swelling behind her ears.'

Mrs O'Riley glanced away, her eyes downcast.

'Is there something wrong?' I asked.

'The ice, doctor,' she said. 'It's so awfully dear.'

She fingered the lace collar of her print dress. She couldn't afford ice? I wondered what Wilbert Robson was paying her husband if they couldn't afford ice. I reached in my pocket, pulled out a nickel and handed it to her.

'Buy some,' I said, smiling. 'We can't have poor Mary suffering without any ice.' I sent them on their way.

I discovered not a patient in my waiting-room, but Mrs Beulah Frith, Henrietta Scott's eldest sister. She was a tall, hefty, efficient-looking woman, with an ample bosom that cleaved the air the same way a dreadnought cleaves the waves.

'Mr Scott asks you to come to the house at once,' she said. Her lips came together like two bloodless worms. This wasn't a request; this was a command. 'He's made a discovery concerning our recent tragedy he thinks you should know about.' Her nostrils flared, as if my involvement had to be tolerated like a spoonful of cod liver oil. 'He was exceedingly anxious that you come right away.'

I found Howard Scott in his parlor, slouching in his wing-back chair, the *Newspacket* spread over his lap and a glass of whiskey on the table beside him. It was not yet noon and he was already drinking.

'Glad you could come, doctor,' he said, too numbed by alcohol to sound anything but indifferent.

He looked shrunken, pale, as if the events

106

of the last week had leached away the life from his body. He offered me a glass of whiskey but I declined.

He shrugged. 'You're not a drinking man, then?'

'Not until the evening hours,' I said.

He leaned forward. I could see he was quite drunk. He lifted a woman's stocking from the side table. The stocking was old, with both heel and toe darned many times. 'This stocking belonged to Charlotte,' he said. He rubbed the material through his fingers. 'I was going through her things, and I ... she has a crawl-space up in her bedroom, where the wall slopes down from the ceiling, and I ... I went in there, I knew she kept a few old things back there, and I...' He held up the stocking, pure lisle hose with double black stitching. 'And this is what I found.' He stretched open the stocking and looked inside. 'Tucked away on a small ledge.'

He reached into the stocking and pulled out a bundle of twenty-dollar bills wrapped in an elastic band. There had to be at least several hundred dollars there. All the bills were new and crisp. I waited for an explanation.

'Exactly one thousand dollars,' he said. He handed me the money. 'If I work twelve hours a day without any holidays for twelve months straight, I'll be lucky to make eight hundred dollars for the whole blessed year.

So I ask you, Dr Deacon, how can a girl of seventeen, a student at the high school with no outside employment, happen to have one thousand dollars hidden away in an attic crawl-space?' He shook his head wearily. 'It's got to have something to do with her murder,' he said. 'I'm sure of it.'

EIGHT

I took the money into custody. I said good-bye to the barber and stepped out on to the porch. I stood there ruminating as I heard him retreat to his whiskey bottle in the parlor. Greed was so often a motive in murder. I wondered if this money did indeed have anything to do with Charlotte's death.

I was halfway down the walk when Bernice Scott jumped out at me from behind a sycamore tree and took a picture of me with her Kodak 'Brownie'.

'Gotcha!' she said.

I pretended to be startled. I could tell she was having fun with me.

'Afternoon, Bernice,' I said.

'Now I'll have you forever,' she said. 'Once you're in my camera you belong to me. I'll take you to my hobby shed and you'll stay there until I say you can go.'

I wondered what made a girl of sixteen behave in such a childlike fashion. She wore a violet shift and a white straw hat with a violet hatband.

'You have a hobby shed?' I said.

She cocked her head quizzically. 'Would you like to see it?' she asked. 'It's around back. I keep all my camera stuff there.'

'I sure would,' I said.

I followed Bernice around the side of the house where Mrs Scott's poppies were just ending and her irises beginning. The shade of the maples back here was pleasant. A hammock was strung between posts, and the Scott horse, an arthritic old mare named Lightning, nibbled contentedly on the grass and dandelions at the back near the whitewashed fence. Bernice led me to a tar-paper shed. The windowless structure leaned a bit to one side but otherwise looked stable. She opened the door and it creaked on rusty hinges. I followed her inside. She lit a lamp and put it behind a piece of tinted red glass. I looked around. I understood. With the red glass, she had turned the hobby shed into a make-believe darkroom.

'Do you own a camera, Dr Deacon?' she asked. I was surprised by her change of tone. She sounded suddenly like a grown woman.

'An old one,' I said. 'I haven't used it in years.'

'Is it like this one here?' she asked, yanking a dusty relic from the shelf.

'No,' I said, 'it's smaller. One of the first Kodaks. I took it to Cuba with me. President Roosevelt wanted me to take some pictures.' She handed me the old camera and I inspected it with interest. 'Of course, he wasn't President then.'

'I think I would like Teddy, then,' she said.

'I think he understands the importance of the camera. He was smart to make you take pictures. Now we'll know about his Rough-riders for all time, won't we? We'll know about San Juan Hill. The camera captures all.'

Again I was surprised, this time by her knowledge of recent political events.

'I suppose that's true,' I said.

'Once you have it on film, no one can take it away from you. I was constantly taking pictures of Charlotte,' she said. 'And now that she's gone, well ... I still have her. She photographs so well. She was so pretty.'

'Yes,' I said, 'she was.'

She took the bulky camera back from me. 'This camera is thirty years old,' she said. 'I found it at the Buffalo Fair last year. It's one of the old paper-positive cameras. I'm trying to fix it, but so far I haven't had any luck. I can't get a decent image out of it. I think I'll parcel it off to Kodak to see if they can repair it.'

'Could I see your photographs of Char-lotte?' I asked.

'I've got hundreds of them,' she warned.

'That's just dandy,' I said.

She opened a drawer and pulled out a paper envelope.

In the envelope were photographs; 'Brown-ie' shots, two and a half inches square, all of Charlotte. One showed Charlotte on a swing; another showed her sitting on a horse;

and still another showed her in front of the Trip to the Moon, the famous adventure ride at the Buffalo Fair last year. I saw the spaceship *Luna* looming behind her. Then I found a photograph of Charlotte standing beside her mother's irises.

'When was this taken?' I asked.

Bernice glanced at the photograph as her hands continued to sift through others.

'Last year,' she said. 'I've got the date written on the back.'

I flipped the photograph over: June 19 1901.

I turned the photograph over and gazed at Charlotte's picture. It showed a sixteen-year-old girl, poised on the brink of womanhood. She wore a white gown which, over-exposed in the sunlight, seemed to glow. Her hair was up, revealing a long graceful neck. She had sharp, intelligent eyes and a maturity which belied her years. Her skin was as clear as a summer day and I saw the locket around her neck, the Greek archer clearly visible.

'Do you mind if I keep this?' I asked.

I was thinking of my investigation. Bernice stopped her sorting and looked at the photograph.

'I like to keep my photographs,' she said.

'Then can I borrow it?'

She looked at me curiously. 'Why would you want to borrow it?'

'I might need it,' I said, 'for my investigation.'

She looked away, a troubled expression coming to her face. 'It's gone, isn't it?' she said. 'It's over.' She continued to shuffle through the photographs. I wasn't sure what she was talking about. 'Charlotte's time is over,' said Bernice. 'We should be thinking of other things now. We should be thinking about what we're going to do tomorrow – and the next day. Tomorrow we could feed ducks at the Park Street bridge. The next day we might go for a bicycle ride to Burkville, where they sell that delicious ice-cream. These are things that Charlotte can't do now. This afternoon I'm going to start pasting her photographs into a photograph album. I have a nice photograph album I set aside for just that purpose. And then I'll put it away somewhere. I've got some high shelves in my bedroom. Maybe I'll put it on one of those. And if people want to look at it, they'll have to ask nicely, and I'll have to consider their requests carefully, and if I think they're sincere, I'll let them look.' While she talked, her hands automatically shuffled through photographs.

'What's this one?' I asked, pointing.

She stopped shuffling.

'Oh, that,' she said. 'That one didn't turn out. There wasn't enough light.'

'Yes, but what is it?'

'It's Charlotte sneaking out of her bedroom window at night.'

With this explanation, the white blotches

sorted themselves into a skirt, the lines joined into a window-frame, and the starburst in the upper left-hand corner became a wall lamp.

'Where was she going?'

'I don't know,' said Bernice breezily. 'She went places.'

'At night? When your parents were asleep?' I asked.

But she was already on to something else. 'What do you think of this one?' She giggled. 'That's me with a tennis racquet. Reverend Porteous lets us use the courts next to the Manse to play. It's flat back there. I don't know how it got so flat, but the ball always bounces true. I'm not very good yet. Roger Robson is giving me lessons. I have a lot of photographs of Roger Robson too. Do you know how to play tennis, Dr Deacon?'

I glanced at the photograph. And I was struck by the rapturous expression on Bernice's face; how she gazed upon Roger with idolatrous eyes. I knew that look. I'd seen it on those girls with the cocker spaniel in the park the other day while they were talking to Roger. It was a look of nervous hilarity. Like half the other girls in Fairfield, Bernice Scott seemed to be in love with Roger Robson.

'Can you remember how many times Charlotte went out at night?' I asked.

I felt I'd stumbled on to something.

She made a face; the same face a cat might make when forced to go in water. 'Why does

114

everybody want to know about Charlotte all the time?' she asked.

'Bernice, please,' I said. 'I think this might be ... why don't you be my guide on this? Why don't you show me how she got down?'

'She was the angel of the glade, wasn't she?' said Bernice, with some jealousy. 'She could fly. Do you want to look at my photographs or don't you? I hardly ever ask anybody back here. You're very lucky, Dr Deacon.'

'Bernice, did you love your sister?'

'If I were going to poison someone I'd have used hemlock. Did you know Socrates died of hemlock poisoning?'

I grew impatient. 'Did Charlotte sneak out several times, or only once?'

Her brow arched. 'Did you ever read Plato's *Phaedo*?'

'I read it in Greek many years ago,' I said.

'Oh,' she said, 'you know Greek. Reverend Porteous knows Greek too. I often catch him napping with a Greek book over his nose. You don't know how much fun I have photographing Reverend Porteous when he's snoring in his sun chair.'

'Did Charlotte ever say where she went?' I asked.

She made the same cat-in-water face. 'I was no more than a dust mote to Charlotte,' she said. 'I have this problem, you see. That's why I have a private tutor. I'm too disruptive.'

I let her talk. And as she talked I surreptitiously slipped the photograph of Charlotte into my pocket. She skipped from one subject to the next, talking one moment of Egyptian pyramids, then about her mother's hats, then about the water stain on the ceiling of her bedroom. She got on to the subject of books, and I was surprised by how well-read she was: Twain, Hawthorne, Dickens, Zola, even Dostoevsky – she'd read them all, told me she spent hours in the public library when all the other kids were in school.

'I can be quiet when I'm all by myself,' she assured me. 'But when I'm around other kids, well, I blow up.'

'Could you tell me about the picnic on Thursday night?'

'Must we talk about that? I find it upsetting.'

'Could you please just tell me what you saw?'

'A lot of self-important young people dancing the Turkey Trot,' she said. 'I was disgusted.'

'Mr Murchison said you were bothered by Richard Lip.'

She finally stopped shuffling through the photographs and looked at me. I could tell there lurked behind those strange grey eyes a formidable intellect. 'Richard Lip's an outcast,' she said. 'Like me. I felt sorry for him.'

'And you gave him a bottle of sloe gin?' I

asked.

'I did.'

'And then Mr Murchison came down and chased him away.'

'Chased?' she said. 'Oh, no, I wouldn't say chased. Mr Murchison was too drunk to do much chasing. He told Mr Lip to move along.'

'And Mr Lip left?'

'Yes.'

'Which way did he go?'

'You're getting tiresome, Dr Deacon. What difference does it make? Charlotte's dead.'

'Please, Bernice.'

A petulant look came to her face. 'He went down to the river.'

This at least confirmed Murchison's story.

'Did you see Mr Early go down to the river with your sister at or around the same time?' I asked.

'What, that insufferable pompous idiot who thinks he's Heaven's gift to the stage?' she said.

I winced. 'The drama teacher,' I confirmed.

No,' she said.

I paused. So Roger Robson was wrong about Herbert Early going down to the river with Charlotte?

'Did anybody else go down to the river with her about this time?'

'No,' she said, 'no one – unless you want to count Mr Murchison.'

117

I felt my eyebrows rising. 'Mr Murchison?'

She shrugged. 'I think he wanted to make sure Mr Lip was safely on his way.'

When I left Bernice I surveyed the outside of the Scott house, in particular Charlotte's bedroom window. She couldn't fly like the angel of the glade but I saw that it was easily possible for a girl as athletic as Charlotte to descend the sturdy garden trellis against the side of the house. Yet wouldn't her parents hear her? Apparently they hadn't. Howard Scott probably fell asleep in a drunken stupor each night. And Henrietta Scott's bedroom was on the first floor near the front; she had to take strong medication for her arthritis, so she too was probably stuporous by the time she went to bed. A nocturnal descent might reasonably be achieved without detection under such circumstances.

But why? Where did she go? And did it have anything to do with the money I had safely tucked away in her sock, or anything to do with her secret pregnancy, or with her murder? And why hadn't Bernice ever told her parents about Charlotte's midnight escapes? My first inclination was to tell the Scotts about them. But then, I decided, what purpose would it serve? It would probably just cause them pain. As I walked out to Milton Street and turned toward Tonawanda Road, I decided to tuck the information away until I could better understand it.

118

NINE

I found Stanley Armstrong in the yard behind the Sheriff's Office where the stables were, sifting through boxes of ash from the Mosely's Ironmongery arson, dressed in soot-covered overalls and wearing a ragged pork-pie hat on his head. The yard was strewn with hay and I saw the rumps of the three Fairfield Police horses over the gates of their stalls. When I told Stanley about the money, he got up from his toil, walked to the rain barrel, and washed his hands and face.

'Let's have a look,' he said.

I stuck my hand in Charlotte's sock and pulled out the wad of bills. Stanley's eyes sprang open.

'By golly, they're new!' he said.

He took the bills from my hand and started flipping through them one by one. A look of unhinged delight came to his eyes.

'Stanley?' I said. 'Stanley, what is it?'

'I don't believe this,' he said, his voice high and tremulous. 'After six months of pain-staking work, waiting all the time for some of this money to shake loose ... I honest-to-Betsy don't believe it.'

He lunged away from me and bounded up the back steps into the Sheriff's Office. I followed up the steps, down the corridor past the rack of shotguns, into the main part of the office, my perplexity diminishing as I began to understand what was going on. I found him sitting at his desk, his spectacles now astride his nose, flipping through a long list of numbers, running his fingers down the columns, his eyes flicking back and forth between the bills and the list, his brow hoisted, his lips forming a small circle of anticipation beneath his shaggy mustache.

'Lord in heaven!' he exclaimed, leaning closer to the list. He looked up at me, his body rigid, reminding me of that frigid morning in Colorado while the two of us were prospecting, when he had struck his pickaxe into the mountainside and found gold. His body was as tight as a spring-coil. 'This is Corn Mercantile money!' he said. 'These serial numbers ... good God, Clyde, do you know what you've done?' His eyes proclaimed, 'Eureka!'

'Really?' I was hardly able to believe it myself.

'You don't know how long I've waited for some of this money to show itself. And now you've found it in a dead girl's sock.'

We drank. We felt we really had something to celebrate. We didn't know how or why Charlotte wound up with Corn Mercantile money, but we drank anyway. The June afternoon mellowed with a golden hazy light. It was like old times; Stanley and me, discussing a case, like it wasn't the canal and Court Street just outside, but the tumbleweed and dusty llanos of West Texas. I was a doctor; I'd had a long, hard struggle to become one, but sitting here with Stanley, in Stanley's office, with the cells behind us and the 'Wanted' posters up on the bulletin board, I was, as if magically transformed, a lawman again.

'We just have to think of everyone she knew,' said Stanley. He tapped the bills on the table, still looking as if he couldn't believe their reappearance. 'It was a brilliantly planned, brilliantly executed burglary using acetylene torches and low-impact explosives. We know the burglary was timed to coincide with the big Corn Mercantile deposit in March, so whoever perpetrated the crime knew when the Corn Mercantile money was coming into the bank.' He gestured at the money. 'Charlotte Scott must have been involved in some way. Either that, or one of the perpetrators gave her this money.'

I told Stanley what Herbert Early had said about Sims and Charlotte Scott, how they were sweethearts.

'Could there be some connection?' I said. 'He works at the bank, after all.'

'I've checked Michael Sims through and through,' he said. 'And I know about him and Charlotte. I admit, now that we've found this money in Charlotte's sock, it might be worth checking again. But I don't think we'll find much. Sims wasn't even here on the night of the burglary. He was visiting his parents in Ohio. When he came back, I watched him for a month, just in case. I never saw anything suspicious. We searched his room at Lillian Lalonde's boarding-house. We told all the merchants in town to watch the money he passed. We even had law officials search his parents' house in Ohio. They found nothing.' Stanley tapped the ash from his cigar on to the floor. 'He's not the type, Clyde – church every Sunday, sings in the choir, volunteers at a soup kitchen in Hoopertown Wednesday and Friday nights. He's bookish. He's got a Victor III phonograph in his room and listens to a lot of opera. He's not a rough sort. Daniel Howse swears Sims couldn't possibly have had anything to do with the burglary. Around the bank, Howse treats him like family. Not only that, but Sims doesn't have the necessary skills. The perpetrators worked with special explosives.' Stanley sat back and took a leisurely sip of his whiskey. 'He's as clean as a washboard, Clyde. I think we're going to have to look elsewhere.'

I got back to the surgery shortly after four and discovered a telegram in my mailbox. I quickly ripped open the Western Telegraph envelope and gazed at the contents. It was

122

from Mr Erskine Mann, the headmaster at the Ashtonbury School for Boys in Boston, my son's boarding-school. The news was good. Jeremiah had finished second in his class. He would be home in three weeks, on the fifth of July.

I folded the short missive, stuck it in my pocket, and ambled up the walk, a beatific grin on my face. Jeremiah. I thought of his large brown eyes, his unruly brown hair, massive locks of it, hair he'd inherited from his mother; thought of his bright smile, and the impish smirk that came to his face whenever he beat me at chess. I entered the surgery, walked past the waiting-room, and went into the front parlor. Dust particles floated in the segmented bands of sunlight slanting through the Venetian blinds. I walked to the mantelpiece and looked at the photographic portrait of my son. In this shot, he was twelve, dressed in knee pants, a jacket and vest, with a small bow-tie. His dark eyes shone luminously at me from the portrait. I felt a sudden wave of tenderness for the boy. I sincerely hoped he would like Fairfield. After living in Cross Plains for most of his life, coming east had been a big change for him.

My eyes strayed to Emily's portrait. I was struck, as always, by the largeness of her brown eyes; the brown eyes she'd given to Jeremiah. In this portrait, her last, she was twenty-seven, a year before she died while giving birth to Jeremiah. I felt my eyes misting over with tears. Every time I thought of Emily, or looked at this portrait, I felt her cold hand reaching out to me, heard her gentle voice whispering to me from where she rested in that bare patch of earth outside Cross Plains. Dead these fourteen years, since 1888, and she still wouldn't let me go. Was it a long time, or a short time? When measured through my abiding love and respect for her, it seemed a short time. Yet, looking at her portrait, with her hairstyle so old-fashioned, and her dress a decade and a half out of date, unaccountably I couldn't help thinking of Olive Wade. I felt a weakening of the tether. The photograph of Emily still pulled, but it didn't pull so hard.

The next day, at noon-hour, I found Anthony King, owner of King's Emporium of New and Used Merchandise, on my front porch. Though he wore a basket-weave vest with a pocket watch and fob, he was without collar and cuffs, and was sweating profusely despite the cool breeze blowing over the porch. He was a man of indeterminate age. He could have been forty, he could have been sixty. He had a bald pate surrounded by wisps of thin mousey hair. A compact paunch with the density of a medicine ball strained against the pearl buttons of his vest. I had on occasion purchased glassware for my lab from the man.

'Afternoon, Mr King,' I said. 'I hope you're not ill.'

'No,' he said, 'not at all.'

His tone was evasive.

'Then what can I do for you?' I asked.

He looked down the walk, and then glanced at my front door. 'Have you not found yourself a nurse yet?' he asked.

'I haven't had time,' I said. 'I'm too busy trying to find Charlotte Scott's killer.'

He nodded, a convulsive dipping of his chin. 'Rightly so, Dr Deacon, rightly so. Poor Miss Scott.'

'It's a shame, isn't it?'

He looked at me cagily. 'Just so, just so,' he said. 'A terrible shame.' He paused, waiting an appropriate second or two before he got to what was really on his mind. 'You knew I traded in all sorts of goods and merchandise, didn't you?' he said.

'I sure did.'

'And that I'm a busy man?' he continued.

I wasn't sure where this was going, but I nodded. 'I'm sure you are,' I said.

Anthony King often prevaricated; one just had to wait him out.

'And that as a busy man I may on occasion overlook a thing or two?'

'You can only try to do your best, Mr King.'

'Yes, that's true,' he said. 'And, lord knows, I'm not perfect. God has yet to make a perfect human being. I'm sure, as a doctor, you know that more than most.'

'We're all just flesh and blood,' I said.

'And so one can't be blamed if one over-looks a thing or two now and again,' he persisted. 'I reckon it's only natural.'

'Mr King...'

'And that's why I didn't get around to reading Saturday's *Newspacket* until today. When I read about that locket ... the one with the Greek archer ... mind you, I deal in all sorts of merchandise, and like any businessman I don't like to take a loss, especially on such a fine piece.'

'You have the locket?' I said, taking a step forward.

He held up his finger. 'Not so fast, Dr Deacon. I didn't say that. I was trying to tell you a thing or two about profit and loss. If a man comes into my emporium and he offers to sell a fine piece of jewelry, and I pay him the princely sum of five dollars for it ... and then I learn that this piece of jewelry really wasn't his to sell...' He leaned forward, the cagey look in his eyes more evident than ever. 'Anyone with a decent moral sense and fear of God can see that it's not me who should lose five dollars. Any patriotic, thrifty American who's ever had the misfortune to—'

'Do you have the locket?' I repeated, my tone hardening. 'Because if you do, Mr King, I suggest you hand it over.'

'Dr Deacon, what I'm telling you here is all

126

hypothetical. And I might add that there's a season for giving, and it happens to fall on and around December twenty-fifth, and as far as I can judge we're still in the middle of June. Yes, sir. This is just a regular business week, and on a regular business week I hate to take a loss.'

I withdrew my pocketbook and wrote him a promissory note for five dollars. 'You know my credit's good,' I said. 'Now, can I have the locket?'

He stood up and pulled a velvet drawstring pouch out of his trouser pocket. He took the promissory note and gave me the pouch. I undid the drawstrings and pulled out the locket.

There it was – unmistakably Charlotte's locket. The gold chain was thick, and the Greek archer was white on a burnt-sienna background. Anthony King looked at the piece with regret.

'And the man who sold it to you?' I said. 'Who was he?'

He looked away, his eyebrows arching in apprehension. Gone was the generally acquisitive and conniving Mr King. Now he looked genuinely concerned.

'Just because a man sells a locket doesn't mean he's a murderer, Dr Deacon. I've dealt with this man for years; he's always bringing in items, and I've grown to trust him. Be-sides, I've got a business to run. I can't be asking the origin of every trade-in. Lord above, I'd scare away half my custom. I'd hate to see this man come to harm. I know for a fact he couldn't have killed Charlotte Scott. For one thing, he's always too drunk to do much of anything.'

'Mr King,' I said, with growing exasperation, 'you know Judge Norris will protect any man in the county if he's rightly innocent. Now, could you please tell me who sold you this locket?'

He looked away, struggled with himself, but finally nodded.

'Richard Lip,' he said. I stared at him. Richard Lip. King said the Chinaman's name with evident relief, as if Lip were just a bad penny he desperately wished to get rid of.

Stanley Armstrong held the locket, bouncing its weight in his palm, letting the chain slip through his fingers like a gold snake, his chin raised as he looked down at the piece of jewelry through his half-frame spectacles.

'Richard Lip,' said Stanley, as if he should have guessed. He put the locket down and continued to stare at it, the skin immediately beneath his left eyelid twitching in a spasm of fatigue. He smelled of ashes, and I knew he'd been digging around the burned-down ironmongery again, exhausting himself in a search for clues he probably would never find. 'I always thought he was harmless, but I guess not.'

I knew the evidence was damning, that it looked as if Richard Lip had killed Charlotte Scott in an act of robbery, and had then sold the locket to Anthony King, but I couldn't easily believe that cyanide would be used in the commission of such a crime.

'Stanley, just because he sold the locket to Anthony King doesn't necessarily mean...' Then I decided that I just didn't know enough about Richard Lip. I had to gather information about the man. 'How old is he?' I asked.

Stanley looked at the big key-ring hanging on the side of the desk. A patina of rust clung to the iron ring like brown paint, worn smooth and shiny.

'He must be about fifty,' he said. He leaned back, stretching out his tall frame, and folded his hands over his flat stomach. 'I never took him for a killer.'

'A Chinese hobo,' I said. 'You don't find them every day – especially in this part of the country, where most everyone has a white face.'

'I believe Mr Lip lived in San Francisco when he first came to America,' said Stanley.

'That's just my point, Stanley. Why would he leave his family and come all the way up here? We have a small Chinese community in Washington and, believe me, they're as tightly knit as a bedjacket. They would never let one of their own turn into a hobo. They got strong family ties. I don't understand how Richard Lip could have become a hobo like that.'

'Clyde, hoboes come in all shapes, sizes, and nationalities these days. We got boatload after boatload of immigrants coming into Ellis Island, and none of them's got more than a few dollars to their name. And maybe Richard Lip did something. Maybe that's why his own kind won't look after him.' Stanley gazed at the locket. 'Maybe he killed a Chinese.'

I saw Stanley was ready to hang the man.

'Stanley, him killing Charlotte Scott makes no sense,' I said.

He leaned forward and opened the locket. 'Look at this,' he said. 'She's got a bit of hair in here. Looks like baby hair.' The blond-white hair was indeed fine, infant hair, and it carried a faint scent of perfume.

'Why would Lip carry cyanide around with him?' I asked. 'It's not something people usually carry around with them.'

'Lip's just a speck of a man,' said Stanley. 'I bet he carries rocks in his pockets so the wind don't blow him away. Mayor Vanduzen's been complaining about him. Looks like he stole a gooseberry pie from Mrs Vanduzen's kitchen stoop around Easter. The Mayor's been after me to get rid of him ever since. I've been moving him along whenever I see him. And I've asked the shopkeepers to shoo him away. We don't want to encourage him.'

'So, in other words, he got hungry and he got desperate,' I said.

'I guess so,' said Stanley.

I scratched my head. Even so, Lip would never use cyanide to rob the girl. It didn't make sense. Why not knock her over the head? To use cyanide in the commission of a simple robbery was ridiculous.

'And you insist on Morley Suggett?' I said. 'A posse, Stanley? You know what that means.'

Out in Cecil Fray's smithy yard I heard a cock crow. The infernal bird had its clock mixed up – it was now four o'clock in the afternoon.

'I'm afraid I do, Clyde.' Stanley looked up from the locket. 'We've got to at least talk to Lip.'

TEN

The next evening, I hitched Pythagoras to my buggy and drove across the Tonawanda Road bridge to Cherry Hill, the wealthier part of town. The sky was bright with the colors of sunset. High overhead I saw seagulls floating on the evening breeze. As I gained the elevation of Cherry Hill I turned around and gazed at my new home. Except for the burnt-out ruin of Mosely's Ironmongery on the south bank near the Milton Street bridge, the scene was idyllic. The maples and elders clustered around the wood-frame buildings and houses, the steeple of the Congregationalist Church vaulted to an impressive copper-green peak high above the canal, and the river snaked like a silver ribbon south along Cattaraugus Avenue. Yet I was hard-pressed to enjoy this quaint view. My stomach fluttered, my hands grew clammy, and I wondered if I had any genuine reason at all to call upon Miss Olive Wade, other than a persistent craving to gaze upon her comely face once more. I convinced myself that I did indeed have a reason. I had to know more about Charlotte

Scott. And Olive Wade knew Charlotte Scott. Olive Wade coached Charlotte Scott with her singing. The Boston heiress must know something of Charlotte's acting ambitions, of her desire to go to New York. At least that's what I kept telling myself as I climbed higher and higher.

Cherry Hill, so named for the abundance of cherry trees lining its wide residential streets, had at one time been a meeting-place of some significance for the Indians of the Five Nations. Boys in the area were forever finding Indian arrowheads among the garden shrubbery and in the capacious pastures where the rich grazed their horses. Miss Wade's house, a large, sturdy three-storey dwelling with green shutters, a green roof, and white clapboard, sat at the extreme north end of Poplar Avenue on a two-acre lot with an adjoining pasture of thirty hectares.

As her private horse-groom came out to attend to my buggy, I grew suddenly subdued. My tongue felt like lead. I'd no idea she lived in such opulence. Why would Olive Wade ever want to come and work for me at the surgery? For that matter, why would she want to work as a midwife?

A housemaid answered the door.

'Was my mistress expecting you, doctor?' she asked.

From somewhere inside I heard the strains of a Chopin nocturne exquisitely played.

133

'No,' I said. I summoned my courage. 'If you'd kindly tell her I've come on a matter of business.' The housemaid arched her brow. 'In connection to the Charlotte Scott case,' I said.

I gave her my hat and riding gloves and she made off toward the back of the house. I glanced around the front hall. The Chopin nocturne ceased. The hall was well appointed with leaf and floral wallpaper, three large indoor ficus palms, and a gargantuan gilt-edged mirror. Paintings hung on the walls – portraits, landscapes, and still-lifes. I heard footsteps coming from the rear of the house. I peeked into the room to my left. I hadn't seen so many books since I'd left the White House. An African violet the size of a full-grown orchid flowered magnificently on the window-sill.

Olive Wade entered the hall. She wore a simple white dress of seersucker, and she had her hair down. I was stupefied. I'd never seen her with her hair down before, and it was the first time I'd ever seen her without a hat. Her hair was like spun gold. It sparkled in the dim electric bulbs from the overhead chandelier.

'Dr Deacon,' she said, extending her hand. 'This is indeed a pleasure.'

'I hope I'm not disturbing you,' I said.

'I was just finishing my afternoon practice.'

I took her hand. Her skin was like silk. I stared at her, trying to determine the exact shade of her eyes. We have a species of blue-bird in Tennessee, up where the mountain people live. Its wing feathers are the rarest shade of blue. Miss Wade's eyes were the same shade. She looked down at her hand. In my scrutiny of her eyes I'd forgotten to let go.

'I'm sorry,' I said, letting go abruptly, as if her hand were a dead rat.

She gave me a patient smile. 'Would you care for tea in the conservatory?' she asked. She nodded at her housemaid. 'Freda, could you have tea prepared, please?'

'Yes, ma'am.'

The housemaid retreated to get the tea.

I followed Miss Wade through the house, trying to regain my composure.

The conservatory was a large glass enclosure appended to the back of the house. The air was thick with the smell of the varied plant life growing there. Hiding behind the blooms of a flowering hibiscus was a small fountain – a cherub pouring water from an urn into a basin. Through the glass I saw Cherry Hill rising to its summit. A single, large spreading oak tree, looking centuries old, grew at the top surrounded by open pasture.

Miss Wade followed my gaze. 'You're looking at the tree,' she said.

'I haven't been up here before,' I said. 'I've been as high as Saddle Road.'

'The Robsons,' she said.

'Yes.'

She sat in a red velvet chair, the hem of her dress falling over the zebra-skin rug.

'I quite like it up here,' she said. I sat on the *chaise longue*. 'That old oak tree, it's rather stunning, isn't it?'

'Stunning, yes,' I said. 'But it looks so solitary.'

'Morley Suggett was up there this afternoon,' she said. 'He had about twenty others with him. My property goes only up to that fence. I suppose they're after that poor Chinese fellow.'

Richard Lip's name and likeness had by this time been gratuitously advertised in the *Newspacket*.

'Why would they meet up there?' I asked. 'I understand Mr Suggett lives on his father's farm in West Shelby. It seems a fair piece to ride just to meet his men.'

'This is the highest elevation for miles around,' she said. 'And from what I understand, this has been a traditional meeting-place for the sheriff's posse. In Boston, we don't have posses. We have a proper constabulary. Criminals are apprehended by properly trained law enforcement officers.'

'I hope they don't hurt him,' I said.

'I hope so too,' she said.

Freda arrived with tea. In fact, it was more like a supper, with smoked beef tongue, a pâté of goose livers, fried oyster-plant, three different cheeses, water crackers, figs, nuts, raisins, and champagne jelly. The tea was a scalding Darjeeling. When I'd filled my small plate with a modest amount of these delicacies, I told Miss Wade of my meeting with Mr Early. I thought it the best way to begin my enquiry into Charlotte Scott's character. I described to Miss Wade how Mr Early had portrayed Charlotte as a headstrong and manipulative girl.

'I believe Mr Early has taken a most immoderate view of Charlotte,' said Miss Wade. 'Determined, yes, but certainly not headstrong; effective in her relations with others, but never manipulative. You see, Dr Deacon, Charlotte Scott had a dream. She wished with all her heart to become an actress.' Miss Wade put her teacup on her saucer and looked at me with those miraculous blue eyes of hers. 'I've never seen such determination in one so young.'

'An admirable trait,' I said.

She looked at the table. 'I suppose so, but...' She frowned, shook her head. 'I can't help thinking ... Charlotte sometimes pushed herself too hard.'

'She sang beautifully in *Angel of the Glade*,' I said.

This was meant as an oblique compliment to Miss Wade's teaching skill, but the compliment didn't register. Miss Wade seemed lost in her own thoughts.

'Charlotte once read Ibsen for me,' she said. 'She did a remarkable Hedda Gabler. I

137

was endeavoring to set up a trust fund to send her to drama school in New York when she was murdered.'

I thought of the thousand dollars in Charlotte's sock.

'And her father was entirely unable to do anything for her?' I asked.

'I'm afraid Mr Scott invested unwisely,' she said. 'Do you remember the Panamanian Land Fraud Scandal a few years back?'

'I do.'

'He was one of the unlucky souls who lost his life savings. Charlotte told me the money was really meant for her.'

'That's an awful shame,' I said.

'Yes, it is. Charlotte cried terribly. She was hoping her father's money might save her from Fairfield. She was hoping the money would send her to drama school. I'm afraid Mr Scott didn't fully understand what he was getting into.'

I took a sip of my Darjeeling, impressed yet also saddened by Charlotte's dream.

'So when her father lost his money, what did she do?' I asked. 'She obviously didn't give up.'

'Heavens, no,' said Miss Wade. 'She was broken-hearted for a week or two but then her ... her determination came back. You see what spirit the girl had, Dr Deacon? She was going to be an actress and nothing was going to stop her, not even her father's financial misfortune.'

'I understand she was fond of Michael Sims for a while,' I said.

A smile came to Miss Wade's face. 'Michael is a sweet man,' she said. 'Quite a few years older than Charlotte, but that didn't seem to bother the two of them.'

'I understand he's fond of opera.'

'Yes, he is,' said Miss Wade. 'He always attends Mrs Vanduzen's musical soirées. I believe he's attempting to learn the violin.'

I lifted a water cracker and spread a small bit of champagne jelly on top of it.

'And she was fond of Roger Robson as well,' I said.

Miss Wade put her teacup and saucer on the teakwood table, keeping her back erect, her shoulders straight, her movements precise.

'I can't say I particularly like Roger,' she said, 'but, yes, they were fond of each other. They were a handsome couple. I think they came together quite by accident. Young people are so often like that, aren't they, doctor? I think each wore the other like a fine suit of clothes. They complemented each other. Whether there was any love between them, I can't say. I found the whole affair frivolous, but young girls are bound to be frivolous from time to time.' She lifted a sprig of parsley and inspected it. 'She certainly didn't talk much about Roger.'

'I see.' I nibbled a bit of my cracker. 'And did Charlotte have any female companions –

any confidantes, besides yourself?'

Up on the glass roof of the conservatory a squirrel scampered by. 'Just Toula,' she said.

'Toula?' I echoed.

'I'm not sure of the woman's last name. She must be four or five years older than Charlotte. I don't know where Charlotte found her. She brought her to our coaching sessions from time to time. The lipstick-wearing came from Toula. And so did the gum-chewing. Toula was rather a rough girl.'

The squirrel jumped from the conservatory roof on to a neighboring spruce.

'Do you know where Toula lives?' I asked.

'No,' she said. 'I hardly knew her.'

Miss Wade was looking past my shoulder. I turned, and from behind the fronds of a large potted palm I saw the flurry of a black skirt as the housemaid quickly retreated.

'You'll have to forgive Freda,' said Miss Wade. 'She's curious about you, doctor. I think we all are.'

I turned back to Miss Wade, wondering how best to answer her veiled enquiry, knowing that here was an opportunity to reveal myself, and thus to gain a greater intimacy with Miss Wade. She was curious about my notoriety. I was the doctor who had tried unsuccessfully to save President McKinley's life last year. She had every right to be curious. Yet the subject pained me; I could hardly speak about it. And, as if in concordance with my pain, Miss Wade's features softened,

140

and a look of compassion came to her eyes; an expression of understanding and concern. I couldn't remember the last time a woman had looked at me that way. I again thought of Emily, how terribly I missed her, and how alone I'd felt all these years without her.

'I assure you, Miss Wade, there's nothing to be curious about,' I said.

A perfect chance to reveal myself, to find in Miss Wade a sympathetic friend, and yet, thinking of Emily, I felt like a sea urchin closing up at the barest breath of danger.

'You were a friend of the President's?' she asked.

'Here we are in Fairfield,' I said, bluntly changing the subject, 'you from Boston, and I from Washington. I have my own reasons for not going back to Washington, but I'm stumped as to why you haven't returned to Boston. With your aunt's passing, I can't imagine why you'd want to stay here.'

Her cheeks reddened, and her eyes grew pensive. I felt I'd unwittingly uncovered a part of Miss Wade that should have stayed hidden. Her eyes glistened and she compressed her full lips as she struggled for words.

'Forgive me,' I said. 'I've been most inappropriate.'

'I'm sorry, doctor...' She looked at her hands. 'I'm just that...' She glanced at the mounds of uneaten food with a kind of hopelessness. 'It's not that there's anything

141

keeping me in Fairfield,' she said. 'It's just that personal circumstances have made it advisable for me to forsake Boston, at least for the next little while.'

She looked at me, and we gazed into each other's eyes, and it was as if a current passed between us, the undeniable voltage of a mutual attraction; not only an attraction, but a deeper understanding, a willingness to extend ourselves for each other. She gave me a nod and a smile, accepting the way I looked at her; maybe even pleased by it. If it weren't for Everett Howse, I would willingly have allowed myself, right there on the spot, to fall in love with Olive Wade. And if it weren't for Emily floating somewhere about me, I would have reached out and touched Miss Wade's hand, let her know without equivocation just how I felt about her. But I couldn't. I let the opportunity slide by, and later, on my way home, I cursed myself for it.

ELEVEN

I was called, in my professional capacity as doctor, to the Early residence the next day to examine Mrs Early; a fortuitous circumstance, as it would give me the opportunity to further substantiate Mr Early's status as a suspect in the Charlotte Scott murder case. I was ushered into his house on Talbot Lane by one of his two servants, a slight girl who couldn't have been more than sixteen, and who introduced herself as Florrie.

'And is Mr Early expected home for lunch?' I asked, as she led me down a narrow corridor toward the sickroom.

'He's always home by noon, sir.' I took out my pocket watch. Half past eleven. That would work nicely. I fully expected my examination of Alice Early to take a full half-hour at least.

Florrie rapped lightly on the sickroom door.

'Excuse me, ma'am,' she said, 'but the doctor is here to see you.'

'Send him in,' called a faint voice.

Florrie opened the door and I entered the sickroom.

I found Alice Early propped up in a narrow cot, her back supported by three pillows, her legs covered with a quilt. She was really a patient of Dr Olaf Thorensen's, but the Norwegian physician was now baffled by the case of Alice Early and had asked me to provide a second opinion.

'Morning, Mrs Early,' I said.

'Good morning, doctor.'

Even this small pleasantry seemed to pain her. I put my bag on the chair and gazed at her, making some preliminary observations. She looked about thirty. Her skin was as pale as talc, and her long straight hair, parted in the middle, hung limply around her thin shoulders in waxy, straw-colored strands. She was indeed plain. What she needed, I thought, was joy. With some joy to animate her face she might be pretty.

'I've read Dr Thorensen's notes,' I said. 'He's been thorough in documenting your illness, Mrs Early.'

'I wish there were some way you could help me, Dr Deacon,' she said, dooming me to failure even before I'd begun, 'but the pain I suffer seems to be of a most elusive sort. Dr Thorensen started by calling it neuritis and, as I understand it, that might account for some of the localized pain I have in my shoulders and in the backs of my arms. As for my headaches, he's still undecided.'

'And have the headaches been getting any

better at all?' I asked. 'I see he has you on salicylate acid.'

'If anything, they're worse.' She looked down at her thin white hands. 'You see, doctor, I worry. And when I worry, my head hurts. I've told Dr Thorensen this a thousand times, but he doesn't seem to have a remedy for it. He says I should take a tumbler of brandy in the evening, but I find that brandy disagrees with me. My headache might disappear for a while, but in the morning it's always worse.'

'What do you worry about?' I asked.

She looked away. The light of the overcast day coming in through the window made her look paler than she really was. Her eyes momentarily clouded with tears. She seemed suddenly shy of me.

'I can guarantee you, Mrs Early,' I said, 'your confidences will be strictly respected.'

'I worry about death,' she said. 'I worry about how, when I die, I might be punished.'

'And why should you be punished?' I asked.

She paused. 'Because of the way I sometimes feel toward Herbert.' She turned to me, a helpless look in her eyes. 'Sometimes I think the most horrid thoughts about him. And that's wrong of me, doctor. He's been so good to me, and so patient. Look at me. I'm twenty-nine. Half the time I'm in this bed; and when I'm up and about, I'm in my wheelchair. My sciatica just won't leave me alone. Have you any idea how excruciating it is?'

I looked down at Dr Thorensen's notes. 'And you've had three flare-ups in the last two months?' I said.

'Can I really blame Herbert for all this pain?' she asked. Her hands absently clutched the edge of the quilt. 'I don't think I can. I only wish he could spend more time with me. He's suggested a companion, someone who could read to me, but I...' She lifted the back of her palm to her forehead, as if she felt suddenly faint. 'I would feel...' She seemed at a loss.

'You don't like the idea,' I concluded.

Her eyes narrowed, and in a quieter voice she said, 'I don't mind the pain so much, I've grown used to it. And every so often I have a good day. And that makes up for a lot. But it's more than just pain, Dr Deacon.' Again she looked away, stared at the roll of Pep-O-Mints on her bedside table. 'I just feel so ... so desolate sometimes. I feel as if I ... I don't belong to anyone or anything. When Herbert comes home at the end of the day, I sometimes think he's a perfect stranger. I know I shouldn't think that. He's only human, but he seems so ... you see those flowers up there?'

I turned. On the bureau there stood a vase filled with long-stemmed yellow roses. I remembered the thirty yellow roses in Charlotte's room.

'They're lovely,' I said.

'I hate them,' she said. 'They represent to me the incarnation of Herbert's hypocrisy.' I turned from the roses and peered at her closely. Did she know something about Charlotte, then? 'He doesn't talk to me about his ideas any more. When I first knew him, Herbert was full of ideas. But now he hardly says anything. He lives in this house with me, but I feel as if I've been abandoned. He never discusses his plans with me any more. These physical maladies of mine would be much easier to bear if every day I didn't wake up to a sense of overwhelming abandonment.' She stopped. Her breast rose and fell with great agitation.

'Maybe you should rest now, Mrs Early,' I said. 'You look tired. I have something that might help you sleep.'

'I might be ill, doctor, but I'm not blind.' She turned away. 'But that's enough of that,' she said. 'Forgive me, doctor.'

'Have you told Mr Early about these ... these dissatisfactions of yours?' I asked.

She looked at me wearily. 'He's been struggling so hard for his recent promotion at the school,' she said. 'These dissatisfactions, as you call them – what are they but the baseless apprehensions of a worry-sick mind? Were I even to whisper about the way I feel, about what I've come to suspect ... I'm without means, Dr Deacon. Mr Early is my sole support.'

'But if you find things so intolerable, Mrs Early, wouldn't it be better to—'

'I still love him, Dr Deacon.' She reached for an embroidered handkerchief. 'He's always hated weakness. It's a pity, really, that we should turn out this way. He tells me I'm entirely blameless. I'm twenty-nine; I have rheumatism, neuritis, and sciatica. God will have His way. Herbert wants to rise in the world. He wants to climb the peaks, Dr Deacon. He's already sent applications to some of the most prestigious colleges in Albany and New York. He wants to soar. Indeed, he deserves to soar. But how am I to soar with him when I'm bedbound all the time? I'm afraid I never will.'

'Mrs Early, the late President McKinley's wife was an invalid as well, and I don't think her condition stopped his rise to the most prominent office of this nation.'

A fragile smile came to her face. 'You're too kind, Dr Deacon. I love my husband, and I wish with all my heart to aid him in his ambitions. But this marriage of ours, it's no longer a thing that grows. And it's certainly not something I should be troubling you with. You're a physician. Your task is to heal my body, not probe the darkness in my soul. The Reverend Porteous visits me twice a week and gives me solace.' She forced a false cheer to her face. 'And just last week Mrs Vanduzen was kind enough to visit. She read to me a most delightful paper she'd written

148

for the Thanatopsis Club on Chinese wallpaper design. Can you imagine? I felt like the luckiest woman in all Fairfield to have the Mayor's wife reading to me like that. What an honor!' There hung about her words a miasma of heartbreak. 'Alas, doctor,' she said, after a pause to catch her breath, 'is there anything you might recommend that Dr Thorensen hasn't already tried?'

I glanced down at Dr Thorensen's notes. I heard the front door open and, a moment later, Herbert Early's voice as he asked Florrie to prepare lunch.

'I think for your sciatica we should try a spray-mist of ethyl chloride on the affected nerves,' I said. 'For your rheumatism, gold salts and a hot poultice. As for your neuritis and headaches...' My mustache drooped around my lips. 'I'll prescribe some pain-killer.'

'Thank you, doctor.'

'Now, what about your varicose veins?' I asked. 'How's the Scheele's Prussic Acid working out?'

I'd ventured beyond my professional calling now. I was probing, in the guise of my professional interest in my patient, Herbert Early's culpability.

She stared at me blankly. 'I beg your pardon?' she said.

I glanced down at Dr Thorensen's notes, pretending to be confused. 'Your varicose veins,' I said. 'Did not Dr Thorensen prescribe—'

'I don't have varicose veins, doctor,' she said. 'I think you must be mistaking me for another patient.'

This, of course, was the revelation I'd hoped for. According to Gordon Wiley, the drug store owner, Herbert Early had purchased a vial of Scheele's Prussic Acid for the purpose of treating his wife's varicose veins. Now she was telling me she didn't have varicose veins. And if she didn't have varicose veins why would Mr Early need prussic acid? Why, by Jim, unless it was to poison Charlotte Scott?

As I left Alice Early in her sickroom and ventured into the corridor, I was accosted immediately by Herbert Early, whose solicitous expression under these new circumstances I found not only disconcerting but duplicitous.

'I'm so glad you've come, Dr Deacon,' he said. 'Please follow me into the parlor. I've asked Florrie to prepare lunch for us. I hope you can stay.'

'I wouldn't want to trouble you, Mr Early,' I said.

'There's no trouble,' he said. 'She's just heating a chowder.'

He ushered me into the parlor. I looked around, bewildered by the room. Why cram artificial Ionic columns against the wall? Why clutter every surface with artificial fruit? And why decorate the upright pianoforte with gilt edges and a velvet antimacassar when the battered old instrument had the prosaic aspect of a box-car? His wallpaper was startling. It depicted scenes of classical antiquity, done in soft yellows and golds, with vistas of fluted pillars, archways, and piazzas.

'You like the wallpaper,' he said.

I nodded dumbly.

'I've spent hours getting this room just right,' he said.

I glanced toward the piano. 'Do you play?' I asked.

'No,' he said. 'That's my wife's instrument. An heirloom. I've added the gilt. My wife used to play, but she can't any more.' He glanced at me with a look of guarded hope. 'Were you able to do anything for Alice?' he asked.

I gave him a run-down of my findings and my proposed treatment.

'I might have changed her medicine, Mr Early,' I said, 'but I don't believe medicine has much to do with it. A patient with an emotional ache confounds an average practitioner like myself.'

He stared at me. He affected great puzzlement.

'Emotional ache?' he said.

I wasn't going to prevaricate.

'I suppose it's because you had to coach Charlotte Scott so thoroughly,' I said.

Two pink spots climbed into his cheeks

and his eyes blazed in astonishment as my meaning became clear to him. Florrie appeared at the door with a steaming tureen of clam chowder and a plate of water biscuits. Mr Early lifted his hand angrily.

'Not now, Florrie!' he snapped.

Florrie, all a-fluster, looked at me, then at her master, gave us a quick curtsey, and retreated to the safety of the kitchen. Several seconds passed before Mr Early regained his wits.

Then he said emphatically, 'That's the most preposterous insinuation I've ever heard.'

I gazed at him intently. I studied him as if he were a specimen. Finally, I sighed, leaned back in my chair, crossed my legs, and pulled out a cigar.

'Do you mind?' I asked.

'If you must,' he said.

I struck a match and lit my cigar. I continued to stare at him through the cloud of blue smoke that drifted from my mouth. He couldn't contain himself any longer.

'Would you mind telling me who...' He sat back, crossing his legs with great agitation. 'What ridiculous charges have been laid against me?' he demanded.

I shook the match, stifling its flame, and deposited it into the ashtray.

'I was raised in Clifford's Bend, Tennessee, Mr Early,' I said. 'Population, 612. In small towns, things usually get said for a reason. I know all about small towns.'

'Then you must know that half the people here are vindictive, narrow, self-serving philistines.'

Not the best attitude, I thought, considering he was going to be the high school principal next year.

'Charge number one,' I said, 'you were down at the river alone with Miss Scott at or around the time she was murdered.'

'That's a lie,' he said.

'Mr Early,' I said, as mild as could be, 'I'm prepared to listen. You no doubt had a good reason for being down at the river with her. Maybe you wanted to talk to her about her performance. Or maybe you wanted to congratulate her.'

He leaned forward, put his hands on his knees, and shook his head, nearly beside himself. 'People in this town envy me, Dr Deacon,' he said. 'I'm a teacher. I love culture. I love books. I love music. I really don't belong in Fairfield. People see me as different, and because I'm different, they're afraid of me. They don't like me, though they won't say so to my face. They show it in other ways, like slandering me behind my back. I was never anywhere near that river with Charlotte.'

I ignored his denial.

'Charge number two,' I said, looking at the ash on the end of my cigar, 'three days before the murder, you bought a vial of

Scheele's Prussic Acid at Wiley's Drug Store for your wife's varicose veins. I know this. I've seen Gordon Wiley's inventory record. When I asked your wife about her varicose veins just now, she told me she didn't have any. It doesn't look good, Mr Early. And I'm waiting for you to explain it to me.'

I took a pull on my cigar and watched his expression quiver with sudden apprehension. 'That's ridiculous,' he said. 'I refuse to be bullied by—'

'Could I see the vial of Scheele's, please?'

I wanted to see how much was gone so I could compare it with how much I'd found in Charlotte's stomach.

'By Jove!' he said. 'You think I murdered Charlotte Scott.'

'Mr Early, the Scheele's, please,' I said.

His eyes went so wide they looked as if they might pop out of his head. He stared at me a moment more then, to my perplexity, lifted his pant leg. A varicose vein the size of an earthworm bulged from his calf.

'I bought the Scheele's for myself!' he said.

'Then why did you tell Mr Wiley it was for your wife?'

'Only old men have varicose veins,' he said. So. Male pride.

'Varicose veins are nothing to be ashamed of, Mr Early,' I said, softening my tone.

'And I swear to you, I was nowhere near that river with Miss Scott.'

I let this go. I didn't want to push him. I

would let the matter gnaw; give the medicine a chance to work. As for the prussic acid ... well, Mr Early's varicose vein was undeniable, like a deep purple welt on his leg. I leaned closer, inspecting the inflammation.

'I don't use prussic acid any more for varicose veins,' I said. I looked up at him. 'I'll have Wiley's clerk bring you some elastic hose. That should give you at least some relief. Put them on while you're still in bed in the morning. And for heaven's sake, get rid of those garters.'

I got up, tapped the ash of my cigar into his fireplace, and turned around. I had no intention of staying for lunch any more. Mr Early stared at me morosely.

'And as I leave, Mr Early,' I said, 'I want you to think about things. Think about what Mr and Mrs Scott and poor Bernice have had to go through. Think about Charlotte. Think about all her dreams. Think about how all those sweet girlish ambitions are gone. And think about your fellow Fairfielders.' I squared my shoulders. 'These might be small-town folk, Mr Early, they might even be philistines, as you call them, but they're still hurting, and that's what you should keep uppermost in your mind.'

PART TWO

A Trip to the Fair

TWELVE

At midnight, as I was getting into my nightshirt, I heard knocking at the surgery door. I put on my slippers and went downstairs. When I opened the door I saw Rupert Scales, the town drunk, standing on the front porch, his face covered with blood, a deep gash in his forehead. He smelled of alcohol, and was carrying a nearly empty bottle of whiskey.

'Sorry, doc,' he said. 'I know it's late but...' He looked at my nightshirt and screwed up his eyes, his head bobbing a few times. 'What time is it, anyway?'

'What have you done to yourself, Rupert?' I asked.

'I hope I didn't wake you,' he said. 'I have this small cut on my head.' The small cut was a two-inch gash. 'I thought it might need a stitch or two.' He leaned forward, bending at the waist, stumbling a bit as he showed me his gash. 'I thought I could get your professional opinion.'

I examined the gash, and then shook my head. 'Let's get you inside,' I said.

I took him by the elbow.

158

'Thanks, doc,' he said. He stumbled into the vestibule. 'Say, doc, I hear you order your bourbon straight from Tennessee.'

'Rupert, how old are you?'

'Forty-five.'

'You're going to run into trouble soon if you don't stop drinking. How'd you get that gash?'

'Now, doc,' he said, 'this gash ain't my fault.' I led him through the waiting-room into the examining-room. 'Frank Jaslowski pushed me. I tripped over the curb.'

I turned on the light. 'Why did Frank Jaslowski push you?' I asked.

'Because Arnie Murchison told him to,' he said, 'that's why.' His tone was querulous.

'So you were at the Parthenon?' I said.

He hoisted himself up on to the examining-table and looked around at the shelves of dressings, gauze, and tissue paper, his eyes bleary, his face streaked with a dozen rivulets of dried blood. He took a sip of whiskey.

'I'm still after Arnie to pay me for the work I did on that racing trap,' he said. 'I've been after him all week. I don't see why he can't pay me. Those boys from Saratoga Springs came by tonight and they got their money just fine. Why can't Arnie pay me mine?'

He gazed at me as if there were no justice in the world.

'Don't get yourself excited, Rupert,' I said. 'I'm sure Mr Murchison will pay you as soon as he can.' I raised my hand. 'Could you give me your bottle?'

'Why?'

'Because I want you to lie down.'

He reluctantly handed his bottle to me. 'Don't spill any,' he said.

'I won't.'

'It ain't no fancy Tennessee bourbon, but it's all I got.'

I put the bottle on the counter.

'Lie down,' I said gently. 'Try to relax. You're fidgeting.'

He lifted his legs with some difficulty and lay down on the examining-table.

'Say, do you think Sheriff Armstrong would let me sleep in the jail tonight?' he asked.

'I'm not sure if he's there,' I said, getting out my suturing needles, thread, and wood alcohol. 'Mrs Armstrong's just had a baby daughter and he's trying to spend as much time with her as he can.' I took a fresh piece of gauze and soaked it with alcohol. 'I'm going to clean you up a bit,' I said. 'Try to hold still.'

I leaned over the man and pressed the alcohol-soaked gauze to his wound. He winced.

'Ouch! What is that stuff?' he said.

'Wood alcohol,' I replied.

A philosophical look came to his face. 'Can you drink it?' he asked.

'Only if you want a quick trip to the next

world.' As I wiped the dirt and blood away, I saw the extent of his gash. 'That looks bad, Rupert. You're going to have a scar.'

He pressed his lips together. 'Dang that Jaslowski!' he fumed. 'He didn't have no right kicking me out of no Parthenon Theater.'

'Were you making a nuisance of yourself?' I put the cloth aside and threaded the needle.

'Of course I wasn't,' he said. 'All I did was ask Toula for a drink. It's a free country, ain't it? And it ain't against the law to ask someone for a drink, is it? And I wouldn't be asking for no drinks if Arnie would pay up.'

I stopped threading my needle. 'Toula?' I said.

Toula, the rough girl Olive Wade had described to me; Charlotte's friend, the girl who wore lipstick and chewed gum.

Rupert looked at me as if he were surprised. 'You don't know Toula?' he said. He shrugged, accepting my ignorance. I think he believed I'd been sadly short-changed in life because I didn't know the mysterious Toula. 'Toula's just about the prettiest girl God ever made, that's all. And just about the nicest.'

How many girls in Fairfield could be called Toula? Not many. I took a chance. 'Charlotte's friend,' I said.

I began nonchalantly threading my needle again.

'That's the one,' he said. He was looking at

the hooked needle with some trepidation. 'Say, doc, this ain't going to hurt, is it?'

'Toula works at the Parthenon?' I asked.

'Oh, sure,' he said, trying to muster his courage. 'Her and Charlotte both.' He tried to get up. 'Actually, I don't think this little old gash is so bad after all.' He was still looking at my needle as if it were the maw of Hell. 'I think I'm just going to put a bandage on it. I shouldn't be troubling you so late like this.'

'Lie down, Rupert,' I ordered. I reached for his bottle. 'Drink this.'

He nodded. 'I guess if anything's going to kill the pain, this will,' he said. And he drank greedily. When he was done, a euphoric grin came to his face. 'Funny how a sip or two makes everything clearer. You go ahead, doc. A few little pokes ain't nothing I can't handle.'

I bent over and made my first suture, pulling the green thread through the ragged flaps of skin.

'And Charlotte and Toula work as dancers?' I said.

'I thought you knew that, doc,' he said.

I executed my second suture. I digested this new information. Charlotte worked as a dancer at the Parthenon. She snuck out of the house late at night and walked across town to the theater to dance. But why? To earn money? To gain experience? Rupert's forehead was a mapwork of premature wrinkles and previous scars. And why hadn't Murchison told me about this?

The next night I went to the Parthenon. One of the gents pointed Toula out to me. She was up on stage dancing with a green feather boa. She was dressed in harem pants, crowned with an elaborate gold headdress, wore not only wrist bracelets but ankle bracelets. The bill-card said: 'CLEOPATRA AND HER FATAL ASP'. As such things went, she made a convincing Cleopatra, possessed all the charm and mystery of Ancient Egypt, with her dark eyes, tresses of black hair, and olive-skinned shoulders. Yet I couldn't imagine the real Empress of the Nile cavorting in such an acrobatic way. I grew convinced that Toula must have had a circus background. She had none of the indulgent curves and superfluities that might make her ideal for employment at the Parthenon; her figure was boyish, muscular, and as hard as a razor strop. She looked more like a trapeze artist.

When she was done, I had one of the waiters intercept her before she could scurry backstage. She looked over the waiter's shoulder and picked me out in the cavernous and echoing theater. She then glanced apprehensively at Arnold Murchison's closed office door. She finally said a few words to the waiter and worked her way through the tables toward me. As she reached me, she seemed to pierce me with her cold green eyes.

'What do you want?' she asked.

She must have had this happen often – a man wanting to talk to her after her performance. Under such circumstances, I could hardly expect unrestrained enthusiasm.

'My name is Clyde Deacon,' I said. I took out my badge and placed it on the table where it glimmered in the light of the small candle. 'I'm investigating Charlotte Scott's murder. I understand you were Charlotte's friend.'

Her eyes narrowed apprehensively.

'I'm sorry, I can't talk to you,' she said.

Her blunt refusal caught me by surprise. She began moving away. I got up and caught her by the wrist.

'Let me go,' she said.

Men at neighboring tables cast curious glances our way.

'I insist, Miss … Miss…' I was hoping for her last name, but she wouldn't give it to me. 'You at least owe Charlotte a minute or two,' I said. 'That's all I want.'

I let go. Her features softened and her full lips came forward in a questioning pout, her eyes glistening with sudden sadness. Even Cleopatra grieved for her dead friend. She glanced toward the bar where Frank Jaslowski, hunched to one side on his shorter leg, stared at us with unconcealed suspicion.

'A few minutes?' she said.

'That's all,' I said.

She hesitated, then eased into the chair across from me. I took my own seat. On stage, a vaudevillian played the trumpet, rode a unicycle, and twirled an umbrella, all at the same time. The gents in the audience weren't impressed. They were waiting for the next burlesque act to start.

'You're the doctor?' she said.

Her English was accented. She sounded Greek. Or perhaps Macedonian. She was anxious, looked like she didn't want to sit with me. She reminded me of a trapped animal who wanted to get away. I couldn't understand why.

'I am,' I said.

'What do you want?'

'You know what I want.'

Toula lifted her elbow on to the paper place-mat and rested her chin on her upraised palm. She glanced at a table of fellows across the way. She then turned her gaze toward the corridor leading backstage.

'I have no idea who killed Charlotte,' she said. 'There. Can I go now?'

The vaudevillian had now cast away his trumpet and umbrella and juggled three red balls while still riding his unicycle.

'Were you good friends with Charlotte?' I asked. But she seemed not to hear. She was watching a loud altercation between a waiter and one of the patrons near the front door.

She quickly grew bored by this. She looked up into the smoky rafters, her eyes narrowing.

'I taught Charlotte things,' she said at last. 'I taught her how to be a woman. I made her understand just what she could do. I made her understand her power.' A defiant grin came to her face. 'I loved Charlotte,' she said. 'Unfortunately, she didn't love me back. Not in the way I wanted her to.' Her eyes, circled by dark eye-liner, were like pieces of jade. 'So, yes, we were just good friends, nothing more.'

It took a moment before I understood her meaning. 'Did she work as a dancer at the Parthenon long?' I asked.

But, again, it was as if she hadn't heard. 'I liked to watch Charlotte dance,' she said, her eyes growing distant. 'She used her arms when she danced. She even used her fingers. Not many girls can do that.' Toula twisted her lips to one side, a tough-girl pose. 'She made men squirm. You don't know how much I enjoyed that, watching them squirm when she was up on stage. She had a real talent for making them squirm.' Then, without warning, her face went perplexingly blank, as if she'd suddenly been struck with a poison dart. 'Can I go now?' she asked.

'Why are you so anxious to get away?'

Toula was looking over my shoulder. I glanced behind me.

Frank Jaslowski was lurching our way. He

was a formidable man, six and a half feet tall, with ox-like shoulders. As he reached our table he said sharply, 'Miss Vassos!'

At least I had her last name now.

She got up, her eyes still blank, her lips slack.

'Yes, Mr Jaslowski,' she said.

And she walked away like an automaton backstage, slyly displaying her contempt for Mr Jaslowski.

I stood up. 'What the devil do you think you're doing?' I demanded.

Jaslowski stared at me, his grey eyes like stones. 'Mr Murchison don't like the girls talking to the patrons,' he said.

And he lurched back to the bar. I stared after him. My first impulse was to knock on Murchison's door, find out the real reason why I wasn't allowed to talk to Toula, and why Murchison hadn't told me up-front about Charlotte's employment here as a dancer. But then I thought I'd better leave it. At least until I had better information. All I had was information from the town drunk. Better wait until I had the opportunity to talk to Toula alone. Then I would be better equipped for a second interview with Arnold Murchison.

I worked all afternoon the next day, made a few country calls late in the day, and didn't get back to Fairfield till dusk. I saw rain clouds moving in from the west. I was just climbing the porch steps when I heard a bicycle bell out on the street behind me. I turned around. It was Olive Wade. Even from this distance I saw that there was something terribly wrong. She came to a stop in front of the surgery, leaned her bicycle against the iron pike fence and, lifting her skirt so it wouldn't drag, hurried up the walk, her face flushed, her lips pressed together, her intelligent blue eyes wide with worry.

'Dr Deacon, you must come quickly,' she said, in a breathless voice. Her hair was flyblown under her tightly tied boater. 'Some men have gathered around the oak tree on Cherry Hill. Forty or fifty at least. I believe it's the sheriff's posse. I heard some shooting. I believe they mean to hang a man.'

I took her by the arm.

'Sit down and rest, Miss Wade,' I said. 'You're out of breath. I'll ride up on Pythagoras.'

When I had Miss Wade settled on the front porch, I hurried into the surgery, unlocked my writing desk, and retrieved my revolver; my Army Frontier Colt model with the seven-and-a-half-inch barrel, the gun I'd used in Cross Plains. I loaded it, shoved a box of ammunition into my pocket, and put on my riding boots. I grabbed my hat, rushed out the back door, and saddled Pythagoras in no time flat. I rode her down the gravel drive at a trot, gave a final wave to

Miss Wade and, once on Culver Street, spurred Pythagoras to a full gallop.

I rode across the Tonawanda Road bridge past the metalworks and climbed Cherry Hill. At the top of Cherry Hill, I bolted along Erie Boulevard. Soon I reached the pasture and summit behind Miss Wade's house. The sky began to spit rain, yet far to the west I saw a break in the clouds; a red band of twilight, the clear air of a fairweather front. I saw horses and men silhouetted against this red band up near the solitary oak tree. As I got closer I discerned the unmistakable outline of a noose hanging over the lowest branch of the tree.

I spurred Pythagoras relentlessly, drew my revolver and fired a few shots in the air. The horses by the tree grew skittish, and the men moved about, anxious, unprepared for this last-minute interruption of their deadly work, some trying to calm their horses, two or three slipping away on horseback into the thick sumac that grew on the west side of the hill. As I drew within twenty feet, I jumped from my horse and fired another shot into the air.

'You boys break this up or, by golly, I'll plug every last one of you,' I said.

I saw a small Chinese man sitting on the ground, badly beaten, the left sleeve half torn off his dirt-covered cheviot coat, his derby lying crushed at his feet, his cheek scraped and bleeding, his lip broken, his eye turning purple. He looked up at me, spoke to me in Chinese, but I couldn't understand a word. The posse stood around, mostly young men in farm clothes, their faces sullen, resentful, half of them carrying rifles or shotguns. Morley Suggett, Charlotte's childhood sweetheart, and the leader of this posse, stepped forward out of the crowd. He towered above everybody else. 'You get on your horse, doctor,' he said, 'and get yourself out of here. We don't want no outsiders interfering with town business. We got a man's work to do here and we intend to do it. Ain't no one going to stop us.'

I stared at him. I understood: I was an outsider; I was from Tennessee; I was a Southerner.

'Morley, son,' I said, 'I'd advise you to step aside and let me take Mr Lip into custody.'

'We already got him in custody,' he said. 'We don't need your help. We know how to deal with this here Chinaman. You get yourself out of here now if you know what's good for you. We spent a lot of horse flesh catching this man, and now he's got to pay up.'

I smiled, but it was my hard smile, the one I used for horse thieves and cattle rustlers in Cross Plains.

'Morley, I'll give you one last chance, and then I'm going to have to take you over my knee.'

Surprised murmuring swept through the crowd. I looked around. I kept my smile.

Some men chuckled. But it wasn't good-natured chuckling. I'd insulted Morley; they smelled blood, and that's what they chuckled about, the prospect of violence, the chance to see me pulverized by the gargantuan Mr Suggett. Here was some entertainment they hadn't counted on; as good as a cock-fight, even better. Morley wasn't chuckling. Morley was scowling.

'Go on, now, doctor,' he said. 'You get yourself out of here.'

I ignored Morley. 'Mr Lip, could you come with me, please?' I said.

This was more than Morley Suggett could take. Like a bull enraged by red cloth, his nostrils flared, his shoulders rose, and he thundered toward me, his hands folding into fists. My own fists came up, and I danced back, jumping to the left, darting around him. He slid on the wet ground and fell. I kept my guard up, waiting for another attack. I glanced around and looked at the other men. Some looked ready to help Morley, one or two even stepped forward, but Morley grunted, held up his hand.

'I don't need nobody's help,' he said. 'You boys stay back. I can handle this man myself.'

The way he held his fists, like great bear paws drooping in front of his chest, I knew he couldn't have had any formal training in the boxing ring. He lumbered toward me again, but I again danced out of the way,

171

placed my feet firmly apart to give myself some good leverage on the wet ground, and launched a strong uppercut into his solar plexus. The boy doubled over, sputtered, gasped for air, his eyes wide with surprise. I thought I had him. But his recovery was quick. He lunged for me, clipping me on the cheek with his fist, knocking me backward over the wet ground, so I had to back-pedal several times to catch my balance. He pressed his attack, lunging again, like a bull moose charging me. He grabbed me by the shoulders and flung me, as easily as he might have flung a rag doll, toward the tree.

I went flying through the air.

I landed with a grunt, looked up, saw him coming again, was struggling to get to my feet, but before I could, he kicked me in the ribs. I collapsed on to my side, winded by this blow, tried to catch my breath, kept rolling away from him, heard some of the men chuckle again, as if they thought Morley had the advantage now, pushed myself up, got to my feet, and let my anger take control; the same anger I'd used to neutralize an artillery position on San Juan Hill. I marched toward Morley with a deadly stride. He took another swing at me, but I dodged out of the way, and punched him in the mouth. I saw the way to work it with Morley. I couldn't give him time to recover. So I punched him again, this time in the eye, then stuck my foot behind his ankle and tripped him into the mud. He went down like a fifty-foot Douglas fir in timber season. Before he even knew what had happened, I jumped knees first on to his stomach, using my whole body like a big fist. The wind rushed out of his lungs, his eyes opened wide, he gasped for breath, and his face contorted with agony. I got to my feet and kicked him in the ribs, didn't give him even a second to recover and kicked him again, as hard as I could, making sure he got my message. As I went to kick him a third time, two farm boys broke from the circle and approached me, their fists coming up. I was tired of this. I wasn't going to take any more of their insolence. I drew my gun and cocked the hammer.

'Just try it,' I said. The boys stopped, stared at me sullenly; they couldn't have been more than eighteen.

'You ain't fighting fair,' one of them said.

'I don't fight to fight fair,' I said. 'I fight to win.'

Keeping my gun trained on the boys, I walked over to Richard Lip and helped him to his feet. He pointed to my cheek and spoke excitedly in Chinese. I reached up and touched my face, pulled my fingers away, and saw blood. Morley's clip on my cheek had broken my skin open, nothing a small dressing wouldn't fix. Morley was still gasping on the ground. I walked over.

'You should be ashamed of yourself, son,' I

said. 'I know you loved Charlotte and all, but the sheriff gave you strict orders not to hurt Mr Lip.'

'We got two lame horses because of him,' he managed to say.

'That don't matter,' I said. 'You still had orders.'

I walked back to Mr Lip. He looked terrified. He had no idea why all these men wanted to hang him. He looked at me as if I'd just descended from Olympus. I glanced at the hanging branch. I reached up and pulled the noose down.

'Somebody lose their rope?' I said. I stared at the noose. 'That's a mighty fine slip-knot.' I looked around at the crowd, my smile slipping away, my true disgust showing through. 'A mighty fine slip-knot,' I repeated, 'only none of you look like sailors.' I was so angry I spit on the ground. 'Matter of fact, y'all look like a passel of cowards.'

I helped Richard Lip to my horse. Morley got to his feet. 'You ain't going nowhere with that there Chinaman, doctor,' he said. 'That Chinaman belongs to us.'

'This man's innocent until proven guilty, son,' I said. I pointed my gun directly at Morley's head. 'And if you're going to argue again, you're going to have to argue with this.'

We stared at each other. I saw that he wasn't a bad man, just heartbroken over Charlotte, just wanting to do something, anything, to ease his pain, to somehow right a wrong that could never be fixed.

'Go on, now,' I said. 'You boys break this up. You go on home now.'

I helped the tiny Mr Lip on to Pythagoras, then got on to the filly myself.

We were halfway to Olive Wade's fence when I heard gunfire; a single loud boom, shotgun fire. An instant later, Pythagoras shuddered and Mr Lip cried out, and I knew we'd been hit. Pythagoras reared up, panicked, and in my ensuing struggle to bring the horse under control, Mr Lip fell to the ground. I glanced back at the oak tree as I yanked on the reins and I saw the posse scattering. Cowards! Dogs! To shoot us when our backs were turned. No wonder they ran. They were infidels, the lot! I brought Pythagoras under control and jumped to the ground.

'Mr Lip!' I cried. 'Mr Lip, are you all right?'

The small man was writhing on the ground in agony, the back of his cheviot coat ripped to shreds by double-ought buck, the blood seeping through his shirt. I got him to lie steady on his stomach and pulled the garments away. Mr Lip's back had at least forty small flesh wounds. He said something to me in Chinese, moaning the words but, by Jim, I had no hope of understanding him. I glanced at Pythagoras. She was settling down, her rump streaming with a modest

175

amount of blood, swishing her tail at the small wounds as if they were no more than fly bites.

'Mr Lip,' I said, 'we're going to have to get you to my surgery.' I didn't care if he understood or not. I thought he might find comfort in the sound of my voice. 'We've got to get that buckshot out of you before you get infected.' I remembered President McKinley, how I'd uttered similar words to the nation's leader the afternoon Czolgosz pumped two rounds into his stomach; how infection had been our greatest fear. 'If we can rake out that buckshot, you might just stand a chance.'

THIRTEEN

Richard Lip's shirt was no more than a rag, torn by lead shot, soaked with blood. I snipped the garment away with surgical scissors and got a better look at the wound. I inspected the ragged and indeterminate nature of the wound, the stippling effect across the ribs, the small bumps immediately beneath the tissue where the lead shot had caused pockets of inflammation to form. I shook my head, thinking of the dozens of pieces of buck I would have to find, and brought the light closer.

'We've got a night ahead of us, Mr Lip,' I said. I got some laudanum from the shelf, put four drops into a glass of water, and made him drink the mixture. It took five minutes, but he finally dozed off.

The big problem with buckshot was retrieving every single piece. Once it entered the body, it spun and twisted as it ate its way through flesh, ending up far from the entrance wound, sometimes burying itself so deeply there was no hope of ever finding it. And if you didn't find it, you risked a pernicious infection. As I retrieved the first piece of lead with a long pair of tweezers, my hand began to shake. I looked at it. This was the same hand that had saved hundreds of young American lives in Cuba. This was the same hand that had retrieved two bullets from President McKinley's stomach. It shouldn't have shook; it should have been rock steady. But it shook, and shook badly – all because of my great sense of failure over the President's death. This was the first gunshot wound I'd treated since President McKinley's assassination. I deposited the first piece of buckshot into a tray, fighting to steady my hand. I was afraid Richard Lip was going to die, just like the President had died.

I worked through the night, keeping myself going with strong coffee. Mr Lip woke a number of times, asked for whiskey, got it, drank it, got drunk, and drifted off again. He wasn't a president; he wasn't even a soldier. He was just a hobo. But I was determined to save him.

As the first light of dawn brightened the surgery windows, I slumped in the folding chair and looked at the recovered buckshot. Thirty-three pieces in all. Surely to God that had to be it. I lifted my fourth cup of coffee, took a sip of the cold brown liquid, then pushed myself up and had another look at Lip's back. I swabbed it clean with alcohol. Lip groaned in his sleep. I checked every little tear and bump with my fingers, squeezed each little wound, hoping to express yet one more piece of lead, the fragment of shot that might conceivably kill Lip, but I found nothing. I was reluctant to dress him. To dress him meant to end my search. To dress him might mean leaving that last fragment of buckshot inside him. But I had to close him. I honestly couldn't see any more shot in there.

I wrapped him up, looping foot-wide gauze around his abdomen several times, fastening it tight with a couple of safety pins. I was still shaky. I lifted Lip – he couldn't have weighed more than ninety-five pounds – and carried him to the cot in my laboratory. I would just have to trust to Providence now.

I didn't sleep. By the time I got washed, in a fresh doctor's tunic, and had breakfast, I already had patients knocking at my door. I phoned the Sheriff's Office but got no answer. So I rang Stanley's farmhouse near Reese's Corners and was told by Camilla Armstrong that Stanley was in Burkville investigating a burglary, and wouldn't be back until two in the afternoon. I explained my circumstances to Camilla, and she assured me she would have Stanley come to the surgery as soon as he got back.

I worked steadily through the morning, every now and again checking on Richard Lip in the laboratory. I was pleased to see he was getting better. I made some porridge and sliced peaches and, much to my relief, he ate everything. I went back to my patients with renewed hope.

Viola White, the town's telephone operator, came at half past ten with a bad case of laryngitis. She was a tall, stringy woman of nearly fifty, a town gossip and a general busybody. I pressed her tongue down with a tongue depressor and had a look. I needed sleep, wasn't in the best mood, and I found Miss White's overbearing manner trying.

'You should give your voice a rest, Miss White,' I said, leveling the advice more like a criticism. 'You've strained it. You've used it improperly.'

'Improperly?' she croaked. She looked at me with puzzled and suspicious eyes. 'How does one use one's voice improperly, doctor?' she demanded.

'By wearing it out,' I countered. 'By using it so much it can no longer function properly.'

She looked affronted. 'And what can I do to restore its proper function?' she asked.

'Rest it, Miss White,' I said. 'Rest it.'

'But how can I rest it?' she asked. 'I must use my voice.' She enunciated her words clearly, and with great affectation. 'There are only three of us, you know. The other girls would have to work twelve-hour shifts if I were to rest my voice, and that wouldn't be fair, would it? Is there not a medicine you can give me for it?'

'There are one or two things I might

prescribe, Miss White, but the best medicine is rest. You sing in the church choir, don't you?'

'Yes,' she said, puffing up. 'I am their lead soprano.'

'Then maybe you shouldn't sing so loud,' I said. I was recalling her piercing performances in the Fairfield Congregationalist Church. 'And maybe you should get rid of that vibrato. I think in a choir you have to try to blend in with the other voices. Maybe you should give the singing a rest for a week. And if you've got to speak, well, just keep it to a low roar.'

'But I can't stop singing,' she said. 'I have a singing lesson this afternoon with Miss Wade. I haven't missed a lesson yet. I'm one of her best pupils.'

'I'm sure Miss Wade will understand,' I said. 'I'm telling you plainly, you might risk permanent damage to that lovely voice of yours if you don't take my advice.'

I often had to cajole my patients into undertaking my prescribed treatments.

'But I haven't missed a single lesson yet,' she said, as if this fact precluded the possibility of missing any future lessons.

'Well ... if you're going to be mulish about it,' I said, 'let's just go ahead and try some tincture of benzoin. You'll find it at Wiley's Drug Store for twenty-five cents a bottle.'

She looked at me as if I'd just made an obscene suggestion.

181

'Twenty-five cents a bottle?' she said. 'But surely that's highway robbery, doctor.'

'Then I'll give you a bottle,' I said.

I just wanted to send her on her way. She lifted her chin, pouting, but seemed mollified. 'Thank you, doctor,' she said, as if she had expected no less.

I got up from my desk and walked down the hall to the back. I opened the door to my laboratory. Richard Lip was now asleep on the cot, his breath coming and going in a steady whisper. I opened the glass cabinet and searched for the tincture of benzoin.

Then I heard footsteps in the hall. Blazes! Miss White was coming down the corridor. The woman had the most astounding gall. To intrude into the private part of the surgery! Before I could stop her, Miss White stood at the door.

'I was just thinking, doctor, perhaps there are some home remedies you might—'

But she stopped. She saw Richard Lip lying on the cot. Her face reddened. She knew exactly who he was.

'Oh!' she said, 'Oh, dear ... I'm sorry. You have a guest. I must beg your pardon.' Her eyes darted to my face, then back to Mr Lip's, as if she wanted to make sure of Mr Lip's identity. 'I didn't mean to intrude, I'm sure.' Her voice sounded fine now.

She quickly retreated. I let her go. There was no point in stopping her. As a gossip, Miss White was a force of nature. And because town sentiment was so strongly against Mr Lip – like Howard Scott, many had roundly condemned Lip as Charlotte's killer with no other evidence but their own blind conviction – I knew I would have a mob at my door in a few hours' time.

Stanley Armstrong stood on my front walk, his bobby hat held in the crook of his arm, surveying the twenty or so curious onlookers who had gathered in front of the surgery. I'd sent my patients home, and now stood on the front walk with Stanley.

'Maybe you should go talk to young Morley,' I said.

'We better get Lip to the jail first,' said Stanley. 'He's not safe here, Clyde. Is he fit to move?'

'He's healing up nicely,' I said. 'He should be on his feet in a couple days.'

'I'll bring my wagon around back.'

'What are you going to do about Morley?' I said. 'Someone's got to pay. We've got assault with a deadly weapon here.'

'But you said Morley wasn't armed.'

'Plenty of others were,' I said. 'You ask Morley to tell you who did it.'

The sheriff shook his head, saddened by my naïvety. I think he knew I was just blowing off steam. I didn't expect any charges. Stanley humored me. 'Those West Shelby boys,' he said, 'they stick together. There's not one of them going to point a finger at another.' He shrugged wearily. 'I'll send Ernie Mulroy over to ask around, Clyde, if it'll make you feel better, but I don't think he'll get far.' He gestured at the crowd. 'Half these people probably want Lip dead anyway.'

I gazed at my fellow townspeople. I didn't recognize many; I'd been in Fairfield only a few months. These people gathered, I thought, the way crowds in medieval Europe must have gathered, thirsting for an execution, gloating in their hatred of Richard Lip, despising him not only because he was Chinese but because he was a hobo.

'I'll bring the wagon round,' Stanley said again.

'See if you can get some of these people to clear off.'

'Let 'em watch, Clyde,' he said. 'They've got a right to watch.'

He walked out to Culver Street to get the police wagon. I went back into the house.

Richard Lip was sitting on the edge of the cot. He was a strikingly small man, no more than five feet tall, fragile-looking, like he was made of glass. His pants were baggy, a couple of sizes too big for him. He had to be about fifty, like Stanley said, and had one of those droopy Confucius-style mustaches. His face was broad and flat, and burnished to a coppery sheen. He had the windburnt look of a man who spent all his days and nights outside. He looked at me with

184

tranquil dark eyes.

'How are you?' I asked.

He nodded, a few eager jerks of his head. He didn't understand a word I said.

'We've got to take you to jail,' I said, speaking loudly, as if I thought it might help him understand. 'You'll be safer there. Can you stand?'

I heard Stanley's police wagon rattle down the drive into the backyard. Lip stared at me blankly. I went up to him and grasped him by the arm. Besides his pants and shoes, all he had on was my dressing, from the waist up, lily-white gauze wrapped around his abdomen. He nodded. He knew what I was trying to do.

Grunting, and in considerable pain, he managed, like a stiff old man, to stand up. A cold sweat covered his forehead, he grew suddenly shaky, swooned a bit, then gagged, as if he were going to throw up. He gained control of himself and nodded, letting me know he was better.

'OK,' he said. 'OK.'

Stanley came inside. Next to the tall, wiry sheriff, Lip looked even smaller.

'Afternoon, Mr Lip,' said Stanley.

Lip looked at the sheriff in sudden apprehension. He reminded me of some strange bird freshly hatched from an egg, his limbs weak and skinny, his eyes bulging at the sight of the sheriff. He turned to me, as if I'd betrayed him.

185

'Let's help him to the wagon,' said Stanley. 'You got anything he can wear?' I lifted a doctor's tunic from a hook and draped it around the small man's shoulders. It hung on him like a white surrender flag.

We helped Lip down the back steps into the wagon. The wagon was black, with a barred window on each side, and had the words 'Fairfield Police Department' stenciled in white along the rear doors. We had to lift him into the back. We got him seated on one of the benches and I stayed in there with him while Stanley went to drive. As Stanley climbed up on to the box and shook the reins, and we rolled down the driveway on to Culver Street, I wondered what kind of a man Lip was, what he'd seen, where he'd been, who he'd known, and what he'd done. He looked old for fifty, withered and tired out. Yet I recognized within him an imperturbable calm, an acceptance, an inborn comfort and ease with the hardships of life. I admired that. Where did he come by such peace of mind? What secrets had he discovered? And was there any way he could help me with my own peace of mind?

'He sure don't look like a killer,' admitted Stanley, once we had Lip sitting at the basswood kitchen table in the Sheriff's Office.

'He's not a killer,' I said.

And I outlined for Stanley my theories about Herbert Early and Roger Robson,

186

even mentioned how Arnold Murchison had been down at the river at or around the time of Charlotte's murder. He nodded noncommittally, then twitched his mustache from side to side as he stared at Richard Lip. From out in Cecil Fray's smithy yard we heard the pounding of a hammer against an anvil.

'His eye looks like it might close up, Clyde,' said Stanley. 'Maybe we should get a beefsteak.'

I sighed wearily. 'Stanley, how many times do I have to tell you, a beefsteak doesn't make a good poultice.'

Lip looked at us both uncomprehendingly.

'Guess he don't speak much English,' said Stanley. He leaned forward. 'You savvy English, boy?' he asked.

Mr Lip squinted. His pain seemed to come back. 'No speak English,' he said. 'Tiny, tiny bit. Speak Chinese.'

'You understand you're under arrest, boy?' asked Stanley. Lip continued to stare at him with blank eyes. 'Sell locket, boy? King buy locket? You kill girl, boy?'

Lip said, 'No speak English.'

'You *kill* girl?' said Stanley, as if emphasizing the word might help.

Lip turned to me. Did he think I could translate?

'The girl,' I said. I made some curvy figures in the air with my hand to indicate Charlotte. 'Kill girl?' I said.

Lip shook his head. 'Me no understand,'

187

he said. 'Speak Chinese.' His eyes brightened, as if he just had a brilliant idea. 'You got whiskey?' he asked.

Stanley and I looked at each other.

'We're going to need a translator,' I said. 'Only where are we going to find a Chinese translator in Fairfield?' We both stared at Lip. I pulled out Bernice Scott's Kodak 'Brownie' shot of Charlotte and showed it to Lip. His face immediately went slack, his shoulders sank, and his face turned pale. He looked up at me, wincing in pain, and said something to me in Chinese, a desperate utterance, but of course I couldn't understand it.

'Look at him go pale like that,' said Stanley.

'Stanley, the man's been shot in the back with a round of double-ought buck,' I said. 'He's got a right to go pale once in a while.'

Stanley rubbed his jaw with his thumb and forefinger. 'I'll show him the locket,' he said.

He walked to the evidence cabinet, opened the door, and pulled out Charlotte's locket. In the flash of afternoon sunlight coming in through the front window, the Greek archer lit up sugar-white against the burnt-sienna background. Stanley showed the locket to Lip. The hobo went even paler.

'Get him the bucket, Clyde,' said Stanley. 'He looks like he's going to throw up.'

I rushed to get the bucket. I put it on Lip's knees and Lip held his head over the rim. He

188

gagged a few times, but then regained himself. Through his thinning black hair – stiff and straight Chinese hair – I saw sweat form on his mottled scalp. And I had to admit, Lip looked like a man who had just been found out.

'You have any luck?' asked Stanley.

'We have one Chinese family living in town,' I said. 'The Cheungs, up on Allegheny. They speak Mandarin. They tell me Lip speaks Cantonese. They're not the same thing.'

Stanley glanced at Lip. 'Well ... can't they parley somehow?' he asked. 'It's all Chinese, ain't it?'

'That's like having a Paiute talk to a Comanche, Stanley' I said. 'It's all Indian, but it can't be done.'

He shook his head, drummed his fingers a few times on his desk, and then glanced at Richard Lip, who stared at us from behind the bars of the middle cell.

'Then I guess we're stuck,' said Stanley.

I felt the color rise in my face. 'I know a man who can help us.'

Stanley took a deep breath and sighed. 'Clyde,' he said, his voice full of warning.

'For the love of Zeus, Stanley, what else can we do?' I said. 'They have any number of Chinese translators at the State Department. If the President can't spare me one, then I should have left him up on San Juan

Hill to die.'

Stanley pressed his hands flat against his desk and glanced at our poker table.

'You can't be troublin' the President of the United States with a domestic murder, Clyde, you know that.'

'I'm not troubling him with a murder,' I said. 'All I want is a translator.'

'And just because you can't find the right kind of Chinese translator in Fairfield does-n't mean you can't find one in Buffalo. Why wire all the way to Washington? I'm sure they must have two or three hundred Chinese in Buffalo, and there's got to be at least one who speaks this here Cantonese.'

'That's what I've been thinking about, Stanley. How much credibility would an-other Chinese have in front of one of Judge Norris's Grand Juries? The minute they saw him, they'd think he was sticking up for Richard Lip any which way he could. I think we need an official translator; someone we can trust to weasel the truth out of Richard Lip, someone who won't go hiding things for him. Especially if Lip turns out to be guilty.'

'Yes, Clyde, but the President?' said Stan-ley. 'Lord knows, Theodore's got his hands full enough.'

'He won't mind,' I said. 'He'll give Henry Lodge a call and we'll have our translator in no time.'

FOURTEEN

I had just finished washing my hands with surgical soap, and was fastening the buttons on my doctor's tunic, when I heard the bell above the surgery door ring. My first patient of the afternoon.

But it wasn't my first patient at all. It was Olive Wade.

She was dressed in a practical grey skirt and a dark shirtwaist, the same clothes I'd seen her wearing the night Camilla Armstrong gave birth to the twelfth Armstrong child. She carried an old Gladstone bag, the leather so scuffed and cracked it looked like the mummified skin of a long-dead Egyptian king, the handle missing and replaced with rope, the nickel-plated snap-locks open and broken.

'Good afternoon, doctor,' she said.

Her voice was soft, sweet, and had the singular effect, as always, of turning me into a simpleton.

'Afternoon, Miss Wade,' I said.

She lifted the bag, a small crease of concern across her brow.

'I believe this bag belongs to Mr Lip,' she

said. 'I found it up near the oak tree while I was out taking exercise this morning. I was wondering if you would be so kind as to bring it to him.'

I took the bag from her. 'Glad to be of service, Miss Wade,' I said. 'Would you like a glass of lemonade? A cup of coffee?'

The corners of her lips turned upward in a divine smile as she regarded me warmly with her gentle blue eyes.

'As much as that would delight me,' she said, 'I'm afraid I must make a professional visit to Mrs North just now.'

I hoped my disappointment wasn't too evident. 'By golly, that's right, too, isn't it?' I said.

'She's in the final weeks of her third trimester,' said Miss Wade. She peered at me quizzically. 'Is Mr Lip all right?' she asked.

Briefly I explained to her the events of the previous night.

'So it's not a serious gunshot wound,' I finished. 'And I fully expect him to recover.'

'That's so good to hear,' she said

I watched her ride away. And I was filled with an unaccountable sadness. I wanted to reach out to Miss Wade; to go beyond the stiff formalities we used with each other. But somehow, when I saw Olive Wade, Emily always lurked in the back of my mind.

Later that afternoon, after I'd finished with my patients, I went to the Sheriff's Office to give Richard Lip his bag. Stanley cocked his head quizzically.

'Olive Wade found it up on Cherry Hill,' I said.

Richard Lip stood at the door of his cell, hands around the bars, smiling, happy to see his bag, looking a lot better. Stanley opened the bag and inspected the contents, checking for weapons.

'I already looked,' I said. 'He's got some old clothes in there, a few photographs, and some mah-jongg tiles.'

Stanley lifted a small jackknife. 'What do you call this?' he asked.

'It's a jackknife.'

'And you want to give it to him?'

'He's not dangerous, Stanley. I see no harm.'

He shook his head. 'No, sir,' he said. 'The jackknife stays here.' He put it on the desk, lifted the key-ring from the hook on the side of his desk, and handed it to me. 'You can give him the rest of it. I doubt he can do much harm with those mah-jongg tiles.'

I took the key-ring and bag and walked over to Richard Lip's cell. He said something to me in Cantonese, and then reached through the bars, wincing in pain from his shotgun wound, his fingers thin and claw-like, looking as if they were made of cinnamon sticks. His smile broadened.

'I've got your bag,' I said.

I opened the cell door. He took his bag, then beckoned me.

'Come…' he said. 'Come…'

I looked back at Stanley. 'What's he want?' asked the sheriff.

'I guess I'll find out,' I said.

I entered Richard Lip's cell, leaving the door open. The man sat on his pallet and foraged through his Gladstone. He pulled out a crumpled piece of paper and a carpenter's pencil. He pressed the paper flat against his bag and drew. He sketched a large curving arc, a few tiny trees, and some picnic tables. I realized he was drawing the picnic ground down by the river. I saw the railroad tracks, the bridge, and the swimming hole. He said something to me in Cantonese again, hoping I might understand him, but I shook my head. He went back to drawing.

I turned to Stanley. 'Stanley, I think you'd better see this,' I said. 'I think he's trying to tell us something about the murder.'

Stanley got up and came over. Richard Lip continued to draw. He drew dots, lines, and arrows, talking all the time in rapid Cantonese; and, yes, it certainly looked as if he were trying to explain something about Charlotte Scott's murder. Finally, I shook my head.

'Mr Lip,' I said, 'we don't understand. Speak English?'

He shook his head, disheartened. 'No,' he said. 'No speak English.'

I turned to Stanley. 'He's not a suspect,

194

Stanley,' I said. 'He's a witness.'

Stanley said nothing. I turned back to Lip. The big smile came back to his face. He reached in his bag and pulled out an old photograph. It was a studio shot of a young woman. She was Chinese, dressed in a traditional Chinese wedding gown. The painted studio backdrop showed a scene of pagodas and mountains, with a few Chinese characters ink-brushed near the top, like a jumble of criss-crossed sabers. Mr Lip tried to explain the photograph to us but of course we couldn't understand. His eyes moistened and he stared at the photograph with deep longing. He finally kissed it and put it away.

He took out another photograph, a group of Chinese children, seven in all, standing at the rail of a steamer. The moisture in his eyes thickened into tears. He didn't try to explain this photograph, he just stared at it. Then he wiped his tears away with the back of his sleeve and looked at us.

'Is that your family, Mr Lip?' asked Stanley.

Mr Lip said something incomprehensible to Stanley. He could have called the sheriff a coyote, for all we knew. He put the photograph of the children away and shook his head to himself. Then his face brightened again. He got up, walked to the bars, and pointed to the sink behind Stanley's desk.

'Give me,' he said.

We both looked at the sink. 'You want the

sink?' I said. 'You want to wash?'

'Give me,' he repeated.

He rubbed his hands together, mimicking the motion of washing his hands with soap.

Stanley shrugged. 'I guess we can let him wash himself if he wants,' he said.

We let Richard Lip out of his cell. He walked over to the sink, holding his arms out from his bandaged body, treading carefully over the plank floor, angling his spine to avoid any sudden pain. When he reached the sink he lifted the fresh bar of buttermilk soap from the dish.

'You want the soap?' I said.

'Ahhh...' he said. 'Soap.' He gave his head a few quick nods. 'Yes, yes. You give me soap.'

Stanley frowned. 'Then go ahead and wash,' he said.

But Richard Lip dodged around us, wincing in pain, his face paling, a dew of perspiration coming to his forehead, and scooped his jackknife from Stanley's desk.

'Now just hold on there,' said Stanley. Richard Lip held up his hand, like a magician telling his audience to wait, that there was more to come. We watched, both of us ready for any wrong move. Much to our surprise, he sat down and carved the soap with his jackknife. Soap shavings fell all over Stanley's floor.

'That soap costs twelve cents a bar,' complained Stanley. 'If he wants to whittle, we could have gotten him a piece of wood.'

I watched the small Chinese man in growing fascination.

'He's not whittling, Stanley,' I said. 'He's carving.'

Richard Lip worked at the bar of soap with the skill and concentration of a craftsman. He used the point, the blade, and the flat of the knife, cutting out precise chunks, slicing away measured shavings, smoothing away rough edges. After ten minutes he held up a meticulously rendered Chinese dragon. I was amazed. Its scales, teeth, nostrils, claws, and wings were all perfect. Lip gave me the dragon. I studied the dragon then looked at Richard Lip. This was no ordinary vagrant. This was a skilled artisan.

'You like?' said Richard Lip.

I nodded. 'I like,' I said.

'Isn't that something,' said Stanley, taking the dragon from me and having a look.

'You give me whiskey,' said Richard Lip.

So that was his game.

'I'm not going to give him no whiskey for some old dragon carved out of soap,' said Stanley.

I continued to stare at Richard Lip. The man had earned it. It was a masterly piece of work, a figure that evoked the mystery and remoteness of his homeland.

'Stanley,' I said, 'give him your whiskey.'

The sheriff looked at me as if I'd taken leave of my senses. 'That whiskey cost me a dollar a bottle,' he said.

'Give him your whiskey,' I repeated. 'I'll give you a bottle of the good stuff later.'

Stanley pursed his lips, arched his brow, drew his chin back, and looked me up and down.

'Are you serious?' he asked.

'I'm serious,' I said.

He promptly opened his desk drawer, lifted out his half-finished bottle of whiskey, and handed it to Richard Lip. Though deeply saddened by my gullibility, Stanley was nonetheless prudent enough to take advantage of it.

By evening, rain fell on Genesee County. I stood on the corner of Fredonia and Cleveland Streets, sheltering under my umbrella. Far in the distance I heard the bell in the steeple of the Congregationalist Church toll a single stroke – resonant, dark, and haunting. The street lights cast weak reflections on the wet pavement. I watched the Parthenon Theater. It was closing time. I was going to try to talk to Toula Vassos again. My mind was unsettled. I saw patrons stagger away from the theater in ones and twos. I kept thinking how she'd acted so trapped, remembered her furtiveness, her reluctance, and how Frank Jaslowski had finally forced her backstage.

At fifteen minutes past one, Miss Vassos emerged through the stage door and hurried down the alley to Fredonia Street. She turned toward Allegheny Avenue. I left my spot across the street and hurried after her. As I neared her, she turned quickly, startled by my approach.

'Doctor?' she said.

'Evening, Miss Vassos,' I said.

She glanced apprehensively at the Parthenon. 'What are you doing here?'

'I thought I'd walk you to your door.'

'No,' she said. 'I'll be fine. I live just up here.'

Lightning flashed distantly in the sky.

'Miss Vassos, I insist. We've got to talk about Charlotte.'

'No, we don't,' she said.

I matched my stride to hers. 'Why are you so nervous?' I asked. She cast another glance at the Parthenon, her green eyes catching a stray gleam from the street lamps. 'I'm not contagious, you know.'

She gazed at me. Without her eye-liner or rouge, she looked about eighteen. 'Please, Dr Deacon,' she said, her voice thick with entreaty. 'Please go.'

She stopped walking. She looked at the Parthenon again. I heard footsteps behind. I turned. A large man in shirtsleeves, a derby, and a vest descended the front steps of the theater. It was Frank Jaslowski. He moved with that lurch of his, barreling across the street like a runaway steam engine, careless of the soupy manure in the gutters. As he mounted the curb next to us, he looked at me murderously.

'Evenin', doctor,' he said. He touched the brim of his hat with his fingers, pushed past me, giving my shoulder a bump with his own, and grabbed Miss Vassos by the elbow. 'You have yourself a good night now,' he said.

I stared in mystification as they both walked away.

I turned around and started back toward town. To my left, over a tall creosote-stained fence, I saw the train yard – freight cars, engines, and Pullmans huddled side by side in the rain. I puzzled it out. Toula wouldn't talk to me. Why? And Frank Jaslowski was watching her, had dragged her away from me. By the time I got to the railroad tracks, I was so buffaloed I turned around and started back. I was going to talk to Murchison tonight, regardless. I wasn't going to wait until I had better information. I was going to get to the bottom of this once and for all.

But as I neared Cleveland Street, I saw activity down the alley beside the Parthenon. A wagon stood next to the stage door. The alley ran with filth, and the air was ripe with the smell of wet manure. The small stage door light, a single bulb in a tin-pan shade, lit the area with a diffuse glow. A man sat on the driver's box of the wagon with a horse-whip in his hand. Murchison stood at the top of the small stoop, holding the stage door open. The rain dripped off his bowler. Two other men, one in a sombrero stetson, the other in a Grand Old Army hat, both in oilskins, carried a large chest out the door, the same captain's chest I'd seen in Murchison's office last week.

Murchison kept glancing out to the street. I was so well concealed by darkness he couldn't see me. The men carried the chest down the few steps to the alley and lifted it on to the back of the wagon. Murchison reached into the stage stoop vestibule and pulled out two rifles. He gave one to the man in the sombrero stetson, and the other to the man in the Grand Old Army hat. These two men climbed into the back of the wagon. Murchison said a few words, the driver shook the reins, and the two brown horses trudged out of the alley at a slow walk.

From my spot across the street I watched the wagon roll south past the Parthenon down Fredonia Street and make a wide right on Hooper Avenue. I followed. Why was Murchison sending out two armed men in the middle of the night with that chest? What exactly was in that chest? And why transport it through the dark and deserted streets of Hoopertown at this time of night when no one would see them? They crossed Tonawanda Road. All the shop windows were dark, and only three or four windows in the apartments above cast pale reflections on the wet street.

I pursued them up Hooper Avenue as they curved gradually north-west toward the river. I stayed well back, keeping close to the shop fronts, stepping softly but quickly over the plank sidewalk. They moved slowly, and I was easily able to keep up. They crossed Ontario Street, Onondaga Street, and Niagara Street. As we neared the river, I saw the burnt-out ruin of the Mosely Ironmongery to my right, a charred framework sticking up out of the surrounding mud, puddles collecting in and among the piles of ash, a few old pieces of machinery rusting in the rain. I heard the creaking of a weathervane on a stable across the street. A grey cat darted in front of me and disappeared down an alley toward some trash bins.

I followed the men and their wagon across Riverside Drive. I saw a bale of hay floating in the Tonawanda River, watched it drift westward, its box-like shape bobbing back and forth in the current. I waited until the wagon got to the other side of the bridge, and when it was out of sight I darted across, keeping my umbrella in front of me, protecting myself from the wind-driven rain.

Once across the river, the land rose, climbed the western slope of Cherry Hill. The street lamps continued for one more block, then stopped. I thought the driver might light a lamp, but the wagon continued upward with no means of illumination. The macadam grew potholed. Halfway up the hill the road turned to gravel. I kept fifty yards back, seeing my way in the scant light of the phosphorescent rain clouds. I discerned the wagon up ahead – a dark shape moving along the road past the final few houses at the edge of town. The road grew worse as it climbed the slope, with dips, bumps, and small wash-outs where the rain nibbled away at the clay. The wagon ruts turned into small rivers and the water pooled in potholes. The soles of my boots quickly became caked with mud, making it difficult to walk. I pushed on, feeling a chill steal over my shoulders as the rain found its way down my collar. In this dark hour of the morning, when a man's fears are apt to be their strongest, I half suspected Murchison's men might have a dead body in that chest.

They finally turned left through a gap in the fence, where a cart track led up the hill. I heard the wagon axles creak as they pivoted westward, and the rattle of the side-boards as the big twelve-spoke wheels shuddered through a particularly deep pothole. I followed the wagon through the gap in the fence. Cherry trees grew all around, what was left of an abandoned orchard. As I followed the men and their wagon further into this cherry orchard, the sound of the rain changed, murmuring against the branches with a steady hiss. Among these trees, the darkness gathered like a bank of pitch, and all I could see were the slight greyness of the sky overheard and, dimly, the wind-tossed branches silhouetted against the clouds.

I followed the men and their wagon further and further into the orchard, discarding my umbrella by the wayside, finding it more a hindrance than a help. The hill rose steeply and the mud underneath my feet grew slippery. I had yet to make an exploration of this particular slope, had never before been to this abandoned cherry orchard. But I knew they were heading toward the old Allegheny Indian caves. A smarter man might have turned back; I had no gun, they had two rifles. A keener tactician might have forestalled; I was outnumbered three to one. Maybe even a schoolboy might have hesitated; it was dark, it was pouring rain, and I didn't know my way at all. But I kept on, gripped by a perverse determination, dumb yet brave, convinced I was about to catch these men red-handed in the act of a felony.

As the cart track narrowed, the branches arched above me, blocking out the sky, and the darkness closed in like a cloud of coal dust. I couldn't see the ground ahead of me. I might step into a well and never know it until I was halfway down. I put my hands in front of me, afraid I might bump into something, or that one of the cherry tree branches might poke me in the eye. I stopped. I listened for the sound of the wagon up ahead but all I heard were the sounds of the wind and rain. Then I heard footsteps immediately behind me. I swung round only to find myself confronted with the dim silhouettes of two men.

Immediately, a fist struck me in the stomach and I doubled over, gasping for air.

'Who's there?' I cried.

I was answered with another fist in the eye. Dots of light shot up into my retina like fireworks, spreading in dull green blips, the force of the blow making them dance and careen like frenzied insects. I swung out, fighting back, but I couldn't see a thing. Suddenly I was pushed to the ground. I grunted, got to my hands and knees. The blunt toe of a workman's boot thudded into my ribcage. Someone, it seemed, was attempting to punt me like a football. I tried to see who it was.

Before I could make out even the vaguest shape, a rifle butt – at least it felt like one – knocked me in the back of the head. I fell face forward into the mud and drifted into the silent and still world of unconsciousness.

FIFTEEN

The next day I hung my 'DOCTOR IS OUT' sign in the surgery window and nursed my shiner with a bag of ice. I sat in my parlor thinking how glad I'd be when my son finally arrived home from boarding-school this summer. July the fifth. It seemed like a long way away. I hoped the Charlotte Scott murder would be behind me by then. I wanted to spend time with Jeremiah. My new Fairfield house was big, and it was empty. I didn't know why I hadn't bothered to get servants yet. I should have at least hired a nurse.

I found myself thinking of my old friend William McKinley, a placid, kindly, and fair man. I still mourned for him. Mourning was a lonely business. I knew how the Scotts felt. I took a sip of brandy. I usually never drank before supper, but today I'd made an exception. My pride was hurt. I'd sparred with Teddy Roosevelt on numerous occasions – we both liked the gloves – and I was proud of my ability in the ring. But here I was, with ice pressed to my eye, bested by a couple of thugs.

I was just putting down my snifter when I saw the sheriff walk through the gate carrying a burlap sack. I took the ice from my eye, walked to the front door and, feeling a keen dejection as I stood there with that ignominious welt across my eye, swung it open.

When Stanley saw my condition, he hid his hilarity poorly.

'You get in a fight with a freight train?' he asked.

'Sir,' I said, holding myself erect, 'a freight train would run from one such as I.'

Stanley couldn't help himself. He guffawed.

'Look at that,' he said. 'It's got all the colors of the rainbow.'

I looked at the burlap sack Stanley was carrying. 'Are you collecting alms for the poor, Stanley?'

'Hadn't you better put a beefsteak on that eye?'

I scowled in frustration. 'A beefsteak is for eating, Stanley.'

'So you lost, huh?' he said. And he guffawed again.

'Sir, I was ambushed.'

Briefly I recounted the events of the previous night: how Toula had tried to get away from me; how Jaslowski had come out of the Parthenon Theater to escort her home; how Murchison had sent armed men up Cherry Hill with a chest; and how I'd finally been ambushed. I could see he was thinking. One sees Stanley think the same way one sees a threshing machine thresh; there can be no mistake about it.

'What do you suppose that was all about?' he asked.

'I believe they were heading for the caves,' I said.

'Why would they bring an old captain's chest up there?'

I then told Stanley everything I knew about Murchison: how he'd been suspended from the track at Saratoga Springs; how he'd doctored the odds on one of his horses; how his bookmakers had lost money; and how he'd been under a great deal of pressure to pay them back.

'His bookmakers were here last Saturday night, according to Rupert Scales,' I said. 'Apparently Murchison was able to at last make restitution.'

Stanley continued to think. Finally, he shrugged. 'I guess we'll have to watch Murchison, then,' he said. He peered at me. 'The men who drove that wagon, did you get a good look at them?'

I glanced away. 'It was dark,' I muttered.

Stanley rubbed his jaw with his hand. 'Your eyes aren't too good in the dark, are they?' he said.

'Darn it all, Stanley, what do you have in the sack?' I said. 'I can see you've brought it for a reason.'

He put the bag on the floor. 'I got bottles,'

he said, opening it.

'Bottles?'

'Every bottle within fifty yards of the railway bridge where Charlotte Scott was murdered,' he said, proud of himself. 'I thought you might run that prussic acid test – you know, the one that turns the cyanide blue. If we can find poison in any of these here bottles, it'll help our case against Richard Lip a whole lot.'

As far as I was concerned, we had no case against Richard Lip. The man was as innocent as a child.

'Stanley,' I said, 'I'll run the tests.' I shook my head, disheartened. 'But let's not convict Lip until we know he did it.'

The courthouse, a building inspired by the Palladian traditions of eighteenth-century English architecture, was made of Ohio stone, had fluted Corinthian columns supporting a pediment, and was just down the street from the Sheriff's Office.

Judge Edgar Norris was in his chambers, out of his robes, sitting behind a large mahogany desk going over some legal briefs. He was sixty, five and a half feet tall, and as he extended his hand over his desk, he flashed a vigorous smile, his cheeks balling up into pink mounds. He squinted at my shiner but made no remark. 'Glad you could come, doctor,' he said. I shook his hand. His grip was firm. 'Please,' he said, indicating the red leather wing-back chair in front of his desk, 'sit down. I know your time is precious, so I'll make this as quick as I can. Can I get you a whiskey?'

'Thank you,' I said.

He poured two healthy shots of single-malt Irish whiskey and slid my glass across the gleaming varnished surface of his desk. He raised his glass. I raised my own glass.

'Here's to luck,' he said.

We both drank. Then we just sat there. I waited.

Finally he said, 'We get five or six murders a year around here, doctor.' Through his window, I saw City Hall rise behind him. Six or seven grackles sat in a row on the roof. 'People around here, they like swift justice. I'm sure you can appreciate that, coming from a small town yourself.' He stared into his glass of whiskey the same way a fortune-teller might stare into a crystal ball. 'We all know each other around here. We're all honest, decent folk. And we abhor murder, doctor, same as most folk.' He shrugged. 'A lot of townfolk ask me, when am I going to put this here Richard Lip on trial? 'Specially now that he's recovering so quickly from his shotgun wound. This Scott murder is a wicked business. People are mighty tore up about it, and they want to see Lip punished. You got him sitting in jail, and townfolk think he should at least be moved to the lock-up down in the basement here, and I don't know what to tell them.' He put his glass down and folded his hands. 'They see Richard Lip in the sheriff's jail, and they ask me, what's he doing there?'

I realized time was now against me, that public opinion had definitely taken a turn for the worse against the unsuspecting Lip, had finally found voice in this county court judge sitting across from me. I had to solve the murder of Charlotte Scott before the town decided to try Richard Lip. I knew if they tried Lip, they would also electrocute him in the new electrical chair. I wondered just how much Stanley had told the judge. I had to stall the man.

'He's not out of danger yet, Judge Norris,' I said, 'not by a long shot. And it's not as open and closed as you might think.'

The judge's eyebrows rose. He looked at the law books in his bookcase, his lips twisting to one side under his bristly mustache. 'Heck, doctor,' he said, 'I'm afraid you're the only one in town who thinks that.' He exhaled. 'I find the evidence mighty damning myself.' He took off his eyeglasses, squinted, looked through the lenses as if he thought there might be a speck on them, and then put them back on. 'He killed her and took her locket. It was murder in the commission of a robbery, plain and simple.' He sat back, pressing his palms against the edge of his desk, the springs creaking as his generous rear end adjusted itself to the contours of his chair. 'Any luck with those bottles yet?' he asked. He was referring to the bottles Stanley had gathered for me. I sighed.

'No,' I said. 'I've got seventeen left.'

'Well, keep at it,' he said. I saw I had an uphill fight. The judge had elections in November. 'The sooner I can take Lip to a Grand Jury, the better.'

The next day, as I sat in my laboratory struggling to distil prussic acid from the remaining bottles – none of the precipitates carried even a hint of the characteristic Prussian blue – I heard the rattle of a horse and buggy outside. Looking out the window, I saw Herbert Early, the high school drama teacher, the man who gave yellow roses to his prettier female students, coming up the drive. I turned off my Bunsen burner, removed my gloves, and walked to the back stoop.

'Afternoon, Mr Early,' I called.

Mr Early waved, an agitated but glum expression on his face. He drove past the back stoop to the stable, snarled at his horse, and jerked on the reins. His buggy came to a stop and he jumped down. Leaving his horse in harness, he approached me, his gait impatient, his arms swinging, his jaw set beneath his light brown mustache. I began to think he might be ill.

'Are you unwell?' I asked, as he reached the stoop.

'I've come to talk,' he said.

212

'And Mrs Early is all right?' I asked.

He stopped at the bottom of the stoop. He looked as if he'd lost weight, and his complexion was sallow. 'The new medicines you've prescribed seem to have made a difference. Thank you, doctor.' Then he noticed my fading shiner. 'Your eye,' he said.

'It's nothing.' I shrugged.

'Am I interrupting your work?' he asked. 'Because if I am I can come back.'

'You've come about Charlotte Scott, haven't you?' I said.

A look of quiet defeat came to his grey eyes. I tried not to get too hopeful. I tried not to think how we might finally let poor old Richard Lip out of jail. We stood there motionless for several seconds, and in the air between us there seemed to vibrate a kind of silent agreement, as if we had just passed a milestone together.

'I have,' he said.

I wasn't prepared for the integrity I heard in his voice. I was expecting a confession, and now I didn't know what to think.

'Come in, Mr Early,' I said.

He followed me inside and we settled ourselves in the parlor. He sat forward in his chair, his knees together, his bowler on his lap, ill at ease. His youthfulness became painfully apparent. Out on Culver Street the ice wagon rumbled by. Bees hovered in and around the lilac bushes just outside the window, and a cicada whirred up in the trees.

Mr Early rubbed his hands together.

'I don't know if I can make you believe me,' he said. A fragile smile came to his face. 'But I guess I'll have to try.' He took his bowler from his knees, placed it on the side table, and picked a piece of fluff from it. Pink spots climbed into his cheeks. 'I lied,' he said bluntly, looking at me with as much steadiness as he could, as if he had just thrown down the gauntlet. 'I was down by the river alone with Miss Scott on the night she was murdered, but not for the reason you think. I'm sorry I lied to you, doctor. I usually don't lie, but my life these past weeks ... I hardly know how to behave any more, I don't know how I could have allowed my life to spin so recklessly out of control...' He leaned forward, every muscle in his body straining as his brow settled into a straight line. 'But I didn't kill Charlotte Scott, no matter what you might think.' His voice had grown firm again.

He sat back. Half a dozen droplets of perspiration formed on his forehead.

'Go on, Mr Early,' I said.

He hesitated. 'You have no idea what it's like,' he said, in the tone of a man who has borne a great burden. 'With a chronically ill wife, you begin to think your life is over, that any chance of romance has disappeared for ever...' He looked up at me with forlorn grey eyes as if, seeing their expression, I might better understand the notion of lost romance. He seemed younger than ever. 'And it's not that I don't love Alice. I do, I love her very much, but I've ... I've had a difficult time adapting to her condition.' He looked down at his hands and fidgeted. 'So much of what I do is dependent on how well Alice feels. And that's more of a restraint than it might seem. I've always had ambitions, you see, doctor, and I ... I just never thought she would become so debilitated.' He looked at me desolately. 'We share no bed, Dr Deacon,' he said, his voice small. 'I'm a young man. I'm surrounded by attractive young female students all the time. I thought I could do it. I thought I could remain true to Alice, even though we...' He shook his head sadly. 'But then Charlotte came along.' His eyes narrowed and his mustache drooped. 'And she was like the sun, Dr Deacon. I looked at her, and she blinded me. I was drunk with her. And I blundered. I blundered badly.'

His face reddened, and a darkness gathered in his eyes, his pupils dilating under the stress of this admission, the veins on his temples standing out.

'Your rehearsals for *Angel of the Glade* brought you into close contact with Miss Scott,' I said, hoping to ease at least some of his discomfort.

'Indeed they did,' he said. 'And her attentions ... well ... I struggled against them for as long as I could. I had to. I was endeavoring to secure the appointment of principal at Fairfield High School. To fall sway to Charlotte's increasingly bold advances ... I knew the consequences would be disastrous.' His shoulders sank and he looked at his bowler. 'In spite of that...' He seemed to be searching his memory. 'I met her by chance one day down by the river, you see, on the footbridge at the end of Talbot Lane, and we started talking, and she took my arm, and I knew perfectly well what she was doing, the flirting and so forth, and I should have walked away, but I didn't.' He paused. 'It was all because of those daisies.'

'Daisies?'

A fond smile came to Mr Early's face. 'She had a bouquet of daisies. She was dropping them one at a time over the rail, and then running to the other side to watch them drift away. A small thing, yet she took such delight in it, and I ... I fell in love with her ... all because of those daisies. You see what a fool I was,' he said. 'I told her I would help her with her career. I told her I would take her to New York, that I would set her up somehow, that I would...'

He trailed off, grew preoccupied, leaned forward, put his chin on his fist.

'Mr Early,' I said, 'did you at any time compromise Miss Scott?'

I was again thinking of Charlotte Scott's secret pregnancy. He looked at me, his grey eyes focusing.

'Certainly not,' he said, annoyed that I should even suggest such a thing. 'The way I loved her ... it wasn't like that. I don't know what she did with Michael Sims or Roger Robson, but with me, it wasn't like that at all.' He leaned back. 'I respected her. She had enormous talent. I was trying to help her ... she kept on talking about my cousins in New Rochelle, how she would be able to stay with them.' He shook his head. 'I wholeheartedly supported her ambition to go to New York. We had a lot in common that way, our love of theater, our belief in education ... I was going to set her up in New York. She would go to drama school. That was our plan. I don't know why I couldn't stop myself. I realized quite clearly that I was jeopardizing my own possible advancement to the position of principal.'

He sank deeper into the Windsor chair, his shoulders sagging on the upholstery, his arms draped over the armrests. He seemed exhausted by all these admissions.

'And then there's Alice,' I said.

He nodded weakly. 'Yes.' He looked up at the ceiling, as if pondering Alice, took a deep breath, and folded his hands over his stomach as he continued to slouch in the chair. 'I still love Alice,' he said. 'She wasn't always an invalid. And now that she is ... well, I love her just the same.'

'You're right, Mr Early, you've put yourself in a good deal of jeopardy,' I said.

217

He looked at me, pleading with his eyes. 'That might be so, doctor. But I still didn't kill Charlotte Scott. I went to the river alone with her on the night of her murder, I admit that, but only because it seemed like a good opportunity to tell her that ... that we couldn't go on, that we had to end it ... I'd finally come to my senses. I told her I wouldn't be able to take her to New York.'

'And how did she react?'

He squinted. 'Oh, you know,' he said. 'She wanted to be alone. She had to set herself right before joining the others.'

'So you left her there?'

The teacher gave me a desultory nod. 'I did.'

'And you expect me to believe this?'

His eyes widened. 'I've told the truth,' he said.

'Yes, but it's more suspicious than ever, isn't it?' I said. 'Now you have a clear motive for killing Charlotte Scott. One word from her, and your career as principal would be over. You haven't exonerated yourself, Mr Early. I'm afraid you've just implicated yourself.'

Later, after Herbert Early had rattled away in his buggy, fuming because his name hadn't been indisputably cleared, I received a telegram from the White House. I smoothed it out and read: 'Dear Clyde. Expect translator June 27. Bad timing. Cantonese translators needed overseas. T.R.'

I looked up from the telegram. June the twenty-seventh. One week away.

I thought of Richard Lip. I wasn't sure if the town would wait that long.

SIXTEEN

The next day I went for a stroll at lunch-time. I put on my summer coat, my boater, and a red string tie, took my ebony walking-stick, and ambled out into the town. I found my way to the Green, a good place to stroll, with several shaded walkways, numerous flower-beds, two fountains, a bandstand, and a multitude of picnic tables. A good place to think. I went over my suspects. Herbert Early? Yes. Roger Robson? Possibly. I thought of the potassium cyanide polish in the housewares room at his father's metalworks factory, and how he could easily obtain some if he really needed to. And what of Arnold Murchison, who had also made his way down to the river on the night of the murder? What about Michael Sims, the book-reading bank clerk, to whom I still had to talk? I thought of the missing Scheele's at Wiley's Drug Store and wondered if Sims might have it. Finally, there was Richard Lip. Had the aging Chinese been responsible for the girl's murder after all?

I was just passing a large weeping willow when I saw Olive Wade sitting on the river bank with Everett Howse. They bantered. Miss Wade laughed at everything Mr Howse said. I wondered how Miss Wade could so easily be amused by this man. I willed myself to think charitable thoughts about the young Mr Howse, but I had a Dickens of a time.

Then, to my chagrin, Miss Wade turned my way and our eyes met. Blast! I'd meant to avoid them. I felt the blood rise in my face. She raised her gloved hand and waved to me.

'Dr Deacon,' she called.

I was caught like a fly in a trap. I saw I had no choice. Politeness obliged me to say hello. I emerged from behind the undulating branches of the willow tree bearing this unwanted contact with excruciating formality.

'Miss Wade,' I said. I doffed my hat. 'I didn't see you there.'

She looked at me closely. 'What happened to your eye?' she asked.

'I don't believe I've met your friend,' I said.

'Oh,' she said. She was surprised that Mr Howse and I hadn't been formally introduced. 'Everett, this is Dr Clyde Deacon—'

'Yes, yes, yes,' interrupted Mr Howse. 'I know who he is, Olive,' he said with the careless tone of a man who believed he knew everybody. He extended his hand. I shook it. I could have gritted my teeth. 'Won't you join us for a glass of wine, Dr Deacon?'

'Well...' I said, '...I really shouldn't ... I should be getting back to the surgery.'

221

I wanted to make this as short as possible.

'Oh, please do, doctor,' said Miss Wade.

Then again, I wasn't going to refuse Miss Wade.

I obediently lowered myself to their blanket, my face sore from keeping my smile in place, and stared at the river downstream where I saw a few old-timers fishing from the Park Street bridge. I glanced at Miss Wade. She was looking at me with unabashed curiosity. I suppose it must have been my eye. I guess she hadn't reckoned me for much of a brawler.

'We were just having the most amusing conversation about the shortcomings of bachelorhood, Dr Deacon,' said Mr Howse. 'Are you a married man yourself?'

The smile slipped from my face like the dead thing it was. 'I'm widowed,' I said.

He paused. 'Oh,' he said, as if widowhood were like freckles or a harelip. 'I suppose it's a close cousin to bachelorhood, then.' He was proud of the way he had neatly joined the two conditions. 'I was just telling Olive what a pity it was that we bachelors must spend all our money on ourselves when we would much sooner spend it on a charming wife and a lovely home.' He laughed. I tried to think gracious thoughts of Everett Howse. 'I was lamenting the hardship of dining out at one's club every night, coming home to peace and quiet, and setting one's hours to suit oneself.' I felt my jaw clenching as I forced myself to be charitable toward the man. 'And I was bemoaning those sad nights of poker and whiskey, and a cigar always at the ready.'

'A sad state of affairs,' I said, squeezing out the words with noble restraint.

He expounded this theme for the next several minutes. His gratuitous use of Miss Wade's Christian name grated. The intent of his performance was to impress upon Miss Wade his eligibility as a young bachelor, and to underline his own desirability as a marriage mate. I found him insufferable; so much so that I finally excused myself, rising to my feet like a jack-in-the-box. Miss Wade gazed at me with unconcealed alarm.

'I should really go,' I said. My Tennessee drawl became pronounced. 'Y'all have a fine picnic now.'

I hurried away toward the Park Street bridge, feeling my face turn red with consternation, wondering how I could have made such a fool of myself. I thought I might turn back and apologize, but reaching the blossoming crab-apple trees immediately before the bridge, I was accosted by Miss Wade. She touched my elbow.

'Are you all right?' she asked.

'Miss Wade,' I said, 'I'm fine. I thank you for your kind enquiry.'

My voice was curt, cold. I simply couldn't stop myself. My charity had been exhausted.

'What's wrong?' she asked. 'Did I do something to offend you?'

I stopped, turned to her. She was dressed in a white shirtwaist and a white skirt, her blonde hair was pinned above her shoulders, and a pink satin ribbon dangled from the hatband of her white straw boater.

'Miss Wade, your company is always a delight, no matter what the circumstance,' I said.

A look of apprehension came to her face. 'Is the circumstance...' She looked to the ground. 'Is it the presence of Mr Howse?'

I forced a smile. 'Mr Howse is a wit and a wag,' I said.

She returned my smile, but it was a wary and questioning smile. 'You really don't mean that,' she said.

'I only mean to be kind, Miss Wade,' I said.

'I value honesty over kindness,' she said.

What could I say about Mr Howse that might be honest?

'He's young,' I said.

'Thirty-one is young?' she ventured.

I said nothing. In my present mood I didn't want to risk a pronouncement on anybody. I was being a humbug, and I knew it.

'I see,' she said. She took my arm, her touch sending waves of pleasure through my body, and we strolled northward to the Park Street bridge. 'You don't like him, do you?' she said.

'Whether I like him or not shouldn't make any difference.'

224

She paused. 'Mr Howse comes to me at a time in my life when I need distractions,' she said, 'that's all. My situation in Boston...' She looked away. I recalled what she'd told me about Boston, how circumstances made it expedient for her to forsake it for a while. I saw her fragility return. I wasn't sure if I wanted to hear about her situation in Boston. 'I didn't come to Fairfield solely for the purpose of looking after my aunt,' she said. She turned to me, her depthless blue eyes catching reflections from the river. She lifted her chin, a trace of defiance coming to her face. 'I was in love with a man,' she said, her voice now challenging. Why was she telling me this? 'A married man,' she added, as if now that she had poured kerosene all over the place she was going to light a match. She was bold and honest, and for reasons I didn't entirely understand she had chosen me to hear this particularly intimate confidence. 'But he couldn't love me back,' she said. 'Wanted to, but couldn't.' I tried to be sympathetic. 'That's why Boston isn't a good place for me right now.'

'A dire circumstance,' I said.

She continued to stare at me. I found myself entranced by her eyes. The predominant blue was marbled with flecks of grey. Her eyelashes, as blonde as her hair, paled to near invisibility. She was trying to establish a concord with me, I saw that, and she was using this confidence as a means to that end.

But I had no idea what to say.

'I'm sorry, doctor,' she said. 'I'm embarrassing you.'

And still our eyes held. There passed between us an understanding, perhaps the concord she wished for.

'Don't be sorry, Miss Wade,' I said.

A smile softened her features. The understanding remained. Her shoulders sank, and she became suddenly businesslike, overtly polite.

'I don't mean to detain you,' she said.

'Miss Wade, I...' She looked up at me. I watched the color climb into her cheeks. She gazed at me with frantic concentration. My head was dizzy with emotion. Yet my words failed me. 'You have a fine afternoon,' I finally said.

She smiled again. Even these lame words hadn't managed to harpoon our concord.

When I left her, I too was smiling from ear to ear. I continued along the walkway beside the river, curving north-west, giddy with delight, thinking of the way she'd looked at me, with that frantic concentration of hers, how she had continued to smile at me even after my lackluster farewell. I concluded that she must indeed have at least some affectionate regard for me; that despite the impediment of Mr Howse, something bright and marvelous might be growing between us. Was it love? After fourteen years of living as a widower, honoring my dead wife with a chaste fidelity, was that dangerous, unpredictable, and glorious flower finally blooming in my heart again? Was Emily at last going to let me go?

I'd just reached the church grounds, engrossed by these speculations, when I saw Roger Robson and Bernice Scott walking arm in arm ahead of me. I stopped. My delight disappeared. I was most perplexed. Bernice Scott and the devil-may-care Roger Robson, together. Was it the heat, or was I truly stupefied to see them like this? I'd never even considered the possibility. Bernice lifted her chin and kissed Roger on the cheek. Gads! He gave her waist a squeeze. I thought of Charlotte's murder. Was the whole puzzle a lot simpler than I thought? They walked across the Talbot Lane footbridge and disappeared behind the elms on the other side. Did it amount to nothing more than sibling rivalry? Could it be that Bernice had slipped unnoticed to the river around the time of her sister's murder? Here they were, Bernice and Roger, lovers in the park. The idea of Charlotte taking a drink from Bernice seemed a lot more probable than Charlotte taking a drink from Richard Lip. I didn't want to believe it. And yet I had to ask myself: did strange little Bernice have a great darkness in her heart?

SEVENTEEN

At the jail the next day, Richard Lip was running a fever. His skin was warm and dry, and as he gazed at me, he was racked by a sudden chill.

'Damnation,' I murmured.

I carefully unwrapped his dressing and saw that many of the small wounds had become infected, were red and swollen, with one or two oozing pus. Then I noticed all the drawings and soap carvings on the table beside his pallet.

'What are these?' I asked Stanley, lifting the drawings.

'He's been on about the river again,' said Stanley. 'I got him a box of soap.'

The carvings were in fact portraits. One was a young woman who bore a striking resemblance to Charlotte Scott. Another was obviously Herbert Early. One had to be Murchison. There were a few others I didn't readily recognize, maybe high school students.

'Stanley,' I said, 'he saw something. And now he's trying to tell us.'

Stanley nodded. 'He's become mighty

stirred up about the whole thing,' he admitted.

We stared at the stricken Chinese man. I marvelled at Lip's heroic and unique attempts to communicate with us. I was at the same time dismayed to see that my fears had come to pass. Richard Lip was ill, infected, like President McKinley, and if his fever kept up he might grow delirious, and he wouldn't be able to communicate with us at all. I cleansed his wounds with wood alcohol, gave him some laudanum, then applied a fresh dressing. Lip dozed off.

I told Stanley about my telegram from the White House, how the translator wouldn't arrive in Fairfield until June the twenty-seventh. Stanley's eyes narrowed speculatively.

'Is Lip going to be all right by then?' he asked.

'You mean, is he going to make it?'

Stanley nodded.

I took a deep breath. 'He's got to beat that fever, Stanley. If he doesn't beat it ... I thought he was going to get better. He was doing so well. But I guess not.' I rubbed my chin, contemplating Lip. 'I want to drive over to the surgery and get him the cot from the laboratory,' I said. 'We might as well make him more comfortable. That might help.'

While we were driving over to the surgery to get the cot, Stanley told me that he had received his own telegram.

'From Sheriff Vernon Stillwater,' he said, 'out in Saratoga Springs. Seems one of Arnold Murchison's bookmakers, the ones you were telling me about, passed some Corn Mercantile money at the track yesterday. Stillwater says the bookmakers swear they got the money from Murchison.' A sly grin came to Stanley's face. 'Now, what do you suppose Arnold Murchison is doing with Corn Mercantile money? Makes you wonder what he had in that captain's chest, don't it?'

I went to the Exchange Bank later that day. In the cool, high-ceilinged marble interior I saw farmers and businessmen standing at the wickets making withdrawals and deposits. I walked to the back of the bank and rapped lightly on Daniel Howse's office door.

'Come in,' called the bank president.

I entered his office. Daniel Howse's three-piece suit looked a decade out of date, his cuffs and collar were made of paper, and the masonic emblem hanging from his fob looked as if it hadn't been polished in years. He was a fleshy man, well into his fifties, with a burnished mole highly visible on his left cheekbone.

'Doctor, doctor, this is indeed a pleasure,' he said.

He pushed his chair out from his desk.

'Don't get up,' I said.

He hesitated. 'Then sit yourself down,' he said, gesturing at the chair opposite. 'What can I do for you?'

'Mr Howse, I'm here on some urgent business,' I said, sitting down. 'Related to the Charlotte Scott murder case. Is Michael Sims here? I've only a vague recollection of what he looks like, and I thought you could point him out to me.'

A look of surprise came to his face. 'Michael Sims quit a week ago,' he said. 'He's in Buffalo now. Got himself a plush job with an accounting outfit.'

I felt my shoulders sink. 'I need to find him,' I said. 'Do you know where in Buffalo?'

His eyes narrowed. 'He's not in any trouble, is he?'

I glanced at the engraving of the National Treasury above Mr Howse's desk. 'He was a friend of Charlotte Scott's,' I explained. 'I need to ask him some questions.'

He took a moment to puzzle through this, then got up from his desk, walked to a filing cabinet, and opened the center drawer. 'Let me see if I can...' He began going through the files, exploring them, seemingly surprised by them, then finally pulled out a small index card. 'Here we are,' he said. 'Michael Sims.' He handed the card to me. 'The Beardmore, on Templeton Street. He shouldn't be too hard to find.'

'And you said he left when?' I asked.

'A week ago,' he said. 'The thirteenth of June.'

Was it a coincidence, I wondered? Or was it something more ominous? June thirteenth. The day after Charlotte Scott was murdered.

I left for Buffalo the next day. Though Richard Lip's condition was serious, it remained stable, and I thought I could risk a quick trip away. I might even find a Chinese translator in Buffalo.

I booked a room at the Monarch Hotel on Ferry Street, not far from the waterfront, and, in fact, not far from the site of last year's Buffalo Pax America Fair, where President McKinley had been assassinated in September. After a supper of stewed lamb I set off to find Michael Sims's apartment building on Templeton Street.

Compared to Fairfield, Buffalo was a metropolis. I saw six gasoline-powered motor cars as I strolled about the streets; five electric ones, and a few pre-1900 models, tiller-driven curiosities that rattled along the roads at fifteen miles per hour. I saw horses, buggies, wagons, hansoms, cabriolets and landaus of every size, shape, and description. Telegraph and telephone poles supported a tangle of wires overhead. Pigeons and sea-gulls flocked in the sky, and far off in the harbor I heard the bellow of a ship's horn. I passed a music store, a photography studio, a dentist's office, a watchmaker's shop, and a chemist's. There must have been a celebration of sorts going on because the streets were thronged with people, all dressed up, and everyone was wearing a hat. Bunting adorned some of the windows.

I continued on, eastward away from the Niagara River, and soon found my way into Templeton Street. Immediately I began to grow suspicious. It was an opulent neighborhood. Smart brownstones lined both sides. How could Michael Sims, working as an accountant, afford to live in such a rich neighborhood? I continued down the street until I stood in front of the Beardmore. It was a lavish building with a dormered roof, elaborate wrought-iron trim, and gleaming windows. Again I wondered how Michael Sims could possibly pay rent in a place like this. How could he live here on an accountant's salary?

I climbed the front steps under the portico and entered the lobby. A chandelier hung from the ceiling, illuminating a collection of richly upholstered sofas and chairs, and the walls were papered with elaborate Egyptian motif wallpaper. Ferns and spindle palms grew in terracotta planters. Persian carpets lay on the dark and immaculately buffed hardwood floors. I got in the cage-lift and pressed the button for the fifth floor. As the cage-lift hummed upward the evidence grew ever more damning in my mind. Michael Sims, in his capacity as bank clerk, received for the bank monies totaling hundreds of thousands of dollars. Michael Sims knew the exact date when the Corn Mercantile money was to arrive. And despite Stanley's lengthy investigation of the man, this new evidence seemed to me to be overwhelming. I was beginning to think that Michael Sims might have had something to do with the Corn Mercantile burglary after all.

The cage-lift doors slid open. I walked down the corridor to Sims's apartment and knocked on the door. I knocked several times but there was no answer. Finally I examined the lock – a simple skeleton-key lock. I took out my pocket knife and, after a few minutes, had the lock picked.

His rooms were as richly furnished as the rest of the building. The Egyptian motif had been continued in here. Busts of Osiris and Ikhnaton stood on the mantelpiece over the electric fireplace. An oil painting of the Nile in a gilt frame hung above the chesterfield. A West African cockatoo, staring at me from a large bamboo cage by the balcony doors, extended its white crest feathers as I approached, shifted a few steps on its swinging perch, and squawked at me. I saw Sims's phonograph and his opera records. Three back issues of *Wild West Monthly* sat on the coffee table next to a bowl of Turkish delight. I lifted one of the monthlies, skimmed the first story – a maudlin and unrealistic tale about a lone marshal defending a frontier town

234

single-handedly against a band of Apaches, as far from my own frontier experience as possible.

I moved into the bedroom. A row of photographs stood on the bureau in an assortment of frames. They were all of the same woman, a stout matron of mature years, her grey hair fixed in tortoiseshell combs, a Bible in her hands. Sims's mother? The furniture was sumptuous: an ottoman, a chesterfield, and a *chaise longue*, all upholstered in silk damask. On the roll-top desk I saw a ledger book. I walked over, turned on the lamp, and had a look. I found a list of expenses: three worsted suits, five silk shirts, sixteen ties, sixteen pairs of socks, five pairs of shoes, twenty silk handkerchiefs, six pairs of gold cuff-links, a gold watch, a gold chain, and a box of Selectos Havana cigars – a rare commodity since the war in Cuba. A few loose receipts lay on the desk beside the ledger book. One was from a flower shop. Mr Sims had spent two hundred dollars on flowers in the last week. Another was from a department store, purchases totalling 312 dollars. The last entry was for a 2,000-dollar deposit receipt, paid in cash, for a new 1903 Panhard luxury motor car. I shook my head, and then I searched the rest of the premises. I knew exactly what I was looking for. And it didn't take long to locate.

I found it in the back of his closet; an expensive alligator Gladstone suitcase full of money – 20,000 dollars, some in hundreds, some in twenties – all the bills wrapped in the distinctive green and yellow bank straps of the Corn Mercantile Cooperative.

Why is it we so often return to the places of our failures?

After I had telephoned Stanley Armstrong in Fairfield and told him what I had found; after I'd contacted Captain Lanny Mullins of the Buffalo Police Department and made all the necessary bureaucratic, tactical, and legal arrangements for Michael Sims's capture and arrest; after I had searched unsuccessfully for a willing Chinese translator in Buffalo's small Chinatown, my feet inexorably found their way to the site of last year's Pan-American Exposition.

Is there anything more desolate than a closed-down fair? Where once crowds had thronged I found only a handful of souls strolling past the shuttered exhibits and boarded-up buildings, solemnly drifting through the fairgrounds the way the dead might drift through purgatory. In the pinkish twilight, the turned-off fountains, fenced-in rides, and locked-up buildings took on the abandoned aspect of an ancient ruin. I saw the Ferris wheel in the distance, unturning, silhouetted against the sky, its topmost seat swaying slightly in the breeze. A seagull squawked overhead, tracking northward, its cry echoing over the empty midway. I caught a whiff of wet canvas and, a moment later, saw a pile of old circus tents rolled up, stacked against a hoarding, looking like a pile of huge cigars.

With deepening melancholy I approached the Temple of Music, the ornate structure near the end of the fairgrounds. When I came within fifty yards of the place, I stopped. I didn't want to go any further. I recalled how hundreds of people had gathered outside the Temple last year on a sweltering September day to shake President McKinley's hand. The building pulled at me. I felt as if I were mesmerized by it. My feet started moving again, as if by themselves. I covered the final distance and stepped inside.

I walked to the end of the Temple, to the exact spot where President William McKinley had been shot. How well I recalled that young Polish-American, Leon Czolgosz, one of the last in the reception line to approach the President, his hand hidden under a handkerchief, his brow covered with sweat. How well I recalled the two whiffs of smoke jumping from beneath his handkerchief, like two deadly jinn released from a lamp, and the two bullets thudding into the President's stomach. The President had clasped his hands to his abdomen, gazed at Czolgosz with affable but questioning beneficence, then fallen to the dusty plank floor. How well I remembered it all, down to the minutest detail, even though I now wished desperately to forget every last bit of it...

Murder cuts me keenly now. Murder dances in my dreams and taunts me. If Stanley were to ask me to solve another murder tomorrow, I wouldn't hesitate.

I operated on William. I removed the bullets. And then I watched.

I should have taken the tremor in William's hands more seriously. I should have counted more carefully how many hours he slept in a day. I should have measured to the minutest fraction his fluid intake. He began to murmur disconnected lines from his favorite hymn, 'Nearer My God to Thee'. He slipped in and out of consciousness. He confused me with Mark Hanna, his chief aide, and thought Mark Hanna was George Cortelyou, his security advisor. He uttered snatches of incoherent prayer. His eyes glazed over. He recognized no one. On September the fourteenth, at two forty-five in the morning, the murderer's bullets did their work. I had my stethoscope pressed to William's chest at the time. I heard his heart stop beating. I straightened my shoulders and, as my eyes misted over, I quietly announced, 'Gentlemen, the President is dead.'

I am a different man because of this. Murder will never be the same to me. It will always be an open wound to me.

It will always be something I try to heal...

Sheriff Stanley Armstrong arrived in Buffalo

early the next day. I sat with Stanley and Buffalo Police Captain Lanny Mullins in the Buffalo Police Department's only motorized paddy wagon. I saw three police officers with shotguns gather in an alley down the street from the Beardmore.

'You don't need shotguns, Captain Mullins,' I said. I thought of Sims's phonograph, his opera records, how he liked to attend Mrs Vanduzen's musical soirées. 'He's not going to give you a fight.'

Stanley grunted. 'Clyde, let the captain do his work.'

'I don't want the boy hurt,' I said.

The captain grinned. He was enjoying this. 'We won't hurt him,' he said. 'Not unless we have to.' One of the policemen down the alley gave us a signal. Captain Mullins turned to Stanley. 'Have you got your papers in order, sheriff?' he asked.

'I do.'

The captain gave us a nod. 'Then up on our longshanks, boys.'

EIGHTEEN

Back in Fairfield, Richard Lip was worse. His skin was the color of an old paper bag, his breath came and went in a painful wheeze, and he was so warm I felt heat rising from his body. A plate of rice and beans sat untouched on the table beside Lip's sleeping-pallet. I hoped and prayed that this was the natural course of the thing, that the fever would finally lift, that the infection wouldn't snatch Lip away as it had President McKinley, but I knew I was only fooling myself.

Stanley stood at the cell door. 'This is something he has to fight by himself, Clyde,' he said. 'There's nothing you or any other doctor can do.'

I reached for the drinking glass and held it to Lip's mouth. He opened his eyes, recognized me, and nodded. I tipped the glass and watched water dribble into his mouth. He swallowed, an arduous straining of his throat, and managed to keep the liquid down. He reached out and put his weak hand on my wrist. He nodded again, grinned, like he wanted to let me know he was all right. I guess he saw how worried I was. I guess he

240

saw President McKinley's ghost lurking somewhere in my eyes. After a few more minutes, he dozed off. I stood up, feeling helpless, and turned to Stanley.

'Might as well have a few words with Mr Sims now,' I said.

Stanley nodded. The strategy had been to let the bank clerk stew for a day before getting a statement out of him. Stanley walked over to his desk and lifted the large key-ring from the side. I left Richard Lip's cell and sat at the table. As Stanley opened Michael Sims's cell door, I watched our new prisoner, a young man of twenty-five, his face a picture of ruinous worry, rise to his feet. He was pale and disheveled from a sleepless night in his cell. He looked ready to talk. Stanley led the prisoner over and made him sit in the chair across from me.

'How's it feel, son?' I asked.

Sims stared at me morosely, dark shadows of exhaustion under his eyes, the straw-colored cow-lick at the back of his head sticking up like a dozen shoots of overgrown grass. He looked as miserable as a rainy day.

'What are you going to do with me?' he asked in a small, meek voice.

My eyes widened. Was he actually scared of me? Did he think I was going to thrash him?

'We're going to ask you some questions, son,' I said, 'that's all. There's nothing to worry about.'

He looked at his hands, tapped them

together a few times, then glanced at the spittoon resting at the foot of Stanley's desk.

'I thought it would be ... I don't know ... I really don't like it here.'

Stanley and I glanced at each other. Stanley cleared his throat. 'Michael, my boy,' said Stanley, 'there's nothing nice about jail. And when Judge Norris gets through with you, you'll be spending twenty years in one.'

Sims's eyes widened in sudden, desperate alarm. I thought he was going to cry. I shook my head. Stanley always offered despair. That's the way we worked it. This was like old times.

'Michael,' I said, 'you don't want to go to jail.' I, on the other hand, always offered hope. 'You don't want to have guards watching every move you make every minute of the day. You don't want to eat bad food and live in a nine-by-twelve cell with three other inmates, and go to the bathroom in front of everybody, and crack boulders from sun-up to sun-down. It's not a picnic, Michael. And you're small. You wouldn't survive even a year in prison, let alone twenty.'

He stared at me, his look of alarm intensifying. 'But if I ... that is, if the judge...' He shook his head, his eyes moistening. 'I mean ... you caught me with all that money, and there's no way I can ... I have to go to jail, whether I like it or not, don't I?'

He gave his cow-lick a hopeless scratch. His already pale face seemed to go a shade paler and his lower lip drooped.

'I think that's true,' I said, philosophically. 'I think Judge Norris is bound to send you away ... at least for a little while.' Now it was time for my little morsel of hope. 'But you want to make that time as short as possible.' I raised my eyebrows, as if I'd just had a thought. 'Say ... Judge Norris might be lenient if you cooperate,' I said. I brought my hand down and drummed the table with my fingers, pretending to consider the idea. 'Maybe you could be our witness. Maybe you could tell us exactly what happened.' His eyes focused on me the way a starving man's eyes might focus on a loaf of bread. 'We're after real lawbreakers, Michael, the common no-goods who put you up to this ... this misadventure.' I leaned forward and put my hand on the young man's knee. 'The sheriff and I both know you're as honest as can be, and that you wouldn't do something like this without some bad sorts putting you up to it.' My eyebrows rose in a sudden expression of optimism. I lifted my hand from his knee. 'You might even come out of this a hero of sorts if you help us catch these no-goods and recover the rest of the money,' I said. 'Judge Norris would like that.' I leaned back in my chair and coaxed a fatherly smile to my face. 'The sheriff and me, we're not in the business of putting bank clerks in jail. We're after real felons.'

The boy, his defenses weakened by a night

in the sheriff's jail, hesitated only as a matter of form – no one likes to be a skunk – then clutched at my little morsel of hope with both hands.

'You know, doctor,' he said, his voice high, his words quick, 'you're right.' He looked away. The relief in his voice was nearly painful to hear. 'I fell in with some bad sorts – real muckrakers – and, heck, I don't know ... they got me thinking the wrong way; turned me right around with their smooth talk and fancy words.'

He looked at me, pining for encouragement.

'And just who are these muckrakers?' I asked. 'You've come this far, Michael, don't disappoint us now. You know we need names. It's not as if we don't have some idea already.' I thought of Sheriff Vernon Stillwater's telegram from Saratoga Springs, how Murchison's bookmakers had been caught passing Corn Mercantile money at the track. I thought of the captain's chest hauled by wagon in the middle of the night up to the caves. 'We just need you to confirm what we already know.'

His brow settled. He took a deep breath, preparing himself. His neck seemed to shrink as he drew his shoulders in, reminding me of the snapping turtles in the mudholes around Clifford's Bend. He was looking for a way out and, by Jim, I'd given it to him. He'd be a halfwit not to take it.

'Arnold Murchison,' he said. The name burst from his mouth like a cork from a champagne bottle. 'Frank Jaslowski.' This name shot from his lips like a rocket. 'Charlotte Scott,' he said.

I glanced at Stanley, who stared steadily at Michael Sims. Charlotte Scott. It surprised neither Stanley nor I that the barber's daughter might have played a role. She seemed willing to do anything, especially after her father's financial ruin, to go to drama school in New York. With the names out, Sims seemed exhausted. His shoulders sank and he leaned back in his chair.

'We found Corn Mercantile money in one of Charlotte's socks,' I said. I took off my bowler and rubbed my hand through my hair. 'After she was murdered. People kill for money, Michael,' I said. 'And the Corn Mercantile burglary ... well, that's a lot of money.'

He saw what I was suggesting. He didn't look like a killer but, even so, my suspicions had at least some justification. His eyes widened in apprehension.

'You think I killed Charlotte?' He seemed aghast at the idea. 'I would never kill Charlotte,' he said. 'I loved Charlotte.'

'You moved to Buffalo the day after she was murdered,' I said. 'Were you running?'

He looked at me, then at Stanley, then back at me. 'I had nothing to do with Charlotte Scott's murder!' he said. 'I moved because I ... Murchison had his plans and he ... I might have been running, but I wasn't running because I killed Charlotte Scott!'

I thought he was going to have a fit.

'Easy now, son,' I said. 'No point in getting yourself all worked up.' I sat back, taking a different tack. 'Just start at the beginning.' The boy looked positively panicked now. I thought I'd better give him a chance to talk. 'That's all we want.' Give him a chance to let off steam. 'Convince me. You say you didn't kill Charlotte. Tell me why I should believe you.'

He looked at me, gave me an angry and defiant nod. 'All right,' he said, his blood still up, his eyes still wide. 'I'll tell you everything. I'll start right at the beginning.' His tone was belligerent now. 'You asked for it, you're going to get it.'

'That sounds dandy,' I said.

You never knew what you were going to get if you just let them talk.

'I got to know her,' he began, 'just after her father lost all that money.' He shook his head and took a deep breath, as if the subject of Charlotte's father exasperated him. 'I knew about her pa's investment, you see, this Panamanian business.' He tried to get a grip on himself, calmed down a little. 'Charlotte came to me at the bank and asked me if I could do anything to help get back the money. I checked over the Panamanian prospectuses for her. I wrote to a couple of the

246

addresses, even telegraphed all the way to Central America.'

'And what happened?' I asked.

'I never got any answer,' he said. 'I knew Mr Scott's money was as good as gone.' A vexatious knit came to his brow, as if he couldn't understand how people could throw away their money like that. 'When I told Charlotte her pa had been swindled, she started crying right then and there. We had to leave the bank.'

'I believe your story so far, Michael,' I said.

'Well ... after that, we got to know each other. I arranged for her to sing at one of Mrs Vanduzen's soirées, and I was in her good books from then on,' he said. He was talking quickly now, as if he were desperate for me to believe him. 'I was helping her, you see. I started doing all sorts of fool things for her: buying her clothes, giving her jewelry, taking her out to dinner all the time. That's when she started talking about this ... this Corn Mercantile thing.' He sighed, scratched his cow-lick again. 'She kept asking me when the Corn Mercantile money was coming in. She asked me about the safe. She took me to see Murchison. And Murchison had all these smooth words for me, like I told you. Took me into his office, kept filling my glass up with whiskey while Charlotte sat on my lap, kissing me, touching me, like we were a married couple.'

'What exactly did Murchison say to you?' I

asked.

'Well ... he said it would solve a whole pack of problems for everyone if we all put our heads together and made a grab for the Corn Mercantile money. He made it sound easy. I'd be the inside man, I'd get twenty-five grand out of the deal. I have debts, you see. We'd hide the money for a year. When a year was up, we'd all quietly leave Fairfield, one by one. All I had to do was give Murchison some information about the safe – its measurements, tolerances, and so forth – tell him when the Corn Mercantile money was coming in, and leave a back window unlatched so they could get inside without causing a lot of ruckus.' His brow furrowed. 'Once I said yes, I knew there was no backing out. Not with a man like Murchison.'

'And Charlotte's share was one thousand?' I asked.

'Five thousand,' he said.

'But we only found one thousand.'

'Like I said, Murchison wanted to hide it for a year. Charlotte asked for hers right away, and Murchison risked giving her a thousand. Charlotte wanted it all, that's true, but I don't know if she got it. I've never seen a girl so stubborn. She was impatient. She couldn't wait for anything. She wasn't afraid of Murchison, like I was. She wouldn't take no for an answer, kept after him for the rest of the money. Murchison tried to ex-plain to her that if the money got out on the street, we ran the risk of getting caught. But he really had his own plans for the money. We all should have seen that. He had people from Georgia he owed money to. He had people from Kentucky he owed money to. He had debts everywhere, and he was using our money to pay them off.'

'You know this?' I said.

'Frank Jaslowski told me.' He looked down at his hands. 'Frank and me had this private partnership, you see. I paid Frank a weekly premium. Frank was going to look out for my interests. Frank came to me the second week of June with two bags of money. He told me Murchison had people coming from Saratoga Springs. He owed these particular people more money than everybody else combined. Frank gave me my money and I left town. Charlotte should have done the same. She threatened to go to the police and expose the whole thing; that's how much she wanted her money,' he said. 'And that's where she went wrong.' Sims looked up at us with dull, unmoving eyes. In a smaller, weaker voice, as if he were thoroughly exhausted now by all these admissions, he said, 'Why do you think she wound up dead in the river?' I felt my blood quicken. What had we stumbled upon here? 'Murchison is old school. I heard him say flat-out he was going to kill her.'

'You're sure about this, Michael?' I said.

His voice grew stronger again, now that I'd

shown an interest. 'Of course I'm sure,' he said. 'Murchison never lets a problem like that get out of hand. Told Jaslowski he was going to poison her. I heard him as plain as day.'

NINETEEN

By evening, a light rain fell. Sheriff Armstrong and I, along with Deputies Mulroy, Putsey, and Loughlin, rode saddle-back up Fredonia Street toward the Parthenon Theater. We hitched our horses in an alley behind Cleveland Street and walked the rest of the way to the theater. We carried shotguns, rifles, and pistols. Passers-by scattered from our path. A cat staring at us from a shop window darted from the window-ledge and disappeared behind the drapery.

We swept into the theater. We marched through tables and chairs, our faces set, our bowlers cocked forward, our shirtsleeves rolled up. On stage, a young woman danced a modified version of the Turkey Trot; the bill-card read: 'THE DANCE OF THE SEVEN VEILS'. Some of the men sitting at the tables spotted us, quickly got up and left the theater through the various fire doors. I looked around for Arnold Murchison and Frank Jaslowski but I couldn't see them anywhere. Though my shiner was nearly gone, I still harbored a grudge for what Murchison's men had done to me up on Cherry Hill last week.

Stanley and I looked at each other.

'Let's check the back,' he said.

We stormed around the proscenium arch to Arnold Murchison's office door. Raymond Putsey kicked the door in. We found no one inside. A spilled bottle of whiskey lay on the table, a half-finished cigar sat smoking in an ashtray on Murchison's desk, and the filing cabinet drawers had been gone through and half the contents taken.

'Looks like they just left,' said Stanley.

'By the stage door?' I suggested.

We filed backstage, our boots reverberating against the plank floor. Half-naked women peered out at us from their dressing-rooms. At the far end of the corridor the stage door gaped wide on to the stoop, swaying in the wind, knocking against the railing. The rain blew into the corridor. We hurried out the exit on to the cramped stage stoop and looked around.

'The stable,' I said, pointing down the alley.

But we were too late. We heard the jingling of bridles, and saw Murchison and Jaslowski burst from the stable on fresh mounts, spurring the animals to a full gallop, leaning forward in their saddles like a couple of racing jockeys. They bolted past us, neither of them looking at us. Donal Loughlin hoisted his shotgun and took aim at the passing men. I gripped the barrel and yanked it

252

downward.

'We want them alive, deputy,' I said. 'They have got a lot to answer for, and they won't do no answering if they're dead.'

Murchison and Jaslowski turned the corner on to Fredonia and disappeared.

'They've got a head start!' said the young deputy.

'That don't matter,' said Stanley. 'We'll track 'em for twenty miles if we have to. They won't get away. Not if I have anything to do with it.'

We jumped over the railing, ran past the stables out to Cleveland Street, crossed the road, and hurried down a narrow walkway between buildings to the alley where we had our horses. We mounted, rode out of the alley, and turned right on to Fredonia. We bolted down Fredonia, hooves splashing through the puddles, and reined in when we reached Hooper Avenue.

'They've either gone straight along Fredonia,' said Stanley, 'or south-east along Hooper.' These were the only two routes out of Fairfield at this point. Stanley tugged on his reins, trying to keep his horse under control. 'Ray, you and the boys ride south along Fredonia. Clyde and me will take Hooper. I don't want no shooting, not unless they shoot first.' His horse cantered ninety degrees. 'Judge Norris needs them alive.'

We spurred our horses and shook our reins.

Stanley and I rode at breakneck speed down Hooper Avenue. As we curved southeast toward the Fifth County Road, clouds thickened above us, the rain pelted harder, and the wind whipped the tops of the elm trees. I saw the white clapboard spire of the Fairfield Baptist Church beyond a grove of poplar, its thin iron cross rising like a roasting spit into the glowering sky. Five ravens flew by, riding the wind.

'If we don't catch them before dark,' said Stanley, 'we're bound to lose them.'

Once across the Fifth County Road, we climbed Lombard Hill. The summer corn bent like a green ocean in the wind. Though not as high as Cherry Hill, Lombard Hill provided us with a good view. We saw farmhouses, silos, and barns; windmills spinning frantically in the gale; and Jersey cows sheltering under solitary maples and elms. Far to the south, on the twenty-first county line, we spotted two men riding horseback; agitated specks in the surrounding corn.

'That's them!' cried Stanley.

'We'll never catch them if we follow from here,' I hollered. 'Let's double back and ride along the railroad tracks.'

The railroad tracks ran south–east. We would cut our distance by heading diagonally. Murchison and Jaslowski, if they stayed on the twenty-first county line, would veer east and intersect the tracks out near the village of Willet. If we could beat them to

Willet, we stood a good chance of catching them.

We bolted up to the Fifth County Road, galloped east, splashing mud everywhere, passed the picnic ground and Richard Lip's bridge, then yanked our reins and heaved our animals up the embankment to the railroad tracks. There was a footpath on either side of the gravel railway embankment. Our horses found the south path quickly, a path so narrow we had to ride single file. Wet sumac and maple pressed in from the right against us. The rail line stretched to a vanishing point ahead of us. As we passed the signal lights at the foot of Erie Boulevard we scared a few drenched seagulls into the air, and clumped over the dead and flattened raccoon they'd been feasting on.

We crossed a trestle bridge. After a mile, the maple and sumac cleared and we got an unbroken view of the cornfields to the south. Pythagoras worked up a lather as I spurred her relentlessly. The sky swirled with grey clouds and the rain came down like steel pellets, soaking right through my vest and shirt.

'There they are!' shouted Stanley, pointing.

In the overcast light I saw our fugitives, far to the south, still on the twenty-first county line.

'They've slowed to a trot!' I called. 'They're trying to save their horses.'

Up ahead we saw another trestle bridge, the final bridge before Willet. All we had to do was cross this bridge and Murchison and Jaslowski would be in our hands. But then to my great alarm I saw the light of the inbound limited to New York flying past Willet; an iron snake looming out of the mist at thirty miles per hour. I saw cinders and sparks fly from its stove-pipe chimney as it charged toward the bridge, heard the snare-drum rhythm of its engine, and knew that if we didn't clear the bridge before the train did, we would lose all hope of apprehending our suspects. I glanced at Stanley. His eyes were wide. He saw our predicament clearly.

He spurred his horse. 'Yaaa!' he cried.

His horse bolted forward.

To Stanley, after months of painstaking work on the Corn Mercantile burglary, catching Murchison and Jaslowski wasn't open to debate. And now that Murchison might be Charlotte's killer, I spurred my own horse yet again. The inbound limited to New York hurtled towards us, its banner of smoke arching from its chimney, its cow-catcher a triangular speck of red in the ruddy glow of its Cyclopsian headlamp, the passenger windows vague squares of light attenuating eastward in a sequence of diminishing size. In a collision – forty tons of hot, pumping steel against the flyweight organisms of horse and man – we stood no chance. Hooves flung gravel every which way. We had to prevail. The locomotive gained speed. We had to win or we'd be crushed. Machine and men drew closer. Up ahead I saw the bridge. A narrow fringe of plank walkway lined each side, the wood now slick in the rain.

'You take that side!' I called. 'Some of this wood might be rotten! We'll even up our chances if we ride on separate sides!' I took the south walkway, Stanley took the north.

Our horses leaped for the trestle, gained the plank walkways, and flew over the first part of the bridge, their hooves knocking against the wood with a steady tattoo of repeated bangs, their manes wet and plastered to their necks. The train was no more than two hundred yards away now. Fingers of mist reached up from the river below. Up on the trestle bridge it was foggy. The train was no more than a bright blotch of light rocketing toward us like a comet out of the sky. Blazes! The inbound limited looked ready to pounce on us. I dug my spurs into Pythagoras one more time. The train bore down on us, an iron monster, no more than seventy-five yards away. The walkways were too narrow. There wouldn't be enough room. Stanley and I were bound to be crushed. And I'd wager the engineer hadn't even seen us yet, it was so foggy. Nearly there ... nearly there ... yes, we were going to make it ... had to make it ... but then I heard a cry from the other side and, looking back, saw Stanley's horse tumble into the middle of the tracks as some rotten planks collapsed beneath it, watched Stanley fall from his saddle, saw him slide on the seat of his pants over the wet wood, eyes wide, mouth open, knees up. He came to a stop, jumped to his feet, and ran to his horse.

'Stanley!' I called.

The train bellowed like Beelzebub as it rattled on to the bridge – the engineer had finally seen us and was sounding his horn the way Joshua's army had sounded their trumpets at Jericho.

Pythagoras darted forward with a sudden burst of speed, dodged around the cowcatcher, and leaped from the walkway on to the muddy path. She grew foot-sure on the blessedly solid ground. I reined her to a stop beside some burgeoning milkweed, fought to keep her under control as the train rumbled by, hoping she would fight her instinct to bolt. I saw the blurred faces of passengers staring out at me. Stanley had to be dead. No one could survive a head-on collision with a Baldwin Locomotive Works 2-6-2 steam engine, the heaviest locomotive anywhere. The luxury Pullman at the end rolled by, then the caboose, its platform lights glaring red, a carman standing at the rail. He waved to me as he passed.

As the limited reached the bridge's halfway point, I prepared myself – I'd seen some grisly carnage in the Cuban conflict. Yet what I found when the train finally clanked to the

258

other side surprised even me. Stanley was gone. So was his horse. Disappeared. Vanished.

I got off Pythagoras and ran on to the bridge.

'Stanley?' I yelled, fearing I'd lost my dearest friend.

Part of the railing on Stanley's side had been smashed away, the supports snapped like toothpicks, the braces shattered into kindling. Had he fallen into the river? I crossed the tracks and peered into the water. With all that mist, I couldn't see a thing. I held my breath, heard the lapping of the current against the river bank, the sound of the rain, the humming of the wind through the trestle's overhead arches.

'Stanley?' I called again. 'Are you down there?'

'Get going, you chowderhead!' he called. 'What in the blue blazes are you hanging around for? They're getting away.'

Relief swept through me.

'Where are you?' I asked.

'Up to my neck in water,' he answered flatly. 'Where else?'

'Is your horse all right?'

'Jessabel's fine.'

'How'd you get down there?' I asked.

'We jumped, of course.' He sounded exasperated, his voice echoing up and down the river. 'For the love of Pete, Clyde, get moving.'

I hurried back to Pythagoras, leaped on to the saddle, and spurred her hard. She ran at a ferocious clip. In five minutes I reached the outskirts of Willet.

The village looked deserted. The sign above the drug store creaked back and forth in the wind and only a few lights shone from the windows of the dozen or so houses. Main Street angled away from the railroad tracks. I slowed Pythagoras to a walk; I didn't want to spook Murchison and Jaslowski with the sound of hooves. When I reached the corner, I looked down Willet's only side street, Elm Street, and saw Murchison and Jaslowski talking to a local farmer while their horses fed on a scattered bale of hay. I reined Pythagoras back, hoping to stay concealed behind a large lilac bush, but she was so testy from being ridden so hard she whinnied, and pranced into the intersection. The men looked up and saw me. Blast and damn!

They ran for their horses. The local farmer looked up in surprise. I spurred Pythagoras yet again. A flash of lightning brightened the sky and I saw the men clearly, Murchison on the left, Jaslowski on the right. The local farmer backed away as I passed. I followed the fugitives beyond the village limits, took out my gun and fired a warning shot into the air, hoping they might stop if they knew they were being fired upon. But they kept going, faster and faster. Then they separated. As they reached a rise in the road, Murchison darted off to the left, out into the field, not caring if he crippled his horse in unseen sink-holes or deep furrows, while Jaslowski kept riding along the road. The move confounded me. As much as I hated to let Frank Jaslowski get away, I knew I had to go after Murchison, especially because he might be Charlotte's killer.

I reined Pythagoras into the young corn, cresting the small rise after Murchison. As I came to the top of the hill, I saw a creek winding toward the Tonawanda in a shallow valley. A farmhouse stood a quarter of a mile beyond, its windows lighted, its green roof slick with rain. I saw Murchison ride straight for the creek. Did he think he could jump it? Did he really have that much confidence in his small, tired gelding? Over the rain, I heard the barking of a farm dog. Lightning flashed again. Murchison galloped straight for the creek, leaned close to his horse's mane, stood in the stirrups. I slowed Pythagoras to a trot, sat up in my saddle, and watched. Murchison reached the edge of the creek. His animal reared up, attempted the jump, but quickly lost altitude and thudded chest-first into the opposite bank. The creature tumbled sideways, pitching Murchison from its back the same way a child pitches an unwanted toy to the floor.

As I came to the edge of the creek, I reined Pythagoras to a stop, jumped from her back, leaped into the water, and ran for Murchison. He pushed himself up, stumbled a few times, and wiped the water from his eyes.

'Up with your hands,' I said, pointing my Army Colt Special at his chest. 'You're under arrest.'

He looked as wobbly as a marionette without strings. But then he threw a handful of mud, concealed in his hand, into my eyes, and I was blinded for several seconds. I stumbled backward, lifting my hand to my eyes. I heard him run toward me. I didn't want to kill him, not with so many questions still unanswered, but I had to defend myself. I raised my gun, ready to fire, but he knocked the gun out of my hand, and it fell into the water. I forced my eyes open. Murchison's fist plowed into my stomach. I bent double, the wind rushing out of me.

'Can't you take a hint, doc?' he said. He threw a quick left jab into my lip, drawing blood. 'I thought you might have learned your lesson,' he said. I guess he meant my beating up on Cherry Hill. He clasped both hands together and, using them like a club, pounded me against the side of the head. I careened wildly sideways over the uneven creek-bed, trying to keep my balance. 'I thought you might have had more common sense,' he said. He lumbered after me and punched me in the stomach a second time. 'But I guess you don't. I guess I'm going to have to kill you now.'

Before he could throw another punch, I

mustered all my resolve, cleared my head and, still bent double, launched myself head first into Murchison's stomach. He grunted as the wind rushed out of his lungs. We both fell into the water. My anger exploded. I got to my knees in the soaking wet and grabbed Murchison by the hair. I lifted his head out of the water and punched him squarely in the mouth, then brought my elbow crashing down on the crown of his head. I grabbed him by the hair again and forced his face underwater. I remembered how his men had punched me so hard in the eye. Murchison flailed. When I knew he must be out of breath, I lifted him up.

'Try this for a hint,' I said. I punched him in his own eye, satisfying myself with the nemesis I so desperately needed, then shoved his face once more underwater.

I kept him down longer this time. He struggled frantically. I wanted to give him a good taste of it. I pulled him up. He gasped for breath. I remembered the rifle butt crashing down on the back of my head. I grabbed him by the hair again, lifted his face, and launched a massive blow to his nose, straight-arming him with a full strike, leaning into it the way Teddy Roosevelt had taught me. Murchison's eyes rolled into his head, his body went limp, and he fell like a dead dog into the water. I grabbed him by the collar and dragged him on to the sandy bank. I forced his arms behind his back and cuffed his wrists. He opened his eyes and groaned.

'How's that for common sense?' I said.

Murchison groaned again. He was in bad shape. But I felt reborn. I felt refreshed. Nothing could boost one's spirits better than having to use one's fists in the apprehension of dangerous criminals.

PART THREE

Treasure Island

TWENTY

Stanley and I tried our usual mix of hope and despair on Murchison, but he wouldn't budge.

'You don't have a thing,' he said. 'A Grand Jury won't trust the testimony of a bunch of crooked bookmakers in Saratoga Springs. And they won't believe a word Michael Sims says. The man was caught with a suitcase full of Corn Mercantile money. And he can say what he wants about poison and murder, but he's a felon, and his word won't be worth two cents to any Grand Jury.'

'So you deny killing Charlotte Scott then?' I said.

Murchison's face settled. He looked at me with the sour menace of a provoked mastiff.

'I don't harm my girls, doc,' he said. 'I never have, I never will. And I sure don't kill them.'

He rubbed the blood from his broken nose with his sleeve. I shook my head.

'You were down by the river at or around the time Miss Scott was murdered, Mr Murchison,' I said. 'I know this. Bernice Scott has told me this.'

'That might be true,' he said, 'but I still didn't kill her.'

After that, he just sat in his cell, as silent as a statue, his arms folded, his chin jutting, and stared sullenly at the wall. I gave up. I was too tired from our fight in the creek to put up much effort. I checked on Richard Lip.

I put my hand to Lip's forehead. He was hot. Too hot. He looked at me but didn't seem to recognize me, said something to me in Cantonese, then turned away, his hair plastered to his head with sweat. I pulled back the covers. His belly was distended, his breath was wheezy. And he shivered violently as the air touched his bare skin. I shook my head.

'He's gone and developed pneumonia, Stanley,' I said. 'I knew this might happen. Maybe we should telegraph Washington. I don't think he's going to make it.'

Stanley pressed his lips together. 'Let's not telegraph Washington just yet,' he said. 'Leroy had pneumonia last year. We all thought he was going to die, but then he pulled through and now he's fine. Maybe the same thing will happen to Lip.'

But I knew Stanley was just trying to cheer me up.

When I got home from the Sheriff's Office, I found a note in my mailbox. It was from Toula Vassos, Fairfield's own Empress of the Nile; Charlotte's friend from the Parthenon

Theater. She'd been here, she wanted to see me, she had something important to tell me, and she would be at home most of the night.

Though Allegheny Avenue was clear across town, nearly a mile away, I let Pythagoras rest. I cleaned myself up, changed my clothes, and went to catch the tramcar. I paid my two cents and headed up Tonawanda to Hoopertown.

I alighted at the corner of Allegheny and Tonawanda, and walked west until I reached Onondaga Street. Though the rain had stopped, the sky was still overcast. It was nearly dark, but I could see the neighborhood well enough in the light of the gas jets. Shabby bungalows lined Onondaga Street. Old buggies rusted against broken picket fences. All the grass had gone to seed. Toula's bungalow had a sway-backed roof. Her porch, running the entire front of the house, was sway-backed as well. The paint flaked off the clapboard in hand-sized chips. I mounted the steps and knocked on the screened door.

'Miss Vassos?' I called. 'Toula?'

Toula emerged from the kitchen at the back. She wore only a light summer shift. Five small kittens followed her. From parlor I heard the scratchy sound of a phonograph playing the 'Anvil Chorus' from *Il Trovatore*.

She opened the door. 'You got my note?' she said.

'I did.'

She looked down at the kittens. 'And did you catch Murchison?'

News traveled so fast in a small town.

'We did.'

She gave me a worried look. 'What about Jaslowski?'

'The sheriff's organizing a posse,' I said.

She nodded, and then gestured down the dim corridor. 'Come in,' she said.

I followed her inside. As I passed the front parlor I glanced in through the doorway and saw two young women, both in underthings, lying on the couch in each other's arms, both rapturous, both unconcerned that I should be looking at them. As a doctor, I wasn't in the least bit shocked. I knew what Toula was, I knew what these women were, and none of them seemed interested in hiding it from me.

'I have some apple cider,' said Toula.

We sat at the kitchen table and she filled our glasses. She looked at me with those exotic green eyes of hers.

'Have you found the chest yet?' she asked.

I arched my brow. 'You know about the chest?'

She looked away. 'Charlotte told me things,' she said. She took a small sip of apple cider. 'And I heard Murchison and Jaslowski talking. About the chest ... about the burglary...'

'We haven't found the chest yet,' I said.

'We're looking.'

'It's in the caves,' she said.

'That's where we're looking,' I said.

Then for the longest time she didn't speak, as if she couldn't speak; this tough girl with the boyish body and the streetwise green eyes was grief-stricken. Her lips came together, her eyes moistened, and a single tear rolled down her brown cheek.

'My dressing-room door was open,' she said. 'And Murchison and Jaslowski...' She wiped the tear away with the back of her hand. 'They didn't know I was there. I came early. I had a gift to give to Charlotte. A ring ... my grandmother gave it to me before I left Europe...'

A baby goat came in through the back door. Toula looked at the goat, her eyes narrowing as the creature scuffed the plank floor. The goat walked to a bowl of milk, sniffed it, and then drank. I waited. She turned from the goat.

'They talked about ... about killing Charlotte...' So Michael Sims had been telling the truth, I thought. Murchison had to be my man. Or was he? I had two witnesses to the conspiracy, but none to the actual crime. 'And I was ... I dropped the ring on the floor. They heard it. They came to my dressing-room. Jaslowski held a knife to my throat. They threatened me. They said if I told anyone, they would kill me.'

The baby goat came over and nuzzled her

hand.

'Would you be willing to testify against Mr Murchison before a Grand Jury?' I asked.

Anger suddenly flew from her eyes like sparks from a grinding stone.

'Anything you want,' she said. 'Now that he can't hurt me I'll do anything I have to.'

I smiled. Murder could taunt. Murder could goad. I saw Toula had learned the sad lesson I myself had been forced to learn at the fair last September.

I spent the next morning at the Sheriff's Office nursing Richard Lip. I said nothing to Arnold Murchison about my conversation with Toula Vassos. Stanley was up in the caves. I was hoping he would find the chest.

I wasn't disappointed.

Early in the afternoon, Stanley and his deputies returned with it, the same chest I'd seen Murchison's men drag up into the hills. They also had Frank Jaslowski in handcuffs. Stanley was smiling like a boy with a nickel in a candy shop.

'We found Frank up in the caves guarding this chest,' he said.

I looked the chest over. 'That's the one,' I said.

Murchison approached his bars and peered at the chest, then glanced at Frank Jaslowski with questioning eyes. Jaslowski just stood there, a helpless look on his face. Murchison finally looked at the floor, a picture of woe.

'Shoot,' he said, defeated.

Raymond Putsey and Ernie Mulroy lowered the chest to the table while Stanley and Deputy Loughlin locked the new prisoner away.

'Ray, do you want to get that crowbar over there?' asked Stanley.

The deputy from Reese's Corners retrieved a small black crowbar from a wooden tool-box and brought it over. Stanley took the crowbar, jammed it under the lid, and broke the chest open. Inside lay three canvas bank sacks. On the underside of the chest lid was a brass name-plate. The name-plate had Murchison's name on it. I turned to the man.

'Guess we won't need the word of any crooked bookmakers from Saratoga Springs after all, Murchison,' I said. 'We got your name right here.' I put my hands on my hips. 'And since you're going to jail anyway, you might as well come clean about killing Charlotte Scott.'

He gripped the bars, his shoulders tensing. 'I didn't kill Charlotte Scott,' he said.

Stanley loosened the draw-strings and up-ended one of the bank sacks. Bundles of money fell on to the table. The bills were fresh, crisp, and wrapped in the paper straps of the Corn Mercantile Cooperative.

'How'd you find it so fast?' I asked.

'I had help,' said Stanley. 'Morley Suggett

rustled up his boys in West Shelby.' I nodded. I turned from the money and looked at Murchison. I walked over to his cell.

'Arnold, friend,' I said. I grabbed a stool and sat down outside his cell. 'Why not make it easy on yourself? If you up and confess to the Charlotte Scott killing, I'll ask Judge Norris to be lenient. I'll ask him to spare your life.'

'But I didn't kill no Charlotte Scott,' he said stubbornly.

'I think you did,' I said. I now told him about my conversation with Toula. 'She says she'll testify. She'll back up Michael's story. She's anxious to see you pay. If you 'fess up now, you might save yourself your life.'

'But I really didn't kill her,' he said, pleading, frantic. 'Charlotte came to me ... yes, sir, that's a fact ... and she asked for a thousand dollars, just like Michael said, that's all true ... and she said she would go to the police, and, yes ... maybe Frank and I talked about it ... you know, about keeping her quiet ... even mentioned poison once or twice...' He let his hands fall from the bars. I sensed Stanley listening from his desk as he counted the money. 'But that's all it ever was. Talk. I felt sorry for Charlotte. I liked Charlotte. She was headstrong, feisty, and downright stubborn, but I liked her. And, yes, Frank and me ... we might have had a conversation or two about keeping her quiet, but they were never serious conversations,

273

especially not after Charlotte told me she was carrying that unborn child of hers. I'm not going to go killing any unborn child. The reason she needed money so badly was so she could get away and have her baby somewhere out of sight. I swear to God, that's the truth. I had nothing to do with her murder. Nothing at all.'

'Charlotte told you about her child?' I said, leaning forward.

'Yes, sir,' he said, desperate now. 'She had no one else to turn to. She wasn't going to get no help from Roger Robson, now, was she?'

I raised my eyebrows. 'Was it Roger's child?' I asked.

'Of course it was,' he said.

I sighed in gratification. 'No one's been able to confirm that for us just yet, Mr Murchison,' I said. 'I'm much obliged.'

'He's the one who killed her,' he said, 'not me.' I felt my back stiffen. 'She came to me with bruises all over her one day, said Roger beat her because she told him she was carrying his child.' I remembered the bruises I'd discovered on Charlotte Scott's body in Mr Wilson's mortuary. 'I don't know why she ever put up with it. I know for a fact Roger Robson killed her. Charlotte told me he was going to beat her dead if she ever came to his doorstep again. Which is what she did. She never knew when to back down. And now she's dead. It doesn't take a genius to figure it out. She was scared. So I risked giving her a thousand dollars. Get her to New York, I thought. Put her on a train and get her out of Fairfield before Roger Robson kills her.' He looked at Stanley counting the money. 'But I guess I was too late.'

'And how long have you known this?'

'Pretty much since the night she was murdered.'

'But you didn't see Roger Robson go down to the river with Charlotte alone?'

'Just because I didn't see him doesn't mean he didn't go. It was dark out.'

'Why didn't you tell us this before?'

He gestured desolately at the chest. 'Why do you think?' he asked. 'The last thing I needed was the law sniffing around my heels.'

I found the devil-may-care Roger Robson standing behind the Robson mansion on Saddle Road smoking a cigarette and sharing a flask of whiskey with Haines, the chauffeur.

'Doc,' said Roger with a smile and a handshake, as if he were glad to see me, 'you couldn't have come at a better time. We've just taken delivery of my new motor car.'

He walked to the five-bay garage and pulled the tarp off a sporty electric locomobile, a two-seater with gleaming fenders and brass headlamps. I looked at the brand name emblazoned in red along the top of the chrome-plated radiator.

'A Stephens?' I said.

I'd read my share of automobile magazines but I'd never run across a Stephens before.

'It's British,' said Roger. 'My father had it shipped on the *Orpheus*.' The *Orpheus* was the Robsons' private ocean-going yacht.

'It looks like a fine piece of machinery, Roger, 'I said, kicking the tire, 'but I—'

'I'm going to have Haines tow it to the streetcar barn tomorrow,' he said. 'Sam Dennison's going to let me charge my battery there.'

I gazed upon Fairfield's second motor car.

'Roger, I'm actually here—'

'Would you like to go for a ride, doc?' he asked. 'We've got enough juice to take her down the road and back.'

He seemed so amiable. I could hardly believe he was capable of killing Charlotte.

'Roger,' I said firmly, 'we have to talk about Charlotte.'

His habitual smile slipped away. 'Oh?' he said, as if he couldn't understand why I would ever want to talk about Charlotte. 'Well ... what about her?'

I came straight to the point. I told him of the infant child I'd discovered during Charlotte's autopsy. I told him about Murchison's accusations. He stared at me, thinking it out, but finally shook his head and grinned, as if he were amused by the charges.

'That's ripe, doc,' he said. 'Arnold Murchison hardly knows me, and now he's treating my reputation like trash.'

I knew that tone. I'd heard it often. It was the tone of money. He took me by the elbow and ushered me away from Haines. Haines pretended to be busy with a tire gauge.

'Murchison claims you beat her,' I said.

'Why would I do that?' he asked. 'And as for killing her ... don't you already have her killer, doc?' he asked, all innocence. 'I thought you had Richard Lip in jail.'

'Richard Lip didn't do it,' I said.

His blue eyes flashed, but there was nothing behind them.

'And neither did I,' he said, his tone careless. He let go of my elbow and put his hands on his hips. 'Oh, I admit, some of Murchison's story is true. The child, for instance.' He shrugged. 'But, even so, I wouldn't kill Charlotte. Why would I kill her? I have no reason to kill her.'

'To spare yourself the embarrassment of her pregnancy,' I said.

'You think I'd let myself get worked up over something like that, doc?' he said. He shook his head. 'You got me pegged wrong, then. Why bother? It's much easier just to deny it.'

I found this despicable. 'You would deny your own child?' I said.

He frowned. 'Doc,' he said, 'all I ever wanted from Charlotte was a little fun. I spelled it out for her right from the start, and she thought that was just swell. By golly, I'm trying to have as much fun as I can while I still have the chance. I'm twenty years old. I'm going to be twenty-one next month. That might sound young to you, doc. But my life ends at twenty-one. I go to New York next month. My father has it all worked out. I have no choice. I go to New York, and that's going to be the end of girls for me. I'm not going to have any girls. My fun's going to be over.'

'But you compromised Charlotte,' I said. 'And you did so without any honorable intentions.'

His frown deepened. 'She compromised *me*, doc,' he said.

'I find that hard to believe,' I said.

He looked up at the sky, where a few stray clouds floated by. 'Then let me spell it out for you, doc,' he said. 'I go to New York next month because my father's got this girl picked out for me there. Her name's Lily Van Plaat. She's going to be my wife whether I like it or not. I've seen her picture in the *New York Times* society pages. She's not bad looking, but she has that dead look all those Fifth Avenue girls have. The Van Plaats are an old and exclusive family, doc, and my father wants me to marry into them, and he's spent a good part of the last five years smoothing the way for me. I don't want to ruin it for him. He doesn't mind me having my fun beforehand. Nothing I do in Fairfield's going to make much difference in New York. But if I were to go ahead and kill someone and then get caught for it, that would mean the end of all my father's hard work. Do you have any idea what my father would do to me if he found out I killed someone?' Roger shuddered theatrically. 'I might as well call him a mugwump to his face. No, sir, you don't want to cross my father. And I'd cross him bad if I did something stupid like that.'

'You're a brash young man who thinks he can get away with it,' I said, unable to control myself.

He shook his head. 'No,' he said. 'Fairfield girls ain't worth it.'

'Speak of them with respect,' I said.

He lifted his hand, stopping me. 'Cool down, doc,' he said. He sighed. 'Charlotte and me...' he said. He shook his head. 'I should have been more careful with Charlotte. She didn't play by the rules. I should have smelled trouble right from the start. Charlotte had certain ideas.' His eyes grew suddenly bad-tempered, something I'd never seen in the young Mr Robson before. 'I'm the kind of fella, I stop when I'm asked to stop. But she never said stop. She told me go right ahead, said it would be all right, that she'd been watching the days. But it wasn't all right, was it? Turns out she'd planned it right from the start. When she told me about it ... about the child ... she immediately thought I owed her the world. She thought I would do the honorable thing. She started making all sorts of crazy demands. Thought she had me cornered. Thought I'd break my engagement to Lily Van Plaat so we could both go to New York and she could go to acting school. Never met anyone so obstinate. But I was obstinate right back. I told her, it's your problem now, Charlotte.' He glanced at me, flashed that smile of his, as if all this were a joke between chums, the same expression I'd seen on his father's face numerous times. 'You go have your child, I told her, but don't bother me about it.' He shrugged, as if he were sick of talking about it. 'And Murchison can say what he likes. But I didn't kill Charlotte Scott. No one's going to believe Murchison. I'm the son of the town's richest man. People are going to believe me over him.'

TWENTY-ONE

By the time Stewart Craven, the Cantonese translator from Washington, arrived, Richard Lip, though still conscious, was close to death.

Mr Craven was a hale man of seventy. As a translator his reputation was unsurpassed, for he spoke not only Cantonese and Mandarin, but half a dozen other Oriental languages. He was a brisk man, despite his age. He hopped into my buggy with the sprightliness of a jackrabbit.

'So you're the man who single-handedly neutralized an artillery position on San Juan Hill,' he said, as I shook the reins.

I shrugged modestly. 'Any man would have done the same,' I said.

'Any fool, you mean,' he said.

As we drove down Court Street, I filled Stewart Craven in, told him about the events of the murder, the pertinent clues uncovered thus far, the purported movements of Richard Lip, Arnold Murchison, and Herbert Early on the night of the murder, my suspicions about Roger Robson, and described to him the geographical features of the murder scene so he would better understand any answers Richard Lip might give.

At the Sheriff's Office, Stanley supplied our distinguished guest with a box dinner of roast pork, hash browns, and beet greens. While Mr Craven ate, I gently roused Richard Lip and gave him a cup of strong sugary tea with lemon.

By eight o'clock I had Mr Lip propped up on some pillows in his cot. Stanley and I wheeled the cot out into the main part of the office. The other prisoners gathered at their bars to watch. We had Lip's drawing and soap carvings lined up on the table. We thought they might help.

'Boys,' said Mr Craven, 'where should we start?'

'Just tell him why you're here and ask him about his movements on the night of the murder.'

Mr Craven complied. When he was done, Richard Lip's eyes grew distant, as if he were searching his memory. Then he spoke. His voice was soft, trembling, but he got his words out. After he was done, Mr Craven translated for Stanley and me.

'He says he first heard music from the picnic ground around eleven o'clock,' said Mr Craven. 'He'd been sleeping under the bridge up till then, and the music woke him. He got up and looked through the trees and saw the picnickers in the picnic ground. He was hungry. He went to ask the picnickers for some food.'

'Ask him what alcohol he saw,' I said.

Mr Craven translated for me. Mr Lip gazed at me with weary, sick eyes.

'He says whiskey,' said Mr Craven. 'And sloe gin. A lot of sloe gin.'

'Did he ask for any sloe gin?'

Mr Craven said a few words in Cantonese. Richard Lip replied.

'He says yes,' said Mr Craven. 'He says he walked through the trees to the other side of the picnic ground where he found a girl sitting all by herself. The girl gave him a bottle.'

Lip pointed to one of the carvings I hadn't at first recognized. I now saw that it was Bernice Scott.

'He says there were a lot of bottles of sloe gin on this girl's table,' said Craven. Craven's face settled, and he gazed at Stanley and me with steady eyes, as if he were preparing us for something. 'He says this girl poured something into one of those bottles from a smaller bottle.' Craven continued to stare at us, making sure we understood the import of what he was saying. 'I guess that's what you're after, isn't it, boys?' he said. 'That sounds like a poisoning to me, all right.'

Stanley and I glanced at each other. Stanley clearly hadn't expected this.

Lip spoke again. Craven translated.

'He came out from behind a tree ... you know, to ask for some sloe gin, and he scared the girl, and she jumped, and she spilled some of whatever she'd been pouring into the sloe gin all over her sleeve.' Lip spoke yet again, squeezing the words out with great effort. 'Then Murchison came down,' said Craven. 'Mr Murchison told him to go away. So he went away.'

'And where did he go?' I asked.

Mr Craven repeated for Richard Lip my question in Cantonese. Mr Lip's response was brief.

'To the river,' said Mr Craven.

'And what did he see at the river?'

While Lip spoke, he pointed at the soap carving of Charlotte Scott and Herbert Early.

'He says he saw this woman and this man at the river,' said Craven. 'The girl was wearing a skirt made out of leaves.'

'That would be Miss Scott,' I said.

'He says they were having an argument. After a while the man went away. The girl got up and paced.'

'Was Mr Lip concealed?' I asked.

Stewart Craven translated, and Lip replied.

'He was sitting behind a bush,' said Mr Craven. 'He wasn't intentionally trying to hide himself.'

I couldn't help thinking of Herbert Early's story, how he had gone to the river with Charlotte Scott to break off what had become his ill-fated affair with her.

'Then the girl from the picnic table came down,' said Craven, 'the one he got the sloe gin from.' Our translator looked at both Stanley and me. 'That would be Bernice?' he said.

'It would,' I said.

'She had a bottle of sloe gin with her,' said Mr Craven. 'The two girls talked for a few minutes and then the young girl gave the bottle to her sister, poison and all, and her sister drank from it.' Craven sat up, put his hands flat on the table. 'Mr Lip says the effect was instantaneous. The older Miss Scott clutched her throat and dropped the bottle. She shrieked at the younger girl, took a few unsteady steps backward, and fell into the water. He says it didn't take much more than a minute before she was dead.'

I gazed at the sickly Richard Lip, who now reminded me of one of those pale salamanders that live in the underground caves of Tennessee and never see the light of day.

'What about the locket?' I asked.

Stewart Craven translated for me.

'He says he took the locket,' said Mr Craven. 'He was so hungry, he had no choice. He knew it would easily pay for the price of a meal.'

The next day, Saturday, a north-westerly pushed out the muggy humid weather. The air, for the first time in a week, felt comfortably dry and refreshing. I was just finishing my breakfast in the sun-room when I heard a knock at my front door.

It was Judge Edgar Norris. He touched his short stocky fingers to the rim of his bowler and gave me a nod.

'Morning, doctor,' he said. 'I was just talking to Sheriff Armstrong.'

His face was serious, his lips set, his eyes staring at me with hard readiness – the judge was here to talk business.

'Morning, judge,' I said.

'I hope you have a few minutes,' he said.

'I sure do,' I said.

The judge looked about. 'Why don't we settle ourselves on that porch swing there,' he said. 'We've got some discussing to do.'

We walked over to the porch swing and sat down.

'Dr Deacon...' he began. The readiness in his eyes softened and he looked perplexed. 'This is a damnable thing, this Charlotte Scott murder.' He tapped his knee a few times with his fingers. 'Sheriff Armstrong told me about Bernice.' He glanced at the purple clematis curling along the porch rail. 'I can't help thinking,' he said, 'Howard and Henrietta Scott have already lost one daughter.' He inspected the Japanese pearl on his tie-clip. 'Now they're going to lose another one.'

I stared at the sundial in the middle of my front yard. 'That can't be helped,' I said. 'Murder is murder.'

'Yes, but...' The judge struggled for words. Out on the street, Mr Scythes rolled by in his milk wagon, the clip-clop of Belle's hooves drifting lazily across my yard on the fresh morning air. 'What about mercy, doctor?' he asked. 'Not for Bernice. For Howard and Henrietta Scott.'

I felt my face settle. 'Judge, we have laws in this country.'

'I know we do, doctor,' he said. 'But Bernice is a ... she's an odd girl. And who knows if she's really responsible for what she does? Anybody can see that there's something wrong with her. She's always been like that, for as long as I can remember, and I don't know if we can rightly consider her in full possession of her faculties. And she ... well, she ain't normal, is what I'm trying to say. It's going to kill the Scotts to have her taken away from them.'

'What choice do we have?' I asked.

'We can just drop it.'

'No, we can't.'

'Yes, but her mother and father ... especially poor old Howard. Think what it's going to do to him.'

'I appreciate that, judge,' I said. 'Just the same, we got laws.'

These words seemed to hit the judge like a slap in the face. I was a country doctor and I was telling a judge about laws. Judge Norris was a big man in Genesee County. Rare was the man who stood up to him. He looked at me as if I had just insulted his mother.

'Fine, Dr Deacon,' he said, all his friendliness gone. 'Then forget mercy.' He leaned closer, the scent of his cologne cloying the air. 'Let's talk about proof, then.' He leaned back again, contemplating me the way a preacher contemplates a sinner. 'As far as I'm concerned, you don't have any. At least, none I can lay my hands on. Oh, sure, you got the ramblings of Richard Lip, but his brain's addled by fever and he's got a back full of buckshot. And then you got that fancy translator of yours from Washington, but who knows if he got the meaning right?'

'I realize that, judge.'

His eyes widened. I could see he was surprised. He hadn't expected me to agree with him. 'Then what are you going to do?' he asked, his tone incredulous. 'I need tangible, physical proof. You haven't given me anything I can show to a Grand Jury yet.'

'Don't worry, judge,' I said. 'I'll get proof.'

He stared at me as if I were Lucifer himself. I knew he hoped my investigation would defeat me. Trying Bernice Scott would make him unpopular, and he had his election in November to think about.

'Good,' he finally said, frustrated by the dead-end he'd met. 'Because right now, to my mind at least, you don't have much more than pig-slop.'

★ ★ ★

Richard Lip died later that morning.

I was by his side. He opened his eyes one last time, said something in Cantonese to me, something I had no hope of understanding, and then stopped breathing.

I put my fingers on his eyelids and pulled them down. I'd lost him after all.

Later that same afternoon I got a call from Howard Scott.

'We're having a picnic in the park tomorrow,' he said, 'and we'd like you to come along. We'd like to show our appreciation for all you've done.'

I guess he'd heard about Richard Lip's death. I guess he thought my investigation was over. Like everybody else in town, he thought Richard Lip was Charlotte's killer. Tragic though it was, I was going to have to set him straight on that. But not before I got the proof Judge Norris needed.

TWENTY-TWO

The next day the sky was as blue as corn-flowers, with dainty white clouds floating from west to east. The first of the summer clover lay scattered like popcorn across the Green. I sat with the Scott family on a couple of old quilts next to the river. I nibbled a piece of peach cobbler. The remains of a ham hock sat on a large silver platter in the middle of the quilt. Howard Scott was with Bernice out in the field helping her fly a kite. Beulah Frith, Mrs Scott's sister, had hired a boat and was on the water up near the Park Street bridge. I sat alone with Henrietta Scott. She poured iced tea from a porcelain pitcher and offered a glass to me.

'Thank you, ma'am,' I said putting down my peach cobbler. 'I'm much obliged.'

She still wore black, an anomaly amid all the blue, pink, and green of the other female picnickers, and a mourning bonnet with veil. She was a full-figured woman, verging on corpulence. I saw the outline of her corset pressing against the fabric of her mourning dress. She looked exquisitely uncomfortable in the exacting undergarment.

'Look at them,' she said, lifting her chin toward her husband and daughter. 'They never used to do anything together. Howard never really understood Bernice before.' I watched the pair. 'They actually talk now,' said Henrietta Scott. 'Howard's shown an interest in her photography. And she's gone fishing with him.'

'I'm pleased they've discovered each other,' I said.

I cringed. My voice sounded flat. Henrietta Scott had no idea what I had to do to them. Here I was, eating home-baked peach cobbler and drinking iced tea, all the while planning my next move against them. Murder was murder; yes, I had to think of poor Charlotte, but sometimes I thought my heart had callouses.

As if responding to my thoughts, Henrietta Scott said, 'Of course we all miss poor Charlotte terribly.' She dabbed at a small bit of sweet curd and caraway at the corner of her mouth with a cloth napkin. 'And we thank you deeply for apprehending her murderer, Dr Deacon.'

Now that he was dead, Richard Lip's guilt had become an article of faith. I continued to watch Howard Scott and his daughter. He was dressed in black as well. Bernice wore her usual violet. She gazed up at the red and yellow kite high in the sky. She showed not a shred of remorse. Howard Scott looked nearly happy.

Then Henrietta Scott said, 'Isn't that Olive Wade over there?'

I looked. Yes, it was Olive Wade, in a blue shirtwaist with puff-top sleeves, a full skirt with a four-yard sweep, and a straw boater with a blue carnation stuck in the hatband, setting off her magnificently blue eyes. Her hand rested on Everett Howse's arm. I looked away, lifted my peach cobbler, and stuffed my mouth as a way to hide my discomfiture.

'I understand they'll be leaving next week,' said Mrs Scott, regarding the couple fondly.

I stopped chewing. I swallowed what I had in my mouth; swallowed it whole, the way a copperhead swallows a young possum.

'Leaving?' I said, choking on the word.

She looked at me in mild surprise.

'Didn't you know?' she said. 'Mr and Mrs Howse have invited Miss Wade to spend July and August at their summer home on Sodus Point.'

I looked down at my peach cobbler but I didn't have any appetite for it any more. I took a large gulp of iced tea. 'And is ... is Everett Howse ... will he be at Sodus Point as well?' I asked.

'Yes,' she said, her smile broadening. 'Those two,' she said, clucking her tongue at Miss Wade and Mr Howse, as if they were a couple of children who were lovingly indulged by the whole town. 'I think we'll hear an announcement before the summer's through,' she said.

I excused myself. I was upset. An announcement before the summer was through. I hated the thought of Olive Wade spending time at Sodus Point with Everett Howse, but what could I do? Nothing. So I struggled to put it from my mind. Even so, my thoughts were anything but charitable toward the junior assemblyman.

As I walked across the Green toward Arlington Avenue, I forced myself to focus on the matter at hand. I had the advantage. And I had to do my duty. I had to strike while the Scotts were still out of their house.

I walked down Court Street to the railroad tracks and followed the tracks north-west up through the town. At Ontario Street I descended the embankment through the milkweed and goldenrod and walked the block and a half to Milton Street. Milton Street was deserted. People were either down by the river or out on the Green. The day was much too pleasant to stay indoors.

At the Scott house I walked around the side garden with a bold gait, passed the sturdy trellis where Charlotte had made her midnight escapes, and came around to the back where I spied Bernice's hobby shed. The family horse, Lightning, swished flies from her rump as she watched me with her big dumb eyes. I climbed the back steps – they needed paint – and tried the back door. It was open. Of course it was open. This wasn't Washington; this was Fairfield. Every-

293

body left their doors open in Fairfield.

I went inside, walked through the kitchen to the hall, and climbed the stairs to the second floor. I found my way to Bernice's small bedroom at the back.

A narrow cot stood in the corner of Bernice's room. Her bureau was scuffed, small, and looked second-hand. A bookcase full of old books stood beside the bed. She had a single framed picture hanging from the plaster above the chimney-piece – a steel engraving of Daniel Webster, a colorless and joyless portrait of the revered old linguist. A riot of Kodak 'Brownie' shots had been pinned to some cork tiles on the wall, at least a hundred photographs in all. Her window was broken. One of the panes had been replaced with a piece of cardboard. A water mark like the outline of an imaginary continent stained the ceiling. Bernice's room was a poor second cousin to Charlotte's room.

I walked across her badly worn Axminster rug to the closet. Inside I found her violet, blue, and mauve shirtwaists. Her closet smelled of mothballs. I also found a white shirtwaist, the only white shirtwaist in there. I took it out and had a closer look. It was made from fine white muslin and had a pleated puff bosom. I recognized this shirtwaist. It was the shirtwaist Bernice Scott had worn the night of her sister's murder.

In my laboratory, I folded a cotton sheet in

four, and placed it on a card table. I spread Bernice's white shirtwaist on top of the sheet. I then went to my lab bench and mixed some dilute sulfuric acid with some green sulphate of iron. I needed proof, something that would stand up to the scrutiny of a Grand Jury – and, by Jim, I was going to get it.

When the green sulphate of iron was thoroughly dissolved in the dilute sulfuric acid, I added a small quantity of potassa. I then sprinkled the resulting mixture on both left and right sleeves of Bernice's shirtwaist. Even though the shirtwaist had most probably been laundered since the night of the murder, I was convinced I'd discover at least trace amounts of prussic acid. She'd spilled some on her sleeve the night of the murder, according to Richard Lip, and I intended to find it.

With the sleeves at last saturated, I now soaked them with the final ingredient, muriatic acid. My eyes widened. A spill pattern in bright Prussian blue appeared on the left sleeve of the shirtwaist.

I had, as Judge Norris called it, tangible, physical proof.

The next day I deferred my morning patients. I met with Stanley Armstrong and Judge Norris in the judge's courthouse chambers at ten o'clock. We all stared at Bernice Scott's shirtwaist. The blue on the left sleeve was, if anything, even darker than it had been yesterday. Though I'd stretched the boundaries of jurisprudence by my unauthorized intrusion into the Scott house, the truth was the truth, and justice had to be served. The evidence was undeniable.

The judge's face sagged, as if Bernice's shirtwaist had just spoiled his day.

'Well...' he said. 'I guess we have no choice, then.' He looked at Stanley. 'Sheriff, I want you to arrest Bernice Scott. And I want you to search her house.'

TWENTY-THREE

Stanley Armstrong and his deputies searched the Scott house the next day and discovered the missing bottle of Scheele's Prussic Acid from Gordon Wiley's drug store in the attic crawl-space behind Bernice Scott's drab little bedroom. The vial was still half full, and the question had to be asked, was she planning to kill someone else? Why would she keep such a damning piece of evidence otherwise?

I pondered this question as I sat at my dressing-table.

Then there was Bruce Farrow's statement. Bruce Farrow was Gordon Wiley's drug store clerk. On closer questioning, he recalled how three or four days before the murder, Bernice Scott had come into the store asking for peach ice-cream. Bruce Farrow had had to go downstairs to the hardwood ice-chest to get it. When he came back up, Bernice Scott was gone. A few hours later he discovered the keys to the prescription cabinet lying on the floor in the back office, and the back door slightly ajar.

This should have been enough. But I was

only partially satisfied. Yes, Bernice had confessed – three lines on courthouse stationery with her signature at the bottom – but she hadn't bothered to excuse or explain her behaviour; hadn't said anything about her relationship to Roger Robson, nor enlightened us about what must have been going through her mind at the time of the murder. What could she have been thinking? We were all still mystified. The question gnawed, and in fact had kept me awake last night.

I shook my head and continued with my toiletry. I was going to visit Olive Wade.

I looked at the items on my dressing-table – the brush of soft badger hair for shaving, the boxwood case for my aftershave colognes, the small tin of Alletaire's pomade for my hair – and wondered if it was worth it. Why care a wit for my appearance if Olive Wade was going to spend the summer at Sodus Point with Everett Howse? Best to pay my final call just as I was.

I went outside, hitched Pythagoras to my buggy, and was soon driving up Cherry Hill.

I found Miss Wade watering her roses with a five-gallon watering-can. The rose-bed was covered with cocoa shells to keep the weeds down, and the air smelled of shell-chocolate. Miss Wade looked up, surprised to see me, and put the watering-can down.

'Dr Deacon,' she said.

Surprised to see me, yet I detected a distinct coldness in her voice. Our previous concord no longer seemed to exist. I felt confused, and I had great difficulty collecting my thoughts.

'I'm just here to ... to pay my respects before you journey off for the summer,' I said.

She inclined her head and smiled. 'How very kind,' she said.

The silence between us lengthened and I was at last obliged to enquire in a most clumsy manner about her travel arrangements.

'I travel by train as far as Seneca Falls,' she said. 'I'll meet Everett Howse in Seneca Falls and we'll travel together by carriage to Sodus Point.'

A precise answer in a tone that was entirely dismissing. In fact, she seemed positively hostile toward me. What had happened to our understanding? Did she not remember our meeting under the Park Street bridge? What had happened to our concord?

'Is there anything wrong?' I asked.

Her blue eyes flashed with barely concealed anger.

'No,' she said curtly, 'nothing at all.'

I scrutinized her more closely. 'Forgive me if I disagree, Miss Wade, but I believe there is.' I couldn't fathom her behaviour. 'Have I done something to offend you?'

She turned away. Her anger disappeared and a pensive look came to her eyes. She gazed across the yard to where two purple martins fussed about the entrance of an extravagant and commodious bird-house.

'You were only doing your duty,' she said finally.

I surmised she was talking about Bernice Scott. I stared at her lustrous blonde person. She took off her gardening gloves and clasped them in her right hand. Then she turned to me, and I saw a look of pity come to her eyes.

'Oh, Dr Deacon...'

'I wish you'd call me Clyde.'

'I feel so terribly for the Scotts.' She struggled to compose herself. I tried to think of something suitable to say, something that might make her feel better, but I too felt terribly for the Scotts. 'And poor Bernice,' she said. She looked at the ground, her eyes moist, and wrung the garden gloves in both hands. 'And ... and...' She lifted her head and stared at me with puzzling desperation, her jaw coming forward, the delicate blue veins on her temples standing out, her face turning red. I was perplexed. One could expect sadness over the Scott affair, yes, but desperation? 'And I...' She let her hands fall to her sides. 'I don't know what you want,' she said. This caught me by surprise. I was not sure what she meant. 'You come to me, you look at me in that ... that way of yours ... and you ... and I know you want me...' My eyes widened as I felt the blood rise to my face. 'And I ... just when I think you're going to do something about it...' she peered at me more closely, '...you back away. You never ... and I can't get through to you because you ... there's this hidden spot inside you, isn't there? A place where you'll never let me see.'

She waited for me to say something but I was so stunned I just stood there like a dunderhead. So she gave up. She turned from me. She lifted her watering-can and sprinkled her Imperial Sunsets, not bothering to put her gloves back on. I looked away, took off my bowler, and scratched the back of my neck.

'Miss Wade, I—'

'I don't know what kind of man you are, Dr Deacon,' she said.

She uttered this like a pronouncement. Though she kept her face away from me I could see she was crying. Before I could stop myself I lifted my hand and touched the back of my fingers to her pale silken cheek. She looked at me. She didn't recoil. She allowed my fingers to remain upon her skin. And I saw that indeed there was some love in her eyes, that the affectionate regard I'd as yet only hoped for was plainly evident in those sapphire orbs, that all I had to do was act on the intoxicating and romantic poignancy of this moment, perhaps kiss her or take her into my arms, and she would be mine. But I couldn't. I felt a great barrenness inside me. I loved this woman and I could see she loved me back. There was nothing, not a blessed thing, standing in our way. But I couldn't do anything about it. She was right. As always, something stopped me; Emily calling me from the bare patch of earth outside Cross Plains.

I finally let my hand drop. I couldn't go on. I had no business here.

'I don't know what kind of man I am either, Miss Wade,' I murmured.

And I walked away. I felt broken-hearted. I knew that when next I saw her I would be addressing the future Mrs Everett Howse.

Upon my return to the surgery, I found one of the County Court clerks, Linford McLean, waiting for me on the front steps.

'It's Miss Scott, sir,' he said. 'She wants to talk to you. She says she won't talk to no one else but you.'

Having spent Monday and Tuesday in the Sheriff's Office, Bernice had now been moved to a basement cell in the courthouse. She would be tried in Buffalo. Judge Norris wasn't going to take any chances with his November election. I put my 'DOCTOR IS OUT' sign in the window and departed for the courthouse with Linford McLean. Once at the courthouse, I was led downstairs to the lock-up by the County Bailiff, Randall Swain, a tall, bony man, nearly seven feet tall, with large hands and big feet. The cells down here were of heavy riveted steel, with only a small eye-slot in the door. The place was as dingy a lock-up as could be found anywhere. The air was close and smelled of unemptied chamber-pots. Mr Swain took a key-ring from his belt and opened Bernice Scott's cell door.

Bernice sat on her pallet in a prisoner's uniform, a simple grey blouse and a long grey skirt. In the dim electric light she looked paler than usual.

'I don't like it here,' she said, even before I had a chance to sit down on the pallet beside her.

I stared at her. 'No,' I said. I sat. I lifted my knee and angled myself so I could see her face. She turned to me, and a look of curiosity came to her eyes.

'When did you first know?' she asked.

She was as affable as ever, and evidently didn't blame me for the part I'd played in her arrest. I looked around at the dismal little cell and saw a half-finished bowl of corn porridge sitting on a tray.

'Are you all right?' I asked. 'They haven't mistreated you, have they?'

'They move me to Buffalo next week,' she said.

'Bernice, I'm sorry,' I said.

A knit came to her brow, as if she were somehow disappointed in me. 'I wish you'd call me Miss Scott,' she said. 'I'm sixteen, you know.'

I felt a deep pity for the girl. 'Miss Scott,' I corrected.

She looked down at her hands. 'Are they

going to electrocute me?' she asked.

'I don't think so,' I said. 'You're a minor, and that will play in your favor.'

'But they're going to make me stay in prison for the rest of my life, aren't they?'

'That will be up to the judge,' I said.

She considered this for a long time. Finally she said, 'I've never cared what people think of me, Dr Deacon.' In the overhead pipes, I heard a trickle of water. 'I've never had many friends and I've been alone a good deal of the time. But I find I like it better that way. Maybe they'll put me in solitary confinement. I wouldn't mind. People don't notice me anyway. People forget about me, even when I'm standing right in front of them. And that gives me a chance to watch them. It gives me the opportunity to observe them. You strike me as a good observer, doctor. Are you?'

I conceded the point. 'I watch,' I said. 'And I remember the things I see.'

'If you know how to watch,' she said, 'if you know how to observe, you're in possession of a priceless tool.' She nodded to herself. 'You find you have power over other people. Watching people makes you smart. I'm actually a lot smarter than Charlotte.'

'I know you are, Miss Scott,' I said.

She looked at me with the most pathetic little-girl look I'd ever seen. 'Not that it's ever made one bit of difference,' she said.

From a cell down the corridor I heard

another prisoner cough, a soft murmuring hack that sounded like the beginnings of pneumonia.

'Your parents love you,' I said. I felt it important that she know this. 'Your father loves you.'

Her eyes narrowed, as if she found the notion incomprehensible. 'Oh ... I don't know...' she said. 'Father was always so wrapped up in Charlotte ... Charlotte was his...' She shook her head, as if at a fond memory. 'As for me ... well ... I'm just a strange little pet, aren't I? I'm just a ... a puzzle to my father. He feels it and I feel it, and we've never tried to hide it from each other.'

'But your mother loves you,' I insisted.

She looked at me, forcing her eyes to brighten with false cheer. 'My mother is too much like Charlotte to feel much of anything,' she said.

This pained me. Up in the corner I saw a spider dart across a spider web and climb on top of one of the pipes. I didn't want Bernice to think she was unloved. She wouldn't survive the reformatory for girls in Syracuse if she thought she was unloved. She would need something to keep her going. I thought of her and Roger walking along the river.

'What about Roger?' I said, now clutching at anything.

Her eyes brightened further. 'That's precisely why you're here, doctor,' she said. 'To

305

talk about Roger.'

She took a strand of hair, put it in her mouth, and chewed for a few seconds. I waited. I saw she was collecting her thoughts. She spat the strand out and brushed it over her shoulder.

At last she said, 'Roger always included me.' She smiled, nodding amiably. 'He always made sure I went with them on their skating parties and on their hay rides. And he was a great card player. He taught me all sorts of games. He used to play patience with me all the time. He was fun to be with. And he was such a good athlete. He gave me tennis lessons. And he taught me how to kiss.' She nodded energetically, as if she were afraid I wasn't going to believe this. 'I insisted on that.' Her smile broadened. 'I don't know how he put up with me. I can be such an insufferable little nit at times.'

I cleared my throat. 'I was under the impression that you and Roger ... that the two of you were ... fond of each other...'

'Oh, yes, Dr Deacon, we were, very much indeed,' she said. Like most young girls, she was enthralled by the notion of love. 'After he got through with Charlotte, he loved me more than I can say. And he ... he ... for the longest time he really meant it.' The smile on her face slipped away like the last leaves of autumn, and a distant look came to her eyes. 'But then he ... he stopped feeling that way toward me. I don't know why.'

These last words came out in a halting manner.

'He's a rogue and a scoundrel,' I said.

A dullness came to her eyes. 'He told me about my sister,' she said, her voice now quiet. 'He told me about her ... their child.' She stared at the dank grey walls of her cell, where moisture beaded up near the top. 'He promised my sister ... well ... things...' She looked at me suddenly, as if she were challenging me. 'You have to understand this about Roger. He lies. He lies all the time. Never trust a word he says. I did, and now look where I am. He made promises to my sister, and he never had any intention of keeping them, and, yes, she made that ... that ultimate sacrifice ... and then he went ahead and said no to her. I was actually happy about that. It meant he would spend more time with me.' She shook her head. 'But of course he didn't realize how my sister could cause such a dust-up over things. Charlotte always gets what she wants,' she said. 'She always has. No one ever says no to Charlotte. She doesn't know the meaning of the word. And that's what Roger didn't know. That's why he came to me. He thought I might help him.'

She looked at me, her eyes freighted with meaning.

'He came to you?' I said.

'Charlotte was going to go to Roger's father and tell him about her pregnancy,' she said.

She rubbed her hands over her knees and contemplated the half-filled bowl of corn porridge. 'He's terribly afraid of his father. Roger wanted me to do something about Charlotte before she could go to his father. He said Charlotte had become a bother. He said if Charlotte were gone, there would be nothing standing between us. He told me he loved me. But that was a lie and I was stupid enough to believe him.' She shook her head and gave me a weak little shrug. 'He said he would take me to California. He said he would love me forever, and never let me come to harm. I became a machine of sorts for him, then.' She took a deep breath and sighed. 'A Charlotte-killing machine.'

He would take her to California. Little Bernice had her dreams too.

'I'm sorry, Miss Scott,' I said.

She got up and fussed with some papers on a small table. She pulled out what looked like a hand-drawn map.

'But I haven't been entirely stupid, Dr Deacon,' she said. 'I talk about watching. I talk about observation. What better way to watch than with a camera?' She straightened her shoulders and gazed at me. 'What's the maximum sentence for arson in this state?'

My eyebrows rose. 'Twenty years,' I said.

'I warned him,' she said.

'Warned who?'

'Roger.'

'Warned him about what?' I asked.

'About breaking promises,' she said. She gestured around at the dank cell. 'Do you call this California?' She shook her head. 'I don't.' She gave me the map. 'So now he has to pay.' I glanced at the map. 'Have you ever read *Treasure Island*, Dr Deacon?' she asked.

'Years ago,' I said.

'You can learn a lot about treachery from *Treasure Island*,' she said. She gestured at the map. 'Think of this as a treasure hunt.'

I looked at the map. 'These are the caves,' I said.

'They are indeed, Dr Deacon,' she said. 'And the cross marks the spot.'

At the Sheriff's Office the next day, Stanley and I looked at the photographs. The cross marked the spot, and these were what we had found up in the caves – photographs. There were seven in all.

One showed Roger Robson loitering in a back alley behind Mosely's Ironmongery. Another, from the vantage point of Milton and Niagara Streets, showed Roger Robson soaking a bale of hay next to the ironmongery with what looked like a can of kerosene. The shadows were long, stretching to the east, cast by the light of dawn, and the images were sharp, unmistakable. Another showed Roger setting fire to the bale of hay with a rolled up newspaper. Smart girl, I thought. She knew she was good at hiding. People didn't notice her, even when she was standing right in front of them. She was like

309

a ghost in the woodwork.

'I bet his father put him up to this,' said Stanley. Stanley flipped through the remaining photographs. Two showed the resulting conflagration of Mosely's, while the remaining three captured the arrival and deployment of the Fairfield Volunteer Engine Company and their steam-powered pumper. 'Dutch Mosely was always undercutting Wilbert on the domestic chicken wire.' Stanley shook his head, put the photographs down, and looked at me. 'And he killed him on nails,' he said.

TWENTY-FOUR

On Thursday, a day before Independence Day, the *Fairfield Newspacket* ran a story about me.

As 'lamentable and tragic' as the Charlotte Scott case had turned out to be, they had to thank 'the good doctor' for getting to the bottom of things. They said I would continue to be a deputy, and would help Sheriff Armstrong from time to time. They also mentioned the ironmongery fire. Citing 'incontrovertible proof', they solemnly announced the arrest of 'our own Mr Roger Robson' and editorialized how, 'on this day before our nation's 126th birthday', the laws of our land had once again, 'without prejudice for rich or poor', meted out justice 'fair and square'.

I ended up using that day's edition of the *Newspacket* as an umbrella. Late in the day, as I rattled home in my buggy after an afternoon of country calls, I held the paper over my head to ward off a steady rain. I passed the Fifth County Road and drove up and over the railroad embankment into town. To my right, beyond the soggy shoulder of

Cattaraugus Avenue, I saw the cemetery. And at the back, where the newest graves were, I saw a lone figure draped in a black rain slicker kneeling next to Charlotte Scott's gravestone.

I reined in Pythagoras and stopped. I stared at the figure for nearly a minute, and then got out of my buggy. I hopped over the flooded ditch and strode across the wet grass toward Charlotte's limestone cross. The box elders loomed over me like sentinels for the dead. As I reached Charlotte's grave, the figure didn't turn, but I recognized him by his great size. It was Morley Suggett, Charlotte's childhood sweetheart, the boy I had whupped so soundly up on Cherry Hill.

I stood beside him. I heard him weeping. Finally, he looked up at me, his face wet with tears.

'I could have made her happy, doctor,' he said.

I put my hand on his shoulder. Bygones were bygones.

'I believe that's so, son,' I said. 'If only she'd had the good sense to see that.'

He turned back to the grave. I reached through my slicker into my vest pocket and pulled out a photograph, the Kodak 'Brownie' shot of Charlotte standing next to her mother's irises, dressed in white, seeming to glow in the sunshine; the one I'd taken from Bernice.

'I want you to have this, Morley,' I said.

He turned around, looked at the photograph, and then nodded gratefully. 'Thank you kindly, doctor,' he said. 'It sure is a pretty one.'

'Isn't it, though,' I said.

And I left him there in the rain, next to his dead girlfriend, contemplating his loneliness, and drove back to town.

The following day – Independence Day – dawned as bright and clear a fourth of July as any patriotic American could want.

At precisely four thirty-seven a.m., Battery A of the National Guard, Fairfield, fired a forty-four-gun salute to Old Glory in the Green, rousing me from what had been the first settled and easy sleep I'd had in the last two weeks. After a leisurely breakfast and several cups of coffee, I set off toward the Green.

At nine o'clock, Mayor Vanduzen, from a special platform, read the Declaration of Independence. Then we had a prayer meeting led by the Reverend Eric Porteous. After a pancake breakfast, the Ladies' Auxiliary Glee Club performed religious and patriotic hymns. As I wandered through the crowd, I was greeted warmly by many of the townspeople, and congratulated. Most of them were sorry about what had happened to the Scotts, but none of them blamed me for the outcome. Even Judge Norris shook my hand and told me what a fine job I'd done, now that he knew which way public opinion was leaning.

At twelve o'clock the Fairfield Cornet Band gave a concert of marching music in the bandstand. Red, white, and blue bunting hung everywhere. We had a mock battle – redcoats against bluecoats. Then came the three-legged race, the hurdle race, the sack race, the farmhorse race, and finally the rowing race out on the river. You could climb a greased pole and win a dollar. You could catch a greased pig and win the pig. At sunset, Mayor Vanduzen released thirteen white doves from a cage, symbolizing the thirteen original colonies of the Republic.

Then at last came the fireworks. Pretty nearly the whole town gathered on the Green. Every kind of firework imaginable was used. There were serpents, pinwheels, flowerpots, cherry bombs, and Roman candles. They set off cannon crackers, skyrockets, silver stars, triple asteroids, and even a seven-star Pleiades. And while the colorful display lit the delighted faces of the townspeople, and the din echoed through the valley, I saw Herbert Early the high school drama teacher wheel his wife Alice to a box elder in her wicker wheelchair. In the changing colors of the fireworks, I watched Herbert Early put his hand on her shoulder. Alice Early had a contented smile on her face. She reached up and put her hand over his. She looked better – even pretty. She'd put her hair up and she was wearing a hat decorated with osprey feathers. She said something to her husband, and he leaned down so that he could hear her over the fireworks. He nodded, then walked around to the front of the wheelchair, and helped her stand. My eyes widened. She took his arm and they walked carefully, slowly, and with the greatest satisfaction in each other, to the nearest flower-bed, where their faces continued to be brightened in the yellows, reds, and blues of the fireworks overhead.

I felt a sudden emptiness inside. I looked around. Couples stood everywhere, men and women together, old, young, and middle-aged. I scanned the crowd vainly for Olive Wade before I dismally concluded that she must have already gone to Sodus Point with Everett Howse. I was alone and I didn't like it. I wanted my wife, but I knew I couldn't have her. I knew, at last, that Emily was never coming back.

'Nothing burns finer than a strong piece of hardwood, Clyde,' said President Theodore Roosevelt.

The twenty-sixth President of the United States lifted his axe and took another swing at the century-old oak tree. A white chunk of wood flew out from the tree and landed in the grass by the President's feet. He didn't have to cut his own firewood, he had people to do that for him, but here was this old oak tree, starting to die anyway, and Theodore

Roosevelt was determined to cut it down, saw it up, and split it into firewood himself.

'I was a fool,' I said. The President took another swing at the tree. He'd been at it an hour already and showed no signs of tiring. 'I had her, Theodore, I really had her. I saw the love plain as day shining in her eyes, and I let her get away.'

'Sounds to me like you drove her away,' he said.

Whack! The axe thudded into the tree.

'That might be so,' I said.

Through the woods to my right, the land sloped down to Oyster Bay and Long Island Sound. I saw my son, Jeremiah, playing with the President's thirteen-year-old boy, Kermit, on the stony beach. They were making Kermit's young black terrier, Allen, fetch sticks. The President stopped chopping and handed me the axe.

'Here,' he said. He smiled, his teeth showing up like two rows of white masonry, his walrus mustache drooping over the corners of his lips. 'I don't see why I should have all the fun.'

Often enough, the President put his Sagamore Hill guests to work like this, thinking they would find it as entertaining as he did. I took the axe disconsolately. My mind was still on Olive Wade, even after all these weeks. The middle of August already, and my feelings for her hadn't diminished in the least.

'It was Emily,' I said.

The President cuffed me jovially on the shoulder.

'Oh, now, Clyde,' he said, 'you've got to shake yourself out of this. You should treat your old heartaches the same way my Quenty-Quee treats his goldfish.' He was referring to Quentin, his youngest son. 'He ignores them, and eventually they die.'

'That advice is easier given than taken, Mr President,' I said.

I lifted the axe and walked to the tree. I chopped. I chopped and chopped, and all my frustrations came out in my swing. The wood chips flew from the tree trunk like startled birds. I was like a locomotive, building speed, swinging faster and faster. By the time I tired myself out, the President was staring at me through his wire-rim spectacles with incredulous fascination.

'I see why those Cuban boys didn't stand a chance,' he said.

From the patio, a butler walked with an even stride down the lawn carrying a silver coffee service and a pile of letters.

'Well, now,' said Roosevelt, 'my mail's here. Why don't we sit down and take a break from this, Clyde? I suppose this old oak tree will keep.'

'Is that sliced cantaloupe the butler's bringing?' I asked.

He winked at me. 'I know you like your melon, Clyde.'

We sat down in two large Adirondack chairs near the fish pond. The butler put the tray on the table between us. Theodore had a special coffee mug about the size of a gravy boat into which he poured a copious amount of the steaming black liquid. He then took the sugar tongs and sank seven sugar cubes into his coffee, one after the other. Caffeine and sugar – no wonder the President had so much energy.

He sat back and sorted through his correspondence.

There had to be about fifty pieces of mail there, from people as diverse as kings, princes, and prime ministers to football players, farmers, and naturalists.

'Say, Clyde,' he said, 'here's a piece for you. Looks like it's from Stanley.'

He handed me the piece in question. Yes, it was from Stanley.

I opened it and began to read.

The sheriff told me Roger Robson had been convicted in the Mosely Ironmongery arson and sentenced to twenty years' hard labor at Leamington. Old man Robson was under investigation for the fire but so far nothing had stuck. I grinned. Roger in jail. I was happy about that. He was, after all, the real reason Charlotte was dead. I continued to read. Bernice, because of her questionable mental status and her young age, had gotten only five years, three of them on probation in her parents' recognizance. Arnold Murchison and his men had received fifteen years for the Corn Mercantile burglary. Michael Sims had cut a deal for five. The Parthenon Theater was now closed, but there were plans to reopen it as a nickelodeon.

On the home front, Camilla was pregnant again. They were expecting their thirteenth child in spring. Gads!

And Olive Wade ... well, Miss Wade had returned home early from Sodus Point, no one knew why. I leaned forward in my chair, clutching the letter like a life-ring. Rumors suggested she'd had a falling out with Everett Howse. I sat back in relief. Oh, glorious day!

The President looked up from his own correspondence. 'You're grinning like a hound-dog getting its belly scratched, Clyde,' he said. 'What is it?'

'It's just this letter,' I said.

I told him about Olive Wade coming home early.

'There,' he said. 'You see?' As if the whole thing had been foreordained. 'This Everett Howse has had his chance. Now it's your turn, Clyde.'

My turn.

But what did that mean? Should I rush off right away? Should I gather up Jeremiah and get the next train back to Fairfield? As the President went back to his letters I stared through the trees at Oyster Bay where the water was slowly receding with the outgoing tide. I had this chance. And in this chance I felt a sudden great trust in Olive. I remembered the love I'd seen in her eyes. And I felt my own love beating in my chest. Decency demanded I remain at least another week with the President. But then I would go back to Fairfield. The sunlight dappled the grove of birch trees at the end of the lawn. For the first time in fourteen years, Emily's cold hand no longer rested on my shoulder. And William McKinley – yes, good old William, dead for nearly a year – had at last forgiven me. It was as if a long and invisible wire now connected me to Olive Wade; a wire that stretched all the way from Long Island back to Fairfield. I had believed that when she went to Sodus Point she would come back as the future Mrs Everett Howse. But now I knew, with the bright and keen passion of a man in love, that our concord remained, that she was mine if I would only have the courage and intelligence to recognize it, and that our long and invisible wire could never be sundered.

As the President said, it was my turn now.

And, by Jim, I was going to make the most of it.